"I've never stayed in one place long enough to call it home. My brothers belong. I don't."

"That doesn't mean they don't think of you as family."

"I don't know if I want to be family to them, or anyone else."

"I guess that would be easier."

"Easier?" Cruz shifted back into a corner of the couch. If he thought it was weird that two people who didn't know the first thing about each other were talking like long-time confidants, he didn't show it.

"Isn't it easier not to take chances?"

"Sounds like experience talking."

"Maybe."

"Is that why you're hiding out here? Had a fight with your boyfriend about what's easier?"

Aria forced out a laugh. "There isn't any boyfriend."

Cruz's appraisal of her this time was frank. "Are all the men in this town blind idiots?"

Dear Reader,

Life continues to be full of unexpected twists and exciting turns in the small fictional town of Luna Hermosa, located in scenic northern New Mexico, as the Garretts and the Morentes discover new loves, old secrets and unexpected adventures. As these heartwarming and heart-challenging tales of love, forgiveness, pain and hope unfold for each of patriarch Jed Garrett's sons, our wish is that you may discover you share some of their experiences within your own life and heart.

When we wrote our first book in the Brothers of Rancho Pintada series, *Sawyer's Special Delivery,* we knew two things: first, we wanted to write a family story about people with imperfect lives finding perfect love; and second, that story needed to be placed in a town that was alive with the things that matter to us—community, friends, fun and familiarity.

For us, as natives of the Southwest, Luna Hermosa has all of those qualities. The Morentes, the Garretts and the women they love have so many of the joys, passions, heartbreaks, flaws, hopes and dreams we all have that we're extremely happy we'll be there with them to tell each of their unique stories.

Nicole Foster

THE BRIDESMAID'S TURN

NICOLE FOSTER

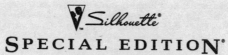

SPECIAL EDITION®

Published by Silhouette Books

America's Publisher of Contemporary Romance

SILHOUETTE BOOKS

ISBN-13: 978-0-373-24926-8
ISBN-10:   0-373-24926-8

THE BRIDESMAID'S TURN

Visit Silhouette Books at www.eHarlequin.com

Printed in U.S.A.

Books by Nicole Foster

Silhouette Special Edition

Sawyer's Special Delivery #1703
The Rancher's Second Chance #1841
What Makes a Family? #1853
The Cowboy's Lady #1913
The Bridesmaid's Turn #1926

Harlequin Historical

Jake's Angel #522
Cimarron Rose #560
Hallie's Hero #642

*The Brothers of Rancho Pintada

NICOLE FOSTER

is the pseudonym for the writing team of Danette Fertig-Thompson and Annette Chartier-Warren. Both journalists, they met while working on the same newspaper, and started writing historical romance together after discovering a shared love of the Old West and happy endings. Their twenty-year friendship has endured writer's block, numerous caffeine-and-chocolate deadlines and the joyous chaos of marriage and raising the five children between them. They love to hear from readers. Visit them on the Web at www.nicolefoster.com.

For my precious daughter Nicole,
Letting go and letting go…
But always holding on to each other.
I love you, Sweetie.

Chapter One

"*I*'*m Cruz Déclan. I'm looking for my father.*"

The first words out of his mouth weren't the ones he'd planned. But nothing in the last two years of his life had gone according to plan. He'd gotten used to—even if he was still uncomfortable with—acting on instinct, making decisions without the luxury of deliberation.

Though he'd had the time to think it over, this decision to come to Rancho Pintada and confront Jed Garrett, the father he'd never known, hadn't been any different.

Showing up unannounced at the wedding reception now seemed overly dramatic, the kind of gesture they made in bad TV movies. Weeks ago, when he'd made up his mind to meet the father who'd abandoned him before he was born, he'd wanted to be done with it and Garrett, by inviting him to his youngest son's wedding, had offered the perfect opportunity.

Standing in the entryway of his father's house, Cruz wasn't so sure about his decision.

He knew without being told the man looking back at him with

a slightly stunned expression was his brother—one he hadn't known existed until a few months ago. It was a disconcerting sensation, recognizing the line and shape of his own features on a stranger's face. It heightened the sense of unreality that had hit him the moment he'd stepped in the door.

The other man recovered quickly and held out a hand. Cruz accepted the brief, firm contact automatically, telling himself it was no more than he'd do greeting a business prospect or a new client, wishing it didn't feel like a lot more.

"Cort Morente. I'm your brother." He stopped, seeming to search for the right thing—anything—to say. "I'm sorry. I didn't… None of us expected—"

"Yeah, I didn't expect, either," Cruz interrupted. "I didn't expect to get a letter and then a wedding invitation from someone I wouldn't know if he walked into me. Even if he does claim to be my father."

"I think we can safely say it's more than a claim," Cort said with a slight smile. "You won't be able to hide your connection to Jed now. When people see you, me and Sawyer together, there won't be any question."

The reference took a moment to sink in and then Cruz remembered from Garrett's letter. There were four of them, all younger than him—Sawyer, Rafe, Cort and Josh. Garrett hadn't told him much more than that.

"I'm not the one who's been hiding it," Cruz said with a touch of acid.

"Fair enough." There was another of those awkward pauses and then Cort said, "Sawyer, Rafe and Josh would want to know you're here."

Cruz said nothing; better that than something he'd regret. No doubt all four of them would be interested in his sudden appearance since Garrett, in his letter, had made it clear his purpose in tracking down his oldest son after thirty-five years was to give Cruz an equal share in Rancho Pintada. He guessed that wouldn't have been welcome news to his recently discovered brothers.

Interpreting his silence as reluctance, Cort added, "This whole thing is a lot more complicated than you know. At least listen to it all before you make up your mind about us. Give me a minute to find them."

He didn't give Cruz a chance to say no and quickly headed into the great room ahead, leaving Cruz at the edge of the throng of wedding guests. A few glanced his way, curious, already speculating. He ignored them, taking a few steps to the side, focusing on scanning faces in the crowd for a clue to the identity of his other brothers or Garrett.

A few minutes later, Cort walked up with three other men, including the groom, who spoke up first. "Leave it to Dad to pull something like this without lettin' any of us in on it." He offered his hand with a grin. "I'm Josh Garrett and Cort's right—no doubt you're one of us."

Cruz thought that of any of them, it was Josh, dark blond and lankier than his older brothers, whom someone might question being related to the rest of them. Then Cort introduced Sawyer and Rafe. Cruz noted the clear evidence of Rafe's Native American heritage and decided Cort was right—it was more complicated than he knew.

"I'm sorry you had to find out about this the way you did. It must have been a helluva surprise," Sawyer said. "But none of us knew you existed until recently."

Rafe gave a derisive huff. "The old man's good for surprises."

"We wanted to find you before Jed did," Cort said. "Maybe we could have eased the shock."

With a laugh, Josh put a hand on Cort's shoulder. "Cort's the family peacemaker," he explained. "But I think even he might have a hard time makin' this family reunion go smoothly."

"And Josh is the hell-raiser," Sawyer added. "Or he was until he let Eliana settle him down."

Rafe smiled a little. "He didn't *let* her—she had him roped and tied before he knew what hit him."

From the moment he'd walked in the door, Cruz never felt more the outsider than he did now. They'd accepted him without question as a brother—although he didn't see as they'd had much choice—but there was obviously a strong bond among the four of them that didn't include him. He had no doubt where their loyalties would be if any one of them sensed he was a threat to their tight-knit group.

It was equally obvious that bond didn't extend to Jed Garrett. "I get the impression none of you are anxious for me to meet—" Cruz stopped, not quite sure what to call the man "—Garrett."

"You won't be, either," Rafe muttered.

The four of them exchanged glances, guarded, with meanings Cruz couldn't decipher.

"Jed's never been much of a father to any of us," Sawyer finally said.

"Maybe not," a rough, gravelly voice spoke up from behind, "but that doesn't change the fact I am." The newcomer, tall, built like a bull, with grizzled hair and hard dark eyes, moved slowly forward to stand eye-to-eye with Cruz. "I see you decided to show up after all."

With an effort of sheer will, Cruz reined in the surge of anger and resentment, never expecting it to be so strong. This was what he'd wanted, to come face-to-face with Jed Garrett after a lifetime of knowing nothing about the man he could call his father.

He looked Garrett straight in the eye and, keeping his voice cool and level, said, "I'll admit to being curious. It's not every day I find out I've got more family than my mother."

"Your mother…" Jed slowly shook his head. "It's been a long time since I saw Maria. Since before you were born. She never told me anything about you. I had to find it out for myself. And I'm guessin' she never told you about me, either."

"Why should she? She was eighteen and pregnant and you couldn't get her out of town fast enough."

"I never promised her anything. But that didn't stop her from expectin' I was gonna give up everything to marry her."

"So why the sudden interest in me now?" Cruz countered. "Am I supposed to believe you've developed a guilty conscience after thirty-five years without one, guilty or otherwise?"

"I got my reasons," Jed answered.

"Now's not the time," Cort interrupted. He put himself in

between Jed and Cruz. "We need to do this some other place, where we can talk without half the town listening in."

"Far as I'm concerned, you all can keep this up for the rest of the night," Josh said. "But I've got a new wife waitin' on me and I intend to get her alone before too much longer."

For several moments Cruz thought it was even odds whether Jed would refuse. Part of him sided with Garrett; he wanted to finish it, here and now. But the idea of becoming the town's front-page gossip any sooner than he had to swung him in favor of Cort.

"Fine," Jed growled, shooting a glare at Cort before fixing his attention back on Cruz. "But I want it to happen soon. I've wasted enough time gettin' the five of you together. I don't plan on wastin' any more."

He turned and started shouldering his way through the crowd, leaving Cruz alone with four strangers he was supposed to call family and the feeling he should have let this part of his past stay secret and buried.

She was really starting to hate weddings.

And not just weddings, either. Holidays, babies, engagements— the whole gamut of happy life-changing family events.

A gust of cold wind rattled the windows of the Florida room and Aria Charez shivered, wishing for the tenth time since she'd come here to escape the festivities that she'd brought a wrap. The bridesmaid's dress blessedly had long sleeves, but the pale gold satiny stuff it was made from wasn't doing much to ward off the chill. Maybe it was someone trying to tell her she shouldn't be hiding to begin with.

It seemed like there'd been so many of these big events in the past months among her friends: Cort getting married and adopting a son; Saul Tamar, Eliana's father, marrying Darcy Vargas; now Josh and Eliana. Even Darcy's wild daughter, Nova, was engaged—Nova, who was probably the person voted least likely to ever settle down when they were in high school.

Not that Aria wasn't happy for her friends; she was. But their happy events had a way of making her maudlin, giving her a sharp reminder she wasn't married, didn't have kids, a significant other or even a pet, and that holidays were never all they were advertised to be.

It shouldn't matter. She had so much and there was so much she still wanted to do.

But it was times like these when she felt a strong tug of longing for fulfillment that her professional success couldn't satisfy; a sense of regret for all the relationships she'd managed to mess up in one way or another and the bad choices she couldn't take back.

It was someone commenting for the umpteenth time on her lack of a date for the reception that had prompted Aria to murmur an excuse and find her way to one of the only rooms in the huge ranch house that wasn't being used tonight. The music and voices from the reception were a low hum here and she could pretend they were far away. She hadn't bothered with lights, just curled up in a corner of the settee near the window and watched the wind scatter ragged clouds across the moon and stars.

The solitude hadn't given her any peace, though, and with a sigh, she decided she'd wallowed in self-pity long enough. Groping for her shoes where she'd tossed them at the other end of the couch, she slid them on and started to get up when the sound of footsteps froze her.

Hoping it was someone who'd gotten lost looking for a bathroom, she stayed still, willing whoever it was to keep on walking. That was all she needed, someone finding her hiding in the dark like a sulky child.

She wasn't that lucky. Whoever it was paused outside the room and then came inside, straight past her to stand in front of the windows and look out at the expanse of land and sky that seemed to run for miles until it hit the mountains.

From his silhouette Aria could tell it was a man, tall, broad-shouldered, holding himself tensely, his hands fisted at his sides. She didn't want to disturb whatever escape he'd come for, but she also didn't want to sit here, unmoving, hoping he wouldn't notice her and then having to explain herself when he did.

She stood up, the silk of her dress softly rustling. He whipped around so fast she jumped and nearly lost her balance.

"Who are you?" he demanded.

"Since I was here first, I should be asking you that question." Aria reached over and flipped on the lamp next to the settee, then almost wished she hadn't. In the dim light, he looked bigger and a bit intimidating, with the expert cut of his suit and short, cropped hair emphasizing his hard, lean build. At first glance, she thought he—dark, good-looking, with an aura of wealth and command—would have easily fit into any high-powered business setting. Yet there was something about him, a touch of the gypsy, sensual and secretive, that roughened his polished edges and made him sexy as hell.

"I'm sorry," he said shortly. He looked her over in one sweeping glance. "I didn't expect anyone else to be here."

"Neither did I." Aria tried for a smile and a light, casual tone. "It's okay. You just interrupted my private orgy of self-pity. Believe me, it needed to be interrupted." A little embarrassed at her honest admission, she hurried to say, "I'm Aria Charez. I don't remember seeing you at the wedding. Are you a friend of Josh's?" He didn't look like one of Josh's usual crowd, but there was something vaguely familiar about his face that gave her the impression she knew him or had seen him before.

"Not exactly." His expression was shuttered. "Cruz Déclan. And I wasn't there."

"Cruz—" Suddenly it clicked. He seemed familiar because he looked like Cort and Sawyer. "You must be—"

"The long-lost brother." His half smile quirked his mouth but didn't reach his eyes. "I decided to make my grand entrance tonight after thirty-five years of being a secret."

"I didn't realize Josh had invited you. I mean, no one said anything…" Aria stopped, not quite knowing how to phrase it without offending him. Everyone had been talking about him and the whole story of how Jed Garrett had seduced an innocent teenager, gotten her pregnant and then dumped her in favor of marrying Teresa Morente and her money. Eliana, one of her closest friends, had told her how Jed had been looking for his oldest son but had been frustrated for the past two years because Cruz, a captain in the army reserves, had been on overseas duty. She hadn't mentioned Cruz might show up tonight.

"Josh didn't invite me. It was Garrett." Bitterness in his voice gave it an edge as sharp and jagged as broken glass. "It looks like my so-called father wanted to surprise my brothers."

"I'm sorry. I can't imagine how you must feel, discovering you have a family you never knew."

"I can't imagine it, either. I'm beginning to believe ignorance is underrated." Cruz walked over to sit on the edge of the settee. Leaning forward, his forearms resting on his knees, hands laced tightly together, he stared at the floor.

She didn't know him well enough to interpret his mood. Carefully, she sat down again at the other end of the settee, her back to the arm so she could watch him. "Did you meet them, your brothers and Jed?" she asked tentatively.

"All of them, and then some. I seem to have become a brother-in-law and uncle several times over on top of everything else." He didn't look at her and long moments stretched between them, tense and heavy with unspoken emotion. Finally, he said quietly, "I thought I was ready for it, but I wasn't. I thought I could control things the first time we met. I couldn't. I just—did it. No plan, no idea what I was getting myself into." He shook his head. "It was stupid. I should never have come here tonight."

Aria couldn't help herself. He was a stranger, saying things to her he'd probably regret tomorrow. But tonight, she felt compelled to offer some comfort, even if it was from a woman he'd likely never see again. "Maybe you just wanted to know your family. I know your brothers wanted to find you when they discovered Jed had another son."

"Why?"

The blunt question caught her off guard. "Because—you're family."

Cruz looked up and the confusion of emotion in his face hurt her somehow. "I'm not family. I'm just a stranger from nowhere. They've all got wives and kids, roots in this place. I've never stayed in one place long enough to call it home. They belong. I don't."

"That doesn't mean they don't think of you as family."

"I don't know if I want to be family to them, or anyone else."

"I guess that would be easier."

"Easier?" Cruz shifted back to lean into his own corner of the couch. If he thought it was weird two people who didn't know the first thing about each other were talking like long-time confidants, he didn't show it.

It didn't feel weird to her, though. Alone, with the illusion of being isolated from the rest of the world, the intimacy between them seemed natural, as if they could tell each other things without fear because it wouldn't matter. No one else would know and tomorrow they could pretend they'd never listened.

"Isn't it easier not to take chances?"

"Sounds like experience talking."

"Maybe."

"Is that why you're hiding out here?" he asked. "You had a fight with your boyfriend about what's easier?"

Aria forced out a laugh, inwardly wincing at the tight, brittle sound of it. "There isn't any boyfriend."

Cruz's appraisal of her this time was frank. "Are all the men in this town blind idiots?"

"No," she said. "Your brothers are good guys, but they're all taken." Leaning her head back against the couch, she stared up at the ceiling. "You say you don't belong, but I grew up in this town and I'm the one starting to feel like a stranger." Cruz stayed quiet, his silence somehow encouraging her to go on more than any words would have. "It's the same old story," she said, trying to make it sound unimportant, mildly amusing. "You know, woman past thirty, alone, clock ticking." She put a hand over her eyes. "I can't believe I just said that. It's ridiculous."

If anything, she expected him to agree. Instead, she glanced over and found him watching her. "It's not ridiculous if it's important to you," he said.

Gazes locked, neither of them seemed able to look away. If things were different, and she was the kind of woman with no qualms about a one-time fling with a stranger, it would be easy for this to turn from confessions and comfort to an illicit encounter in Jed Garrett's Florida room.

She wasn't, and Cruz was everything she'd sworn to stay

away from—hot enough to melt her resolve, wickedly attractive and carrying enough emotional baggage for a group.

The way he looked at her, though—intently, silently acknowledging the odd intimacy between them—gave her the sensation of taking a step into what she thought was a shallow stream. But instead she found herself over her head and upside down in the deepest part of a river. The feeling chased through her and she shivered.

Cruz noticed and, easing out of his jacket, flipped it over her shoulders. "Next time you decide to hide, you should pick a warmer room."

"All the warm ones were taken. Thank you," she said, glad he'd mistaken the reason for her tremor. She pulled the jacket more firmly around her, wrapping his scent around her along with the fabric.

"Do you want to go back to the party?" he asked.

"No. Not yet." She wasn't ready to give up this interlude so quickly. "But if you want to—" She made to slide off his jacket, but Cruz stopped her.

"No. Not yet."

Aria smiled at his intentional echo. Leaning back into the couch again, she hesitated then said, "Are you going back?"

"Back where? Out there?" He jerked a thumb behind them.

"I meant wherever you call home."

"I don't call anywhere home. Last week was the first time I'd seen my apartment in over three years. I spent most of that time in a tent in the desert and I can't say I've got any burning desire to go back to that."

"Are you staying here for a while?"

He dragged a hand over his neck, his sigh heavy with frustration and uncertainty. "I'm not sure. I should be getting back to my life. I've got a company to run in Phoenix, a couple of jobs I need to start working on. Apart from the fact I'm not used to staying in any one place too long. But…" The pause extended so long Aria began to think he'd decided not to say anything more. Then he shifted on the settee and said, "I came here expecting to confront Garrett and then get out. I didn't expect to care about having brothers. If anything, I thought they'd resent a stranger showing up with a claim on this ranch. Except—they weren't like that. It would have been easier if they had resented me. I could've dealt with that. I'm not sure how to deal with the situation now."

The bewilderment in his voice hit a chord in her. He didn't strike her as a man who easily revealed his weaknesses and yet he'd willingly made himself vulnerable to her. Before she could stop herself, she slid closer and gently laid her hand against his neck, her thumb lightly rubbing against his jaw. She let her touch speak, not wanting to minimize his feelings by spouting clichés.

Cruz looked at her, his eyes almost black in the dim light. "Aren't you going to tell me it'll all work out, to just give it time?"

"No," she said softly. She let her hand slide away. "I know better than anyone that there aren't any guarantees it will. Sometimes time makes it worse."

He laughed, and it sounded like a substitute for crying. "Any other woman would be telling me what I want to hear."

"I'm not sure I have anything to say you'd want to hear."

"Don't be too sure," Cruz said in a low, rough voice she could almost feel like a touch against her skin.

A loud burst of applause and cheering abruptly intruded into their sanctuary, turning them both toward the door. Josh and Eliana must be getting ready to leave and Aria realized she'd been away much longer than she intended.

"I should go," she said. "I was Eliana's maid of honor and they'll be wondering where I am." Cruz stood up with her and she slid off his jacket, handing it back to him.

Suddenly she felt awkward, uncertain of what to say to him when before the words had come easily. But it was one thing to say things here alone, in the bare light, another to walk back into a crowded room and realize she'd been saying those things to a stranger.

"Would you like a few minutes' head start?" he asked, all cool politeness as if he'd put on the facade of control and strength along with his jacket.

"It's not necessary," she said, matching his tone. "I doubt anyone will notice us."

Cruz gestured her out the door ahead of him, but before she stepped out in the hallway his hand on her arm stopped her. "Thanks for listening," he said softly and before she could guess his intention, bent and kissed her.

It started as a light brush of his mouth against hers. But the moment he touched her, she was back in the illusion of being alone in the world with him and the boundaries that should have been between them were gone.

From one heartbeat to the next, his hand slid into the fall of hair at her nape and hers found its way to his shoulder, her fingers curling into the hard muscle when he deepened his kiss from a casual gesture to a sensual caress. If he hadn't backed away first, slowly releasing her as if he wanted to keep his hands on her as long as possible, she might have convinced herself she *was* that kind of woman and forget any qualms.

"Is that my reward?" she managed to ask, the catch in her voice betraying her attempt to sound unaffected.

Cruz smiled a little. "No, I just wanted to. It seems to be my night for doing things without a plan."

Quickly turning, he strode off in the direction of the festivities, leaving Aria standing there, alone again. "You're welcome," she whispered.

But she wasn't sure if it was in response to his thanks or an invitation.

Chapter Two

As many hotel and motel rooms, from bottom-of-the-barrel to
five-star, as he'd been in over the course of his wanderings with
his mother and his career as an engineer, Cruz decided he liked
this one least.

It was the nicest hotel in Luna Hermosa, a centuries' old reno-
vated adobe monastery full of charm and history, but he'd scarcely
been able to sleep a wink in it since he'd arrived. It wasn't the
fault of the hotel management. They'd gone overboard—at his
brothers' request he suspected—to treat him like visiting royalty.

The problem was him.

He was used to juggling dozens of balls in the air, but some
of the new ones recently tossed his way were prickly. He'd been
prepared for an uneasy, even angry, reunion with his family. The
last thing he'd expected on arriving in Luna Hermosa was to have
a strangely unsettling encounter with a woman. Since the night
of the wedding reception Aria Charez had haunted his disturbed
dreams—and had been the subject of some new daydreams as
well. His body seemed intent on reliving every sensory memory

of her: the soft tangle of dark curls wound through his fingers; the curve of her body hugged by the smooth silk of her dress; the warm spicy musk of her perfume that clung to his coat hours after he'd left her; the feel of her generous mouth yielding to his…

Cruz ruthlessly shoved aside the remembrances. This morning in particular, he didn't need the extra distraction. He was meeting with his brothers in a couple of hours, to talk about the ranch and Garrett, and he needed a clear head. The emotions connected with that meeting would be enough without stirring disruptive thoughts of a woman he'd likely never see again into the mix.

Closing the heavy carved pine door to his room, he headed downstairs to an enclosed patio where breakfast was being served. The rich smell of coffee, with a hint of cinnamon and chocolate, wafted to his nose. It was a Mexican blend he'd already come to look forward to each morning and even the expectation of one familiar thing these past days had helped calm his restless mood.

"*Buenos días,* Señor Déclan," a stout little waitress in a neat black dress, her graying hair pulled back in a sleek knot, greeted him, coffeepot in hand. "Would you like to sit near the back window again?"

"Yes, please, if you don't mind."

He followed her to *his* table at the back of the room. He liked the view of the mountains in the distance, saffron sun just peaking over their jagged azure tips.

"What would you like today?" she asked, pouring his coffee.

"Those eggs I had yesterday were great, on the flour tortilla with that sauce on top."

A broad smile lit up her face. "You like our huevos rancheros? With green chili sauce? And beans on the side?"

"Sure, why not?"

She smiled proudly, as though the recipe were her own, then cocked her head to one side, studying him. "If you don't mind my saying, you look like your brothers, especially Sawyer."

Cruz nearly choked on his coffee. "Did someone go around town with a megaphone? How did you know they're my brothers?"

The woman laughed. "No, no one told me, although anyone who knows Sawyer and Cort would see the resemblance. I knew who you were because of your last name. I used to clean house for several families here in town. When the Morentes or one of the other families would have big parties, they sometimes hired me for the night or the next day to help out. I met your mother when she worked for Jed Garrett."

"So you know that whole story," he said, not trying to disguise his bitterness.

She nodded. "I felt so sorry for your mother…and I always wondered what became of her. And of you."

"My mother is fine. She's an amazing woman who's managed to survive Garrett and the rest of what life has thrown at her."

"I am glad to hear that. She was so young, so hurt, when she left." The woman paused, looking past Cruz out the back window, then brightened a bit. "Did she come here with you? I would love to see her again."

"Of course not." It came out a little too harshly—more so because of his guilty conscience. He hadn't told his mother why he was making the trip to New Mexico. She'd assumed it was business and he had let her believe it since the alternative would have been a confrontation and accusations he wasn't ready for.

Cruz tried to soften his tone for the benefit of the waitress, who was looking at him curiously. "She won't ever come back here. She lives in Phoenix now. The only problem is she's alone too much. My business is there, but with my work I travel a lot, so I'm not often home."

"I'm sure she understands."

"She does, but without any other family, the days can get long for her."

"Well, if you decide to move here, I hope she will think about coming back. She would have many friends, me included."

Cruz didn't want to offend the woman, but it was all he could do not to flatly state his mother would rather move to hell than come back to Luna Hermosa. The pain of the rejection and humiliation Jed Garrett heaped on her still haunted her so much she could scarcely mention the place. And there was even less a chance he would ever call it home. "I'll tell her I met you," he offered.

"*Gracías*. Tell her Estella Lopez still remembers her." She smiled, pleased with his promise. "Be right back with your breakfast."

"Josh obviously won't be here." Sawyer closed the doors to the library/study against the squeals of his two sons coming from somewhere else in the large hacienda. Rafe, Cort and Cruz had made themselves comfortable on the big leather couch and chairs that encircled a Mexican carved coffee table. "But he's already said he'll go along with whatever we come up with."

They hadn't even started the discussion about their family situation and what was to become of Rancho Pintada after Jed died, but already Cruz felt as if he didn't belong here.

"We need to catch you up on Jed's master plan," Rafe said, his words sharp-edged with sarcasm.

"Thanks for trying to include me and I suppose I should know. But I feel strange being a part of this at all."

Cort smiled. "We figured you would, but you have a stake in this. You've got as much a right to be here as any of us. Besides, we wanted to get to know you better."

Uncomfortable with his brother's sincerity, Cruz found he couldn't echo the feeling yet. Maybe he never would. "I appreciate that," was the best he could come up with.

"Cort said he told you it was complicated, but for now, I'll try and give you the short version, at least where the ranch is concerned," Sawyer began. "Jed's been sick for a while and for whatever reasons, he got it into his head he wanted to split the ranch five ways between us. We don't know how you feel about it, but of the four of us, Rafe and Josh are the ranchers. The last thing Cort and I want to do is raise cattle or bison. The only investment we have in the place is that Jed's our father."

"Sawyer and I plan to sell our shares to Rafe and Josh after Jed's gone and can't give us any grief about it," Cort continued. "Actually—" he glanced at Rafe, smiling a little "—we'd be just as happy to hand them over outright, but somebody's too stubborn to accept it."

"Don't start with that again," Rafe said gruffly. "You know you'll lose."

"I keep hoping I can wear you down." Cort laughed at Rafe's muttered, "Not going to happen," then turned back to Cruz. "We wanted to clear it with you before we put anything into writing."

Cruz sat silent a moment, considering. "Are you asking if I want to sell my share, too?"

"No," Rafe said. "It's one-fifth your ranch. You can do what you want with it. We just want to make sure you don't mind if Cort and Sawyer sell to Josh and me."

Disbelief pricked at Cruz. He could hardly believe four strangers, brothers or not, were treating him as an equal partner in all of this. They didn't have to include him, much less give him a voice with equal weight to theirs. "Whatever you want to do is fine by me. Don't take this wrong, but I don't see that my opinion matters one way or the other. It's all—" He stopped, shook his head. "It doesn't seem quite real to me, if that makes any sense."

Sawyer nodded. "Why don't you take time to think it over? We don't have to resolve this today. Take a few weeks and get a feel for the place."

"I don't need a few weeks to know I have no intention of ever living there, if that's what you're thinking."

Rafe looked at him intently. "I can see why you'd say that, after what Garrett put your mother through. He pulled a similar stunt on my mother. It was a little more complicated, though. She was married to the man I thought was my father at the time."

With all the twists and turns in this story, Cruz was beginning to feel he needed to start taking notes to keep it all straight. "I'm sorry," he said, knowing how inadequate it sounded.

"Yeah, well, nothing I can do to change it. And if Garrett hadn't fathered me I would have grown up on the reservation instead of the ranch and I'd have never met Jule."

"Your wife, right?"

Rafe smiled proudly. "Wife and the love of my life."

Sawyer laughed aloud. "Did you get that on tape, Cort?"

"Damn, we forgot the recorder again," Cort said with a laugh.

"It was your day to remember," Sawyer said. "Nobody's ever

gonna believe he says things like that if we don't have the evidence." For Cruz's benefit, he added, "Two years ago, before Jule came back to town, we were convinced Rafe had never learned how to smile. So now when he goes all mushy on us we have to give him trouble about it."

Cruz leaned back into the couch, beginning to feel more relaxed with his new brothers. At the same time, their easy camaraderie touched off a feeling he couldn't quite name—a longing, a need he didn't recognize ever having before now. What would it have been like to grow up with them? To have the same deep roots in this place? The experience was so far out of the scope of his youth as a loner, always the new kid in town, he couldn't even draw a mental picture.

"Excuse me." Sawyer's wife, Maya, looked into the room. "Aria dropped off the plans for the children's ranch earlier today. You were going to look them over while you're all here, weren't you?"

As she stepped into the room, Cruz took his first real look at Maya. The wedding had been such a flurry of new people, he hadn't taken time to sort one face from the next. Maya was petite, pretty, with a gorgeous head of the most unusual shade of reddish-gold hair he'd ever seen. Cruz thought his brother a lucky guy. She came in to sit on the edge of Sawyer's chair, barefoot, in faded jeans and a hippie peasant blouse that shaped the prominent curve of her belly. Sawyer had told him they were expecting their third child, a daughter this time, and from the look of it, it was going to be sooner than later. Maya seemed completely at ease with herself and her husband's brothers, and Cruz liked her lack of pretense. From what he'd heard and seen, Cort and Sawyer's grandparents were wealthy and the two of them had inherited a good portion of the family fortune. But the Morente money obviously hadn't bought this woman's down-to-earth soul.

Tossing the plans on the table, Maya turned to Cruz. "If I'd known you'd be here, I would have asked Aria to stay. This is really her project. And I'm sure you'd like her."

"Ignore her," Sawyer said as he pulled his wife close.

"She's getting as bad as her mother is about trying to play matchmaker."

Maya looked up at her husband, an impish grin on her lips. "Well, my mother was right about us, wasn't she?"

"And Laurel and me," Cort added, fueling the fire.

Rafe grimaced. "The whole town was right about Jule and me. It just took me a while to figure it out."

Everyone but Cruz laughed. He knew they thought it was because he didn't know their histories. They had no way of knowing it was the mention of Aria's name that replaced his tentative feelings of ease with an edgy tension. The strange closeness to her he'd felt that night lingered like an illness he couldn't shake.

He stared blankly as his brothers unrolled the architectural plans for something on the coffee table, unaware Maya had her eyes on him.

Part of him wanted to see Aria again to discover if their odd intimacy was real or simply a result of emotions that had pushed too close to the surface for comfort. The other, more familiar, rational side of him was warning him to stay away from a woman who had the potential to screw up his world more than it already was.

"Aria's the architect. She's had this idea for years to build a ranch for children with special needs," Maya said, her words jolting Cruz from his reverie.

He blinked. "Sounds—interesting."

Maya smiled. "We understand you're an engineer."

Oh, no, don't go there. If this was heading where he thought it was, he was determined to derail it here and now. "Yes, but most of my work is large projects—sports stadiums, amphitheaters, libraries, art museums. And I travel a lot. My company has done projects in Europe, Hong Kong, Canada and Australia, and we've recently landed a job in Japan."

"Pretty cool gig you got there," Sawyer said.

"I'm sure this project wouldn't be any challenge at all then," Maya said, ignoring her husband's interjection. "You wouldn't mind looking over the plans, would you? Aria's been struggling a bit with a few of the details and I'm sure she'd appreciate your opinion."

Cruz doubted it and from the looks his brothers exchanged, he got the impression they shared his skepticism.

None of them appeared ready to jump in and rescue him from having to flat-out refuse Maya, though. Already he was learning a couple of valuable things about his new family. First, his brothers stuck together. And second, whatever their wives wanted, evidently they got. Not this time, though. He wasn't about to get suckered into working on someone else's project. Especially not Aria Charez's. And, especially not in this town. He'd be back in Phoenix long before they ever broke dirt on their ranch.

"I'm sorry, but I couldn't do that," he said firmly. "I don't think the architect would appreciate me interfering. I know I wouldn't."

"You don't know Aria. She wants more than anyone to get this project moving. It wouldn't take much of your time and it's so important to the community. We don't have anything like this for these children. This summer, Josh helped them set up a temporary site out at Rancho Pintada and I wish you could have seen the changes in those kids. It was amazing."

Cruz held back a wince. Damn, the woman was good at making him feel like a jerk for not offering a couple of hours of his expertise. Poor Sawyer didn't have a prayer saying no to this woman. He glanced at his brothers, vainly hoping for some help. Rafe shrugged and Sawyer made a helpless gesture.

It was Cort who finally said, "We're not asking for you to do anything, really. Since you're the expert though, we just thought we'd ask you for your comments about the design."

"This whole thing is surviving on donations," Rafe added. "We take free advice—free anything—wherever we can wring it out of someone."

Sawyer looked pointedly at Maya. "Or more accurately, guilt it out of anyone."

She smiled innocently at him before fixing that smile back on Cruz. "If you want me to call Aria, I'm sure she'd come back over."

That he didn't want. He was too unresolved about his feelings and he didn't want his brothers and Maya looking on while he tried to pretend they'd never met. Maya would see through that in ten seconds.

"No, that won't be necessary," he said coolly. "I'll take a look at the plans, but I'm not sure how much help I can be."

"Thanks. We really appreciate it." Sawyer spread the plans out on the table and gave him a quick rundown on what Aria had sketched out.

Cruz listened with increasing interest, and with a growing admiration for Aria's skill in architectural design. Her drawings were practically flawless. Her perspective, though far different from his, was unique and showed a distinct talent. So, not only was she gorgeous, she was smart, too. It would have been so much easier if he could have dismissed the entire plan as a mess and excuse himself from going any further with this than he already had.

"So, any thoughts?" Cruz found Cort was watching him intently when Sawyer finished.

"Well, off the top of my head, I have to say first that your architect knows her stuff."

"She's won several awards around New Mexico for her green designs," Maya said.

"I can believe that."

Rafe leaned back a little, searching Cruz's face. "But?"

Cruz shrugged. "It's a different style than mine, that's all. As I told you, the projects I've worked on are nothing like this. I think the green building trend is admirable, but some of the engineering aspects just aren't practical."

"That's interesting," Sawyer said. "Maybe you should talk to Aria. We don't want to build something that won't work."

Cruz put up his hands in a gesture of backing off. "Like I said, I don't want to step on any toes here. She knows what she's doing. It's just some of the systems she's set up here aren't the ones I would use."

Cort began to roll up the plans. "Aria might appreciate your insights."

"Or not," Cruz said flatly. "Besides, I'm not going to be here long enough to get involved in this."

"I'm sorry to hear that," Maya said. "We hope you'll change your mind, don't we?" she asked, glancing from brother to brother, her eyes asking for support.

"We hope you'll stick around long enough to let us show you none of us took after our father," Rafe muttered.

Everyone laughed and Cruz relaxed a little, glad the topic had shifted away from Aria. "I'll just take it a day at a time for now, how about that?"

Sawyer looked satisfied. "Fair enough. We can't ask for more than that."

Cruz outwardly smiled, but inside his uneasiness grew. He was starting to think they had a lot more in mind for him than they'd revealed. If those plans included persuading him to refocus his life around a new family and a ranch he couldn't have cared less about, they were doomed to disappointment.

He knew where he was going and although his three years of overseas combat might have thrown him off course for a while, eventually, he'd get back on track. And that track didn't include a permanent stop in Luna Hermosa.

Aria wondered if she'd ever been more uncomfortable than she was at this moment.

Standing in Cort and Laurel's living room, she tried to keep any expression off her face as Laurel introduced her to the one man she hadn't expected to see again.

"I'm glad you both were able to make it this afternoon." Laurel motioned to Aria. "Cruz, this is our architect, Aria Charez. Aria, this is Cort's brother, Cruz Déclan."

Simultaneously, they answered, "We've met."

Laurel looked back and forth between them, confused. "I didn't realize—"

"We met at Josh and Eliana's wedding the other night," Aria explained. She deliberately kept it short and without details and hoped Laurel wouldn't press for any other explanation.

"Ah, I see." Laurel's expression said she didn't and Aria knew her friend would have all kinds of questions later. But, blessedly, for now, Laurel refrained from asking any of them in front of Cruz. Instead, she led them into the kitchen. "Help yourselves to coffee, tea, cookies," she said as she set out a spread of afternoon goodies. Aria and Cruz took seats as far as possible from each other at the large kitchen table.

"Thank you. You didn't have to go to this trouble. We won't be long," Aria said, with a sideways glance at Cruz.

Cruz's expression was unreadable. "She's right. I've got a full schedule today, but Cort, Rafe and Sawyer wanted me to take a look at these plans."

"I'm afraid it's going to be a bit of a madhouse here because Cort's in Albuquerque and I'm holding down the fort. Cort started law school in September," she added for Cruz's benefit. "He's there three days a week. Days like these, I really miss having him around. Sophie and Angela are both wound up this afternoon."

"Your daughters?" Cruz asked.

"Not yet, we're in the process of adopting them both. It's been an adjustment, though. Our son, Tommy, always said he wanted siblings, but the reality of having two little girls running around the house isn't what he expected. But he's getting used to the idea."

"How is Tommy?" Aria asked as she reluctantly unrolled the latest version of her ranch plans, only half listening to Laurel's answer. How had this happened, she and Cruz Déclan thrown together by his family and her friends? She was definitely less than delighted about him suddenly being a part of the project. Who was he anyhow? He didn't know what she had in mind for the ranch or how long she'd dreamed and worked and planned to create this design.

And that was only part of the problem. Almost as disconcerting was her memory of their first meeting. It had been unsettling to say the least and after that night she certainly never expected to have to deal with him again. The fact that they met at a time when she was vulnerable enough to open up to a total stranger and spill out her insecurities was enough to make her flush. She didn't dare look directly at him now or that's exactly what would happen and he'd see how exposed she still felt.

What had come over her that night? Typically extremely wary about revealing too much of herself to anyone, especially a stranger, and after having sworn off men—again—altogether after her last disastrous breakup, she couldn't explain what had possessed her to treat Cruz Déclan like a confidant. And to top it off, she'd let him kiss her. What was wrong with her?

Distracted by her own thoughts, she wrestled with the stack of curled-up papers she was trying to smooth out onto the table.

"Need some help?" Cruz's deep, smooth voice sounded too close to her ear. He'd stood and moved next to her to place his hands on the ends of the papers so she could smooth them flat.

"Thanks." His scent teased her, a light, masculine cologne that refreshed the memory of the scent that had lingered on her dress the night of the reception. Her fingers trembled as his brushed over hers. If he saw, he didn't show it.

"No problem, it looks like these plans have a mind of their own."

A scream and a wail came from down the hallway and Laurel's head jerked around. "Now it starts. Their cartoon is over and they're bored, so guess what? Time to fight. Excuse me, please, just go on without me." With that she gulped her coffee, grabbed a couple of cookies and made a dash toward the escalating noise.

Left alone with Cruz, Aria instinctively moved away a little. For the first time that day, he smiled, a slight twist of his mouth. "Afraid I'll bite?"

"Of course not. I'm just giving us room to work."

"Right." His raised brow mocked her attempt at confident casualness. "Then let's get at it."

Annoying man. He made her feel as if he could look straight through her. He'd done that to her the first time they'd met and he was doing it again. Was it a deliberate power ploy on his part? Or was he as perceptive as his dark eyes seemed to reveal?

Cruz began to go over the plans, contributing little in the way of his own opinions, mostly asking questions. She answered, her thoughts only superficially on his words.

Part of her drifted back to the night of the wedding when she'd wondered the same things about him. Was it simply her mood then or was it something else that made it so easy to feel an instant bond with him? There was no denying he was dangerously hot, handsome and the kind of guy who always wound up breaking her heart.

But there appeared to be a lot more to him than good looks that separated him from other men she'd gone out with. Traces of a hard and challenging life were written in his eyes. The results of it were there, too: strength, resolve, past pain, pride and sincerity.

Inwardly she held back a sigh. All those qualities were what she'd dreamed of finding in a man, but she had practically given up. The good-looking guys she'd fallen for in the past turned out to be little more than that—often a lot less.

"So," he was asking, "you're building this on what used to be a sheep farm?"

Aria forced herself to concentrate. "Yes, Josh bought the property from the Ramos family. It definitely presents some architectural challenges. Particularly since I've designed a green structure—straw bale construction, grey water system, wind energy and so on."

"I see that," Cruz said, doubt in his tone.

"Do I hear a 'but'?"

"One or two, maybe."

"I know this isn't anywhere near what you're used to working on. I'm also guessing that you got roped into this by your brothers."

"Yes. And yes." He paused, the corner of his mouth lifting in a half smile. "But now that I've had a chance to look closely at your ideas, I'll admit, I'm intrigued."

She crossed her arms over her chest. "You didn't say impressed."

"That, too, although I wouldn't build it this way."

Now he was starting to irritate her. "No one is asking you to build it. This is my project. You're under no obligation to be involved."

Cruz held up his hands in a placating gesture. "I'm not criticizing. I have some differing views, that's all. I'm just offering an opinion or two, if you'd like the help. At least for the short time I'm here trying to figure out what this family of mine is all about. This could be a nice little diversion."

An inquisitive lift of his brow made her wonder if he meant her or the ranch project. Conflicting emotions, attraction versus possessiveness about her pet project, flashed through her. They didn't go unnoticed.

"I meant this project is something completely different for me than for you, obviously," Cruz explained.

"You're right, it's not a 'nice little diversion' to me. And if you're going to put your two cents in on it, then at least take it seriously."

"I never said I didn't," he came back, stiffly. "I'm sure this will be an educational opportunity, a chance to learn about building methods I'd never be able to use. The projects I work on are too large to incorporate the extent of green building you're able to do here."

"I wouldn't want to bore you," Aria muttered. His attitude was getting on her nerves. He was probably the kind of guy who had a woman in every port, so to speak. Exactly the kind of man she didn't need to be involved with, on any level.

Cruz was beginning to look frustrated. "Bored is the last thing I expect to be. May I take a copy of these back to the hotel? I'd like to take a closer look at them."

"Sure. You can have this one." She began rolling up the sheets with her drawings on them.

"I'll jot down a few comments and questions then maybe we can get together again soon to talk."

"As long as you realize I'm only listening to your comments out of courtesy for your brothers."

She saw a line in his jaw tighten, but his smile was all smoothness and ease. "Of course. It's your baby."

"Good." Aria pasted on a smile. "Then we understand each other."

But even as the words left her lips, she knew it was a lie.

Chapter Three

"This isn't going to work."

Aria pushed both hands into her hair, briefly pressing her palms against her temples. She never should have agreed to this. "Are you just now figuring that out?"

Cruz shot her an irritated look. "I meant this." He jabbed a finger at a section of the drawings they were looking at.

"What's wrong now?"

They'd been at it for over an hour and most of that time they'd spent arguing. It had been clear from the start they had completely opposite ideas of what the children's ranch should ultimately look like: she on the side of environmentally friendly and practical; he lobbying for innovative and eye-catching. Consequently, they hadn't made much progress.

It didn't help that when Cruz had called her a couple days after their meeting at Cort and Laurel's to set up a time to go over the plans together, she'd impulsively asked him to meet her at her new house. She'd gotten tired of living and working part-time in Taos, part-time at her dad's, and decided to move home and office to a house she'd found in Luna Hermosa. The move was taking longer than she'd planned and the place was a mess of boxes, bags and piles.

Cruz, obviously one of those annoyingly organized people who categorized and filed everything, had eyed the chaos with a raised brow that questioned her ability to find the drawings for the ranch, or anything else for that matter. When, after several minutes of scrabbling around her office, she produced them from underneath a stack of file folders, he'd wasted no time in throwing out various reasons why she needed to make changes.

Just like now.

"For starters, this part you're calling classrooms isn't very attractive," he said. "You haven't given much thought to how it's going to fit in with the landscape."

"I've only had access to the site for a couple of weeks," she retorted. "And I'm not trying to build a piece of art. I want this to be functional and energy-saving."

"Does it have to look like a barracks to do that?"

"I wasn't aware it looked like a barracks, as you so charmingly put it."

"Look—" he leaned forward in his chair "—I know this is your pet project and you've put a lot of thought into designing it, but with a few changes this could really be something special. For example, if you alter this a bit…" Pointing to another section of her drawings, he grabbed a pencil and a piece of paper and made a quick sketch to illustrate his idea.

Aria moved closer to get a better view, impressed despite herself at his quick grasp of her overall concept and how he could translate his own visions into crisp, clear working plans. She just couldn't quite quell her resentment at his interference in a project she'd dreamed of her entire career, especially when he had no intention of sticking around to see it completed.

But when she took a closer look at his suggestion, she reluctantly admitted it might be an improvement. "That could work," she said grudgingly. "But I'm not sacrificing the solar panels just because you want it to be prettier."

"I'm not asking you to sacrifice anything," Cruz said. "You asked my opinion—"

"*I* didn't ask your opinion."

"And you don't want it, either."

"I didn't say that."

"You didn't have to."

Aria sighed. This wasn't getting them anywhere. And it wasn't helping move the project forward any quicker, which had been the plan from the start. "Okay, I'll admit I can be stubborn sometimes—"

"Sometimes?" Cruz sat back in his chair, his mouth a twist of disbelief.

"—when it comes to anyone else messing with this," she finished as if he hadn't interrupted. "But you aren't exactly a poster boy for compromise."

"Not one of my favorite strategies," he said. "But if we're going to come up with something workable, maybe we both need to try it. I like a lot of what you've come up with. I just see some problems."

"Well, some of your ideas don't suck."

That drew a half smile from him. "I think that has to be the worst compliment I've ever gotten."

The tension crackling between them eased and Aria found herself smiling back. "Sorry, I'll try and do better next time." Stretching to ease the stiffness in her lower back, she said, "I don't know about you, but I could use a break. Why don't we give it up for the day? If you're not doing anything tomorrow, we can drive out to the site and you can get a better idea of the landscape."

He looked as if he wanted to argue but instead nodded curtly. "Tomorrow's fine. I'll take these back with me and look over them this evening to see if I can come up with any *compromises*."

As he pushed away from the drafting table and started gathering up papers, Aria asked, "You're still at the hotel?" His "yes" was more sound than actual word, his focus on neatly stacking the papers in the case he'd brought. "I thought you might be staying with one of your brothers or your—with Jed."

"They offered," Cruz said. "Or more accurately, Garrett

insisted. But I don't intend to give him any ideas I'm interested in that ranch."

"Your brothers—"

"Have got their own families and lives to deal with. I'm better off where I am for now."

The idea of him being alone in an impersonal hotel room when he was already coping with being the outsider, in town and among his own family, bothered her. Fighting the warning sense she was about to get herself more involved with him than she needed to be, she stood up and handed him a folder, drawing his eyes back to hers. "If you don't have other plans, I was going to order takeout. You're welcome to stay and share. If you don't mind Chinese, that is." When he looked a little taken aback, she quickly added, "I'm sorry I can't offer you home cooking, but I seem to have misplaced my entire kitchen somewhere in this mess." She gave a rueful glance around the clutter of the office. "And it's going to require more energy than I've got right now to get myself ready to go out."

Cruz seemed to consider either her offer or her appearance; it was hard to tell which from the way he studied her. The intent way he had of looking at her made her feel self-conscious and aware that in her faded jeans and woolly green sweater, with her hair haphazardly pulled back, she probably fit right in with the rest of the décor, or lack thereof.

"All right," he said finally. She blinked and he laughed. "Now there's a first. I managed to catch you without a comeback."

She flushed, annoyed at herself for letting him surprise her. "I just didn't figure you for the stay-at-home type."

"I'm not. But not for the reasons you think. A social life hasn't been high on my agenda the last couple of years."

Aria could have kicked herself for forgetting where he'd been. "I'm sorry. I didn't think."

"It's okay," Cruz shrugged it off. "I didn't have much of a social life before my tour of duty in Iraq."

"Are all the women around you blind idiots?" she said, echoing back at him his words from the wedding reception.

He smiled, a slow, suggestive curve of his mouth that, for the first time, struck her as genuine, without layers of bitterness or tension. "It's not been one of my priorities."

She left that alone until she'd ordered dinner for both of them and they were sharing her living room couch, splitting the bottle of wine she'd managed to find while they waited for the food to be delivered. When she'd been rummaging in the kitchen boxes for glasses, Cruz had started a fire and now, mellowed by the warmth and the wine, Aria picked up the conversation from where they'd dropped it earlier.

"So what are your priorities?"

"Survival's taken precedence for the last three years. I guess before, too, but in a different way."

"I've never thought of engineering as dangerous. Just where are these buildings of yours?"

"Yours is the most dangerous project I've worked on. I'm pretty sure you wanted to throw something at me earlier."

"Maybe." Giving herself an excuse to look away, she took a sip of her wine. "We seem to rub each other the wrong way."

"Do we?" His low, rough-edged voice suggested answers that had nothing to do with them being opposites in their approach to work.

Throw something at him. See what that wine tastes like on his mouth. Her mind and body kept fighting over which way to go. The answer she settled on didn't satisfy either side. "Sometimes."

Cruz finished the last of his wine in one drink. "You don't sound too sure of that."

"I'm not."

He gave a huff of humorless laughter. "Me, either."

They were getting too close to admitting things that could only get her into trouble. Trying to pretend they hadn't gotten sidetracked into dangerous areas, she said briskly, "You were telling me about your priorities."

"Was I?" he asked with a slight smile. "Are we swapping histories, or am I the only one who gets to confess?"

"I'll bet yours is more interesting than mine," Aria told him, figuring it was probably the truth.

"I doubt it." Staring at the flames, he seemed to be lost in memories. "You already know about Garrett. My mother left here before I was born. When I was growing up, we had nothing. She moved us around constantly. I went to three different schools for sixth grade alone."

"I know how hard that must have been. Not personally," she amended, since he knew she'd lived most of her life in Luna Hermosa, "but my parents took in a lot of foster children, my dad still does, and most of them had been bounced around for years from place to place. My sister and I were lucky. Things were always chaotic at our house, but we had stability, our parents were always there for us."

"My mom was always there," Cruz remarked sharply, his expression hardening. "She was just a kid herself when she had me and she sacrificed everything to raise me on my own. I didn't make it easy for her, either."

Treading carefully, Aria tried for a teasing note. "So does that mean you were a wild boy like Josh?"

That, at least, relaxed the tight set of his shoulders and he settled back a little farther into his corner of the couch. She liked seeing him like that, the long, lean lines of his body at ease, comfortable again with her—or as comfortable as they could ever be with each other with the undercurrent of awareness running through everything they said and did. "I don't know about Josh, but I was in trouble a lot, fights mostly. Being the new kid most of the time, I always had something to prove."

"You seemed to have turned things around," she said lightly.

"I got lucky," Cruz said shortly. "In high school, I had a teacher who got me interested in engineering. He made me understand I needed a plan if I was going to get anywhere. It also made me realize it was my turn to take care of my mother. So I joined the army to pay for college and when I got out, I started my own company, had a few early successes and built it up from there."

"You make it sound so easy. I doubt it was." He'd managed to overcome the handicaps of his birth and upbringing and make something of himself through sheer determination and talent. It hinted again at layers to him that would take a long time to fully explore and that intrigued her, despite herself. It would be so much easier to dismiss the electric attraction between them if she could write him off as shallow or discover some flaw that would be fatal to anything more than a one-weekend fling. "I'm surprised with everything you have going on that you stayed in the reserves."

"I made a commitment," he said, casually, as if it was only to be expected.

The doorbell interrupted them and Aria, reluctant to leave their conversation, went to retrieve their dinner. Cruz waved off her apology for not having a dining room table and seemed as at ease eating off her coffee table as he would have in an elegant restaurant. The dinner conversation was light and unimportant, him telling her about his business in Phoenix, her giving small details about Luna Hermosa.

"What about you?" he asked, when they'd finished and were working on the last of the wine. "You've heard my life story, tell me yours."

Aria tucked her feet up under her and smiled. "There's not a lot to tell. You know I grew up here and now it looks like I'm back permanently. If I can ever get organized," she added. "I was splitting time between my dad's house and an apartment in Taos, but since the ranch project has finally taken off, I decided I needed to be in Luna Hermosa full-time. Hence, the mess."

"What got you started on this project? Growing up with all those foster kids?"

Aria nodded. "A lot of them were kids with special needs, like Eliana's brother, Sammy. Kids like that should have a place where they can feel accepted and safe. They don't always get that in a regular school. I see kids like Sammy and the rough time they have and I just want to make it better for them." Hearing herself heading toward another of her fund-raising speeches, she winced. "Sorry, I have a bad habit of trying to recruit everyone I meet for my private crusade."

Cruz stretched his arm over the back of the couch, relaxing into almost a slouch in his corner. "There's nothing wrong with that. It's admirable. The way you talk about kids, I'm surprised you didn't follow your parents' example and have a houseful of them yourself."

Suddenly uncomfortable, it was her turn to stare at the fire. He'd managed to find the one topic she'd been trying to avoid for years now. "I've never met anyone that made me want to give up being single." That was true, in a way. "And I don't intend to ever be a single parent." She stopped herself from adding that growing up with a single parent, in her view, wasn't best for a child. Considering how defensive he got talking about his mother, she didn't want to risk getting his back up again. "How about you? Haven't you ever been tempted to have your own family?"

"Apparently I have one now," he remarked wryly. "I've got enough to deal with without adding those kind of complications. Besides, I'd never consider becoming a father unless I knew I could commit to putting my family above everything else. I don't see that happening with work, and all the traveling, and now this mess here." His mouth quirked up at the corner. "I've gotten used to being a gypsy. I doubt I'd be good at settling down in one place and I would never want the kind of life I had growing up for any child of mine."

His last words struck her more than anything else he'd said. She had to stop herself getting in any deeper with him than she already had. She'd done this too many times, believed the first tentative beginnings could grow into something good, only to end up disillusioned, disappointed or dumped.

She'd promised herself it wouldn't happen again. He might be a great package with depth, intelligence and a body to fantasize over, but he had issues on issues, and he was as good as gone. He wasn't the man she needed.

She just wished she could stop thinking of him as the man she wanted.

The house was warm and inviting, a welcome contrast to the sharp, cold grayness outside, but Cruz was trying to come up with a polite way to escape.

He hadn't given it much thought when Aria asked him to take a look at the ranch site with her. He'd assumed they'd be alone, and of anyone in Luna Hermosa, his newfound family included, he preferred her company. She wasn't comfortable to be with—they argued, and when they didn't, they talked about things better left unsaid. She was stubborn and opinionated. But she was also intelligent, honest and empathetic and he felt he could talk to her without wondering if she'd use his vulnerabilities to gain some advantage.

Most unsettling, he wanted to be her lover.

But the problem this afternoon was they weren't alone. Josh and Eliana were back from their Mexican honeymoon and were finishing their move into the house on the ranch property. Cruz and Aria hadn't been there for five minutes before Eliana pulled Aria off to a back room to ask her opinion about renovations, leaving Cruz with Josh.

Any awkwardness in the situation seemed lost on Josh. He invited Cruz into the roomy kitchen for coffee and they spent a few minutes looking over the property survey, Josh showing him the area where the children's ranch was going to be built. That done, the conversation strayed into Josh and Rafe's plans for expanding Rancho Pintada onto Josh's new property, a topic that reminded Cruz he'd been in Luna Hermosa almost two weeks and he hadn't even begun to sort out his family issues. The only thing he had managed to accomplish was getting tangled up with some charity project and too close to a woman who was making his already complicated life more difficult.

"Rafe tells me you might be willin' to sell us your share," Josh said over his shoulder as he got up to refill their coffee mugs. Settling back in his chair, legs stretched out in front of him, he cocked his head to one side, assessing Cruz with a long look. "You sure about that? You don't have to decide right now. Who knows, you might figure out you've got a hidden passion for ranching."

Cruz had to laugh at that. "Not likely. I've never been on a horse in my life and the closest I've been to bison or cattle is dinner. I don't plan on staying around here long enough to learn, either."

"You sound like me. I used to swear the last thing I wanted was to be tied down to this place." Josh smiled to himself, as if the memory amused him. "I spent most of my life tryin' to get to the top of the rodeo circuit. All I wanted was that bull-ridin' championship, and once I got that, I figured there'd be no lookin' back. I was gonna put Luna Hermosa in my rearview mirror for good. I nearly did, too. If you'd told me six months ago I'd be happy settling down and lettin' Rafe work me ten hours a day, I'd have called you *loco*."

"I guess I don't have to ask who changed your mind," Cruz said.

"No, but I'll tell you, Ellie's the last woman I expected to fall for. One day she was just the friend behind the cash register at the tack shop and the next, I was lookin' at her and realizing she was everything I wanted and knowin' I was ready to do anything to get her."

Or give up anything? Cruz wondered. He couldn't envision being willing to sacrifice everything, to change his entire way of living, for one woman. It seemed his brothers, though, had all come to that. They knew how to be part of a family. He had no clue. A small part of him was envious. His brothers had everything he'd wanted when he was a kid and had quickly come to learn he could never have.

Aria and Eliana came back into the room, saving him from having to devise some noncommittal answer to Josh's confidences. Aria frowned a little when their eyes met and Cruz wondered what she saw in his face. He hoped he didn't look as unsettled as he felt.

In the next moment, she turned, smiling to Josh and Eliana. "I hate to rush, but I need to get back to my office soon. I have an appointment with a client at noon. If we're going to take a look at the site, we should get going."

Cruz was more than willing to go along with her. But after saying their goodbyes to Josh and Eliana—Aria promising to come back again when she had more time—he followed her back to her SUV, waiting until they were inside before saying, "You didn't mention you had an appointment. We could have done this some other time."

"I don't. I lied. You looked like you were ready to bolt and I thought I'd give you an excuse to leave." She paused, searching his face for a moment before asking, "Did something happen with Josh?"

"Not really. I'm just not very good at doing the family thing."

"Yet. You'll figure it out, if you decide you want to," she said, pulling onto a narrow dirt path that led away from the house.

"Trust me, your brothers weren't always good at it, either." His skepticism must have shown because, flicking him a glance before fixing her eyes on the road, she smiled. "You wouldn't know it to see them together now, but it's only recently they've been this close. Sawyer and Cort have always been tight, and Cort's tried for years to fix what's broken in his family. But it took Sawyer and Rafe over twenty years and Cort nearly getting himself killed before he and Rafe could be in the same place without a fight. And Josh—well let's just say before he and Eliana decided to fall for each other, I think Josh's idea of family was his horse and whoever was buying the next round."

He didn't doubt she was telling the truth. It seemed so at odds, though, with what he'd witnessed that he had a hard time reconciling the two versions of reality. "I'll have to take your word for it. But thanks for rescuing me and for the pep talk, even if I have my doubts about figuring it all out."

Pulling the truck to a stop, Aria turned to face him. "I suppose that depends on how much you want it."

Cruz cocked an eyebrow at her. "So you think I get everything I want?"

"Probably," she said with a teasing smile. "You look the type."

Wrong. He followed her lead and got out of the SUV, walking a little distance from the vehicle to look at the spread of land in front of them. If he got everything he wanted, he'd have had her in his bed by now, because it had been a long time—if ever— since he'd wanted a woman like this, with a burning, hungry desire that consumed all logic and common sense.

"You're not listening." Her voice pulled him out of his thoughts. Aria was eyeing him with barely concealed impatience, her arms folded over her chest. "If you didn't want to do this, why didn't you say so?"

"Sorry, it's not that. I'm just a little distracted this morning." *By you.*

He didn't want to be. He wanted to categorize the night they'd met and kissed as a moment of impulse, a one-time event born of heightened emotions that would never be repeated. Unfortunately, he couldn't dismiss it so easily.

"Do you want to see my plans and compare them to the survey?" Aria asked, already walking back to the SUV. Fishing around in the backseat, she produced a roll of papers and spread them out over the hood.

Cruz moved next to her, only half listening, as she tucked her hair behind her ear, leaning over to compare points on the drawings and the survey. The simple gesture drew his eyes to the curve of her cheek where a soft dark curl had escaped her touch and brushed her skin. Acting on impulse he shifted a fraction closer—close enough for the warm musky scent of her perfume to become a sensual tease.

He didn't realize she'd stopped talking until he found himself looking her straight in the eye and saw his feelings reflected there—uncertainty, desire, the struggle to deny it.

"I shouldn't," she said so softly he was sure it wasn't meant for him. Shaking her head, breaking their locked gaze, she abruptly began gathering up the papers.

"Aria—"

"No, don't." She held the papers to her chest like a shield. "I mean it's…" Her hand fluttered up in a helpless gesture as she groped for words. "It can't be—anything."

Quickly moving away from him, she jerked open the back door of the SUV, threw the papers in and slammed the door shut, making for the driver's seat. Not thinking—because if he thought about it, he would walk, run away now—he moved faster, putting himself in front of her, stopping her escape.

"It's already something," he said roughly.

"What?"

One word and he couldn't answer. He didn't know.

Instead he reached for her at the same instant she stepped toward him and neither of them tried to pretend this wasn't exactly what they'd both wanted from the start.

Her mouth met his in a surge of heat and it was all gone: complications, family, the fifty good, sensible reasons why this shouldn't happen.

There was only her.

Chapter Four

There was only him. His mouth—hot, demanding, pure seduction. His body—long, lean, muscled, wanting her as much as she wanted him. She matched him in passion, and as their limbs entwined, what she felt sank beneath the surface, penetrating deep into her soul.

But even as she tasted his lips, his mouth, his neck, she wondered how this could be possible, how she could feel so much so soon for someone she barely knew.

It couldn't be real—and it definitely couldn't last. It was only a moment, or two or three, between two vulnerable people. She struggled hard against the rising heat of desire between them, reaching for reason, willpower, something to give her the strength to break away from him and flee this crazy fantasy even if it meant tumbling back into the cold truth. At least there she understood the rules.

He saved her the trouble. With a ragged breath, Cruz drew back, eyes clouded, confused. "What the hell are we doing?" His voice was gravely as she grasped for clarity.

Aria caught her breath and blinked hard as if the motion would bring some new vision of enlightenment. "I—I don't know," she said on a whisper. "I…it just—happened."

"Define *it*."

"Um—" *no, dangerous* "—maybe I'd better not."

"I'd definitely better not." He searched her eyes, her face, gently brushed a lock of hair back behind her ear. "Aria—"

"I hope you aren't going to apologize," she interrupted more sharply than she intended.

Clearing his throat, Cruz rubbed at the back of his neck. "No, if I said I was sorry, it would be a lie. Let's just chalk this up to both of us being in a strange place emotionally right now, okay?"

"Good idea." She feared her smile came off a bit too bright, but he didn't seem to notice as he released her and turned to face the land behind them. Her lips were still imprinted with the sensual memory of his, and once his back was to her, she brushed her index finger over them, as if she could preserve the feeling for a little longer.

But he was already back to business, directing his attention to the barren field sprawled in front of them. "It looks like you've got your work cut out here," he was saying while she was occupied with the view of his jeans molded to his firm backside. "You're going to have to do some serious leveling over there—" he gestured "—and on that stretch at the far side, too."

Prying her eyes away, she managed to say, "Probably," and when he looked at her with a raised brow, hastily added, "Yes, of course. I know that."

"Apparently you don't find the view inspiring."

You have no idea. His determined avoidance of the tension thrumming in the air between them emboldened her to answer, "It depends which view you're talking about."

"I was talking about that one," he said with a quick jerk of his head toward the open field. Then his eyes shifted to appraise her slowly, and suddenly his facade of cool control, never as strong as she imagined, broke.

He made a quick motion and before she knew how or why, they were back in each others' arms again, kisses hotter by each heartbeat, his hands roving her back, down to her waist and below to the small curve at the base of her spine. Her hands learned the shape of his body through the heavy leather of his coat. If only they had chosen a better place than an open field in cold December to indulge illicit desires.

Probing the soft hollows of her mouth with his tongue, tasting, suckling, he drew her kiss deeper into his. She fell willingly, scarcely breathing lest their bond break even for an instant. They wound themselves together in long, plunging kisses and touches that had an edge of urgency, an almost desperate need to have as much, feel as much now, because this might be their first and last chance.

It was that thought, unwelcome as it was, that sobered her, yanked her out of the passionate fog, made her feel the cold all the more keenly. How many decisions had she made in haste, how many times had she chosen to act on her passions and impulses, to trust in what seemed like promising beginnings, only to end up with painful regrets and a bruised heart? So much for her vow to herself that she wouldn't do this again, leap headfirst and blindly into another involvement. It had lasted, what…five minutes with him?

Aria abruptly broke away, wanting to blame Cruz for being so damned…everything, but knowing she had herself to blame, again. "I'm sorry," she said, annoyed at the tremor in her voice. "I can't do this—" *ever, say ever* "—right now."

"Now who's apologizing?" he muttered. Turning away from her a moment, he linked his hands behind his neck, leaning his head back into his tightly laced fingers, pulling in a deep breath.

"I didn't mean it that way," she told him, although she didn't know, exactly, what way she did mean it.

"I know." He swung back around to face her. "It's just that neither of us knows what to do with this. And I'll be honest, it's a complication I don't need at the moment."

She winced. "What I've always wanted to be, a complication."

With a frustrated gesture, Cruz started to retort, stopped, and shook his head. "Neither of us is going to say the right thing right now. And obviously we're not going to get anything more accomplished here." He glanced at his watch, and from his frown, Aria guessed he was irritated at having lost track of time.

"Are you late for something?" she asked.

"Almost. I have a conference call with my partner in Phoenix, in thirty minutes."

"You should have told me."

"I didn't expect to be this long."

"Nor did I," she said stiffly. Afraid of adding anything else, certain it would be something she would regret, she spun around and let herself into her SUV, leaving him to follow.

On the short drive back, Cruz tried everything to quash memories of the moments they'd just shared and ignore the uncomfortable awkwardness. He had to get a grip on this situation, on his rampant desires and conflicted emotions. He'd been honest, if not particularly sensitive, when he'd told her she was a complication he didn't need. What he did need was clarification, answers, closure with Garrett and his brothers. In fact, a discussion of his erstwhile father would probably be the perfect cold shower right now. Besides, anything was better than the uneasy silence between him and Aria.

"What can you tell me about my father?" he abruptly asked.

She glanced from the driver's seat, surprise flashing over her expression, before fixing her eyes again on the road. "Jed? Probably not much more than you've already heard from your brothers. I'm sure they've told you the family history."

Cruz leaned a little forward and idly fiddled with the heat and radio buttons. "An abbreviated version. I feel like there are pieces missing."

"I'm certain there are, and some of them none of you will probably ever know. Jed is a puzzle all on his own, and I'm sure there are things he's done that he'll never tell anyone."

"Or even admit to himself."

She gave him a sideways glance. "If I'm out of line tell me, but are you talking about your mother?"

Tension twisted in his chest, tightening his jaw and the muscles at his temples. He thought back on what Jed had done to his mother, abandoning her when she was a pregnant teenager, so he could chase after the Morente fortune. Cruz hadn't known the details then, growing up. But he remembered wishing countless times he could wring the neck of the stranger who had left his mother broken-hearted, penniless and bitter.

"I'm sorry, I've upset you. I shouldn't have asked."

"No, it's okay," he answered, pushing down his anger to that dark place where he'd kept it contained for so long. "I *was* thinking of my mother. If I told you how many ways, how many times growing up I thought of killing my so-called father, you could have me locked up for life."

Aria gave a huff of humorless laughter. "Believe me, you'd have company. I'm sure Rafe, Sawyer and Cort have all felt the same at one time or another. Rafe and Sawyer in particular. Jed's always treated Rafe like one of the ranch hands, and worse, he physically abused Sawyer until Teresa Morente finally took Sawyer and Cort and left. Cort got the least of it, but only because Sawyer was older and always protected him from Jed."

Cruz had suspected as much about Jed from the bare details his brothers had given him and in some ways, it seemed his father, in refusing to acknowledge him, had done him a favor. At least he'd been spared growing up with a man who drank and then took his frustrations out on his sons. That didn't make it easier to accept, but it did give him a new sense of kinship with his brothers, a fellow feeling that united them against Jed's manipulations now. "Josh seems to have gotten off with the least damage," he finally said.

"Del had a lot to do with that, I think. She's not my favorite person, but I don't think she would have stood for anyone messing with her baby boy. Josh probably suffered most from benign neglect and some heavy guilt trips."

"He seems happy enough now. They all do."

Aria smiled. "It just took them a while. In some cases, a long while. I mean look at Josh and Eliana, they practically grew up together but it took them forever to figure out they belonged with each other. Rafe and Jule were about as bad."

Cruz stared out the window a minute then turned back to look across the SUV at her. "At least they did figure it out."

"I suppose it's a lot more than you can say for most people."

The comment struck a little too close to home and he felt his defenses rise. "Are you insinuating something?"

"Not at all," she said, glancing at him with a slight frown. "It's just human nature to screw things up, isn't it?"

"The verdict is still out on that one as far as I'm concerned, but you can speak for yourself," he teased, and thankfully, she seemed to take it in stride.

"Unfortunately, I've got the track record to prove it," she said. "But, hey, there's always tomorrow to get it right, isn't there?"

He flashed back to the dugout where he'd recently spent way too much time waiting for the next round of enemy fire to be his last. "Not always."

"I'm sorry," she said softly. Pulling the SUV into the closest parking space on the hotel lot, she stopped and shifted to face him. "That was stupid of me. I keep forgetting where you've been for three years."

"It's okay." Cruz forced a small smile. "You haven't had the experience of not knowing whether you'll see the sun rise again. You're still counting on having tomorrow to fix things. You've still got hope."

"Is yours gone?"

He looked at her, then beyond her, then far beyond her, back to the chaos in the streets, the endless, fearful nights, the scenes that still haunted him. "No," he said quietly, "I think it's just temporarily misplaced."

His last encounter with Aria had given Cruz back something else he'd misplaced since he came to Luna Hermosa—his determination to quickly resolve his family issues and get back to Phoenix. And so it was late afternoon two days later that he found himself on the doorstep of Rancho Pintada, assuring himself he was ready for this meeting he'd called with Jed and his brothers, ready to settle things and move on.

A flustered housekeeper, arms laden with Christmas decorations, answered the door and led him into what appeared to be a den, separate from the expansive great room. Jed, settled in an oversized leather recliner, puffing on an expensive cigar, waved him inside.

"Come on in, boy, we're all here but Cort. He had some damned test or something to finish this mornin'. He said to start without him."

Sawyer stood to shake his hand. "This meeting is long overdue, isn't it?"

"That's what I thought," Cruz said. "I'm hoping this isn't a big mistake."

Rafe shifted into a corner of the leather sofa to make room for Cruz. "Ought to be entertaining, anyway. These little family meetings always are." He and Sawyer exchanged a look and Cruz had the impression they'd done this before and that *entertaining* wasn't exactly the right adjective.

From across the room where he was leaning against the frame of the oversized picture windows, Josh laughed. "That's not what you usually call 'em," he teased Rafe, grinning at the scowl Jed threw his way. He glanced outside, at the low overhang of gray clouds. "Look, it's startin' to snow. We oughta be havin' a white Christmas."

The housekeeper, who'd been patiently waiting beside a coffee table laden with drinks and snacks, cleared her throat to get Cruz's attention. "Can I get you something?"

He turned to the older woman, who looked eager to get on with her decorating. "No, thanks, I can help myself."

With a nod, she turned and scurried out of the room, closing a set of heavy pine pocket doors behind her.

"It's good you made up your mind to settle this," Jed told Cruz between puffs. "Shows you got some of my get up and go in you."

Cruz narrowly refrained from telling Jed that having any part of him in his blood was a curse not a blessing. Jed looked tired, pale and drawn; his illness was obviously taking its toll, and though Cruz held no softer feelings for the man, it wasn't in him to be deliberately callous. "I asked everyone here because I'm going back to Phoenix shortly and I want to get some things straightened out before I do."

A loud noise came from the doorway, and everyone turned to see Cort stride in, his hair and down jacket dusted with snow. "Sorry I'm late. Traffic out of Albuquerque was miserable."

Tossing his jacket onto the back of a chair, he grabbed a handful of cookies and a cup of coffee and took a seat next to Sawyer. "So, did I miss anything?"

Sawyer snagged one of the cookies. "Not yet."

"I was just saying that I have to get back to Phoenix," Cruz repeated. "But before I go I need to wrap things up here."

"Fair enough," Cort said.

Cruz felt a little uncomfortable with all eyes on him, his brothers' curious and questioning, Jed's suspicious. He immediately shoved the unfamiliar feeling aside, irritated with himself. It wasn't as if he were unaccustomed to being the focus of attention; he held command positions in his business and throughout his military service, and was used to taking the lead and accomplishing what he set out to do.

Nothing before though, had prepared him for the emotions tangled up with this particular business. While he wanted it over and done with so he could get back to his life, at the same time, he was plagued by a strange reluctance to dismiss all ties to his newfound family. More importantly, he couldn't shake his preoccupation with Aria. His thoughts about her bordered on obsession and he didn't like it. He needed to get her out of his head, out of his life, so he could pick up where he'd left off three years ago. His firm needed him, his mother needed him and he needed the straightforward simplicity of a work routine with no personal complications.

Armed with that resolve, he turned to face Jed. "I know you want to divide the ranch between the five of us. I can't claim to understand your reasons, but I'm declining my share."

Jed didn't answer for a moment, reaching over to the side table to tip his cigar into an his ashtray. "I suppose this has to do with your mama."

"It's not your business," Rafe interjected harshly. "She stopped being your business when you turned your back on her."

Cruz gave his brother an appreciative glance for coming to his defense. "My mother doesn't know I'm here. It's better it stays that way."

"You're probably right about that," Jed said. "Maria always

did have a helluva temper. And the woman could hold a grudge longer than anyone. Still does, I'd bet, against me anyway."

"I don't think anyone could blame her," Sawyer said.

Jed ignored him and eyed Cruz hard. "Maybe not. But she didn't do you any favors, draggin' you all over the place and keepin' your brothers a secret. Fact you haven't told her about this little trip of yours tells me she can't lay the past to rest, even now."

Cruz's impulse was to jump to his mother's defense. A small part of him, though, recognized the truth in Jed's bluntness, because although he empathized with his mother, supported her, he couldn't deny that he resented being lied to and kept in the dark about his father and brothers all those years.

"I did what I had to do at the time," Jed said into his silence. "I'm makin' no apologies to anyone for those choices back then. But that was then and this is now. And now, I'm doin' the best I know how to do right by all of you."

"Maybe you are," Cruz said. "But, frankly, for me it's too late. I have a life elsewhere. I don't want or need a piece of this ranch."

"How about a family?" Cort asked quietly.

The question struck Cruz hard. His brothers were the one factor in all of this that made it difficult, if not impossible, to simply hand over his share of the ranch and walk away, never looking back.

"Like it or not, you can't change who you are," Rafe said. "If anyone knows that, it's me."

"I don't—" Cruz stopped, trying to come up with something that made sense, that pulled all the pieces together and made it easy to understand. "I can't stay here. I'll keep in touch, but this isn't where I belong."

Sawyer eyed him critically. "Are you so sure about that?" He paused, studying his new brother. "Or is there another reason you're so hell-bent on getting out of town?"

"You mean it's gotta be a woman?" Josh said with a laugh. He flipped a knowing look at Cruz. "Come to think of it, you have been spendin' a lot of time with Aria."

Cruz felt as though he were suddenly on the witness stand for a crime he hadn't yet committed, but, guilty or not, wished he had. "It's got nothing to do with her," he lied, getting skeptical looks in return that had him resisting the urge to squirm. "I've got to get back to my business. My partner's been running things for over three years now. If I don't make an appearance soon, I might not have a company to go back to."

"We can respect that," Rafe said. "Can't we?" He shot a meaningful look to each of his brothers.

"Sure," Sawyer answered, "but that doesn't mean there can't be room in your life for something, or someone, else."

"Seems we've been waitin' a long time to get to know you," Josh added. "It would be nice to be a whole family for once," Cort seconded.

"What the hell do you think I've been tryin' to do for the last two years?" They all turned in surprise to Jed, who glared back, shaking his head. "This isn't so much about the ranch, not anymore. It's about me, wantin' to see my sons together before I die. And I don't give a damn whether the five of you believe that or not."

"I'm sorry, Aria, but you missed him." Eliana's eyes were sympathetic. "Cruz left yesterday for Phoenix."

A dozen different emotions flooded her at once, tightening Aria's throat. She'd called Cruz's hotel this morning, on the pretext of asking him a question about the ranch plans, only to find he'd checked out the previous afternoon. Thinking he'd decided to accept one of his brother's offers of hospitality, it had never occurred to her that he would leave without so much as telling her goodbye.

"I'm surprised," she managed to say.

The little girl holding her hand tugged at her. "Does that mean I don't get to ride with Josh?"

"No, honey," Eliana assured her, "Josh will still take you for a ride on Star. But right now he's feeding the bison with Rafe, so why don't you and Aria have a cup of hot cocoa while we wait?"

Feeling a strange numbness, Aria followed Eliana from the foyer into the warm kitchen. A blazing fire from the huge country-style kitchen fireplace cast a soft glow over the room and spicy *piñón* and cinnamon scents filled the room. Evie, the foster child Aria had brought with her from her father's house, took a seat in front of the fireplace. Kicking her feet excitedly, she declared, "I *love* hot chocolate. Can I have marshmallows in it?"

"Of course, sweetie," Eliana said. "And we put cinnamon and chocolate flakes in it, too. Does that sound good?"

Evie beamed. "Oh, yeah." She glanced up to Aria and, cupping her hand around her mouth, whispered, "She's nice."

Sitting next to her father's new ward, Aria smiled and stroked her blond hair. "Yes, she's very nice."

A minute later, Eliana handed two steaming cups of fragrant hot chocolate to her guests. "I'm sorry you hadn't heard about Cruz," she said, once Evie was engrossed with her treat. "I would have thought he'd say something to you before he left."

"Me, too." Taking a sip of the delicious concoction, Aria felt it calm her nerves. "I guess I shouldn't be surprised. I expected he'd leave sooner or later. He made it clear from the start he didn't belong here." Feigning nonchalance she added, "It's fine. The last thing I need is to get burned again."

Evie sipped her cocoa then set it down and ran to grab a stuffed toy from a basket of toys set beside the fireplace. She glanced back at Eliana, silently asking for permission.

Eliana smiled at her. "Go ahead and play with any of those. I keep them just for special guests like you." Turning back to Aria she said, "Josh and I wish Cruz would give this place and all of us more of a chance. We really like him. From the little time I spent with him, I'd say he's something special."

"He's successful, if that's what you mean."

"That's part of it. But there's a lot more to him than meets the eye. Although what meets the eye is nice, too."

Aria couldn't help but laugh. "Why, Eliana Garrett, you're a married woman."

"Married, not blind."

"He is good-looking," Aria had to admit.

"Gorgeous is more like it."

She sighed. "Okay, gorgeous."

"And smart."

"And smart."

"And—"

"Okay, okay, I get it. Enough already."

"So?"

Aria looked up from her cocoa. "So what?"

"So what are you going to do about it? About him?"

Aria's heart skipped a beat and for one insane second, she wished she could say she was going to run after Cruz and ask him to come back. To give them time to get to know each other. To explore the crazy, hot passion that flared between them every time they got close enough to look into each other's eyes.

Instead she gathered up what common sense she could lay claim to and armored herself with it against that very real temptation. "I'm not going to do anything about it," she said firmly, as much to convince herself as her friend. "If there ever was anything between us, he's made it clear that it's definitely over. That's the end of it."

And, ignoring Eliana's doubtful expression, she tried hard to believe it.

Chapter Five

Someone was talking, but the words had become a drone, sounds that didn't translate into anything that made sense. Cruz caught himself staring at the papers in front of him and wondering what he was supposed to be approving, deciding and contributing.

"Cruz, you with me here?"

Looking up into Derek Randall's dark face, creased with concern, Cruz squashed the impulse to answer honestly. Impatient and irritated with himself, he avoided the questioning looks he was getting from the other five engineers in the conference room. "Yeah, sorry, you were asking me about—" He stopped, realizing he had no clue and hoped Derek would fill in the blanks.

"The Toronto project? I think it's worth going in with a lower bid if we get the contract."

"Fine, go ahead." He wanted to say it was Derek's call. His friend had been effectively running Cruz's company for the last three years. Cruz's role had been limited to sporadic e-mails and calls, neither of which had been a good substitute for being on the job. He'd hoped by getting back to Phoenix and convincing himself he'd settled what he could in Luna Hermosa for the time being, that he could step back into the skin he'd once been comfortable in at both work and home.

Instead, he'd been restless, out of sorts, finding it hard to concentrate. He blamed it on not being able to sleep. The bouts of insomnia had started in Luna Hermosa but there, he'd put it down to the family issues, and the unsettling encounters with Aria Charez, figuring it would get better once he was back in familiar territory. It had gotten worse. His attempts to sleep had been repeatedly broken by nightmares that left him shaking and sweating and he'd taken to running at all hours of the night, trying to escape the persistent feeling of being trapped, with the walls closing in around him.

A sharp crack to his right jolted Cruz. With a quick jerk and duck he spun around, instinctively fisting his hand around a weapon that wasn't there.

One of the engineers stared back at him, frozen in mid-gesture of bending to pick up the pieces of the coffee mug he'd inadvertently elbowed off the table onto the tiled floor. "Uh, sorry, I …"

All eyes fixed on Cruz. His colleagues were pitying, uncertain, taken aback. It felt like a waking nightmare. Shoving to his feet, he strode out of the room and kept going, taking a back door out of the building to the alleyway behind it. He stopped finally, closing his eyes and leaning against the rough wall, his heart pounding and breathing hard, as if he'd run miles.

What the hell is wrong with me?

He stood there seconds, minutes; it could have been hours, until he heard the door open again. Even then, he didn't bother moving or opening his eyes.

"Hey, man, are you all right?" Derek's voice came hesitantly.

"Apparently not."

"I guess that explains why you look like crap and you haven't done much more than take up space since you got back."

Derek's bluntness pulled Cruz upright. Derek stood a few feet in front of him and he met the other man's eyes squarely. "Anything else you want to add?"

"Yeah, there is. I don't know what's going on with you—the war or something that happened during that little mystery trip of yours to New Mexico, whatever—but it's pretty obvious you aren't ready to jump in and pick up where you left off." Derek paused, giving Cruz the chance to explain or answer and when he didn't, he pressed on. "I've managed to keep things going this long. I think I can handle a few more weeks without you."

"I know you can." He trusted Derek completely when it came to the business. They'd been roommates at Texas A&M together and Derek had been the first person he'd called after he'd finished his first six-year stint in the army and decided to launch his own company. He'd never had reason to regret his decision. "But you shouldn't have to."

"Probably not and you shouldn't have had to spend the last three years in some hellhole getting shot at. If you ask me, I got the better end of the deal," Derek said with a brief smile. "Look, Cruz—take some time off. You're not doing yourself or anyone else any good being here. Get away from here, go somewhere. Go back to that little place in nowhere New Mexico. Give your head a rest for a while."

Cruz doubted a trip back to Luna Hermosa would be as stress relieving as Derek seemed to think. Not with his family problems. *Not with Aria there.* Today's little episode had made it all too clear he wasn't ready to resume work yet. He rubbed at the back of his neck, not looking at Derek, and said, "Yeah, maybe you're right."

"Now I know you're screwed up," Derek said, clapping him on the shoulder. "You never give in that easily. Hell, you never give in at all."

"Like you said, I need a break." He met Derek's eyes again. "Thanks. For all of it."

Derek waved him off. "Just do me a favor and relax for once. Take a couple of deep breaths, enjoy the holidays."

He muttered something noncommittal as he and Derek started back in the building. But Cruz wondered if after everything he'd been through in the past three years, he'd ever be able to relax again.

* * *

He pulled himself together enough to give his okay to a couple of projects Derek wanted to push forward with and then got out. The urge to stuff some clothes in a suitcase and just leave, take the nearest highway with no particular destination in mind, was strong. The only thing stopping him was remembering at the last moment he'd promised to have dinner with his mother.

It ranked among the last things he wanted to do right now. He felt guilty for even having the thought; she hadn't seen much of him since he'd gotten back and he should want to spend time with her. She was the person he was closest to. He could tell her about this morning and she'd listen and sympathize. But the idea of telling her repulsed him to the point he almost called her and said he wasn't coming.

On the drive to her house, he tried to dissect his feelings, but all he came up with was a mixed-up mess of shame, anger and confusion. Since he'd been a kid, he'd always been able to handle things. He'd never leaned on anyone, just did what he had to do and for a long time now his mother had depended on him, instead of the other way around. He wasn't about to confess to her that he felt like he'd been knocked flat on his back and didn't have a clue how to get up.

He also didn't have a clue how to keep her from knowing something was wrong, and she proved the strength of her maternal instincts within the first ten minutes of his arrival.

"Things didn't go well today?" she asked, almost casually, not looking up from the tea she was pouring into tall glasses. Handing him one, she settled back into her chair on the small shaded patio, her expression saying she wasn't about to accept lies for an answer. Small, on the thin side of slim, her stature wasn't formidable; her temper and stubbornness were.

It amazed him that she still had the ability to force honesty out of him when he least wanted to give it. But after the lies that had led to his conception and her humiliation at the hands of Jed Garrett, Maria Déclan had determined she would never be deceived again, even by her own son.

"Not especially," he said carefully. "It's going to take some time to get back into the routine."

"You haven't given yourself much time. You weren't back two days before you left again. And since you've been back, you've scarcely said more than three sentences to me and to say you've been in a foul mood is generous."

The accusation was plain. Knowing it would upset her, he hadn't told her where he was going or why. That had upset her, too, but Cruz frankly dreaded telling her he'd gone to Luna Hermosa and met Garrett. Upset wouldn't begin to describe his mother's feelings about that. But it was only a matter of time before she got the true story out of him, and he just didn't have the energy to keep it from her any longer.

"I was in Luna Hermosa," he said flatly. "I met my father."

It was the first time he'd ever seen his mother shocked speechless.

"I didn't go looking for him. It was the other way around. I also found out I have four brothers. You never told me." The last statement came out unexpectedly, with an edge of bitterness.

Maria ignored that, fixing her attention on his meeting Garrett. "All these years... Has he changed? I can't picture him any other way, but it's been so long..."

Cruz didn't know what to say, what she wanted to hear. "I wouldn't know, would I?"

"No," Maria said. Her face hardened. "I never wanted you to. What I do want to know is why he decided to find you. And why you bothered to let him."

"He's sick, dying maybe. He wants to split the ranch up between the five of us. I told him I wasn't interested."

"I'm surprised he isn't trying to find a way to take it with him to Hell," Maria said bitterly. "That piece of land is the only thing Jed Garrett ever loved. He left me because getting Teresa Morente's money for his precious ranch was more important than you or me. Don't think for a minute he gives a damn now." She got up suddenly, started an agitated pacing across the patio, pausing only to break off one of the roses that was draped from a hanging pot. Shredding it between her fingers, she asked sharply, "You aren't planning on going back, are you?"

He hadn't thought about it, he'd been trying to avoid thinking about it, but he heard himself saying yes before his brain caught up with his mouth. Maria whirled around at him but Cruz raised a hand against her inevitable protest. "My… brothers invited me to spend the holidays with them. The invitation included you."

"I'll never go back there," Maria spat. "Especially not while Jed Garrett is alive. I don't know why you'd want to, either. I don't understand why you went in the first place."

"They're my family," he told her, thinking of his brothers, not Jed, when he said it.

"Jed Garrett and those men have never been your family, not now, not ever. It's always been just us. Those men you keep calling your brothers don't care about you and if they're anything like their father, that damned ranch will be the only thing that matters to them."

"It isn't like that." Rubbing at his neck, Cruz felt the tension crank up another notch, twisting his gut and pushing hard against his temples.

"It's exactly like that! You're just trying to pretend it's not. You know it is or you wouldn't have lied and gone behind my back to track them down."

"I didn't tell you because I knew this was how you'd react. I'm not sorry I went. But I'm sorry I hurt you."

"It's a little too late for that," Maria snapped.

"Look," Cruz said as he got to his feet, "I understand why you don't want to go back. I'm not asking you to. You'd planned on taking that cruise with that travel group of yours before you knew I was coming back. Why not go ahead with it?"

Maria was silent for a moment then sharply nodded. "Why not? There doesn't seem a point in staying here for the holidays when you've obviously made other plans." Flinging down the crushed rose petals, she swept past him into the house, leaving him to follow.

Dinner was short and tense and Cruz felt a guilty relief an

hour later when he escaped. He couldn't rid himself of the feeling he'd betrayed his mother and would continue to betray her if he went back to Luna Hermosa without her. *If...* The whole of the drive back to his apartment, he told himself he hadn't really committed to accepting his brothers' invitation, to going back.

But suddenly he was unable to see himself doing anything else.

I should have gotten the puppy.

The totally random, ridiculous thought went through Aria's head as she stomped the snow off her boots and pushed open her door, arms weighed down by half a dozen shopping bags and one large, unwieldy box that kept threatening to slip out of her hands. A week before Christmas and as usual, she'd waited until the last minute to finish her shopping and now she was cold, tired, damp from the snow melting on her hair and coat, and irritated with herself for putting off the job until it became a detestable frenzied search for everything she needed.

She blamed her current state of chaos on the puppy. One of the animal shelters in Taos had been holding a holiday adoption event at the plaza and she'd been sorely tempted by a small, scruffy-looking ball of brown fluff that had looked at her with big hopeful eyes. Only the fact she was packing too many bags and was in a rush had stopped her from scooping up the puppy for her own.

It probably wouldn't have been too practical, given everything she had going on in her life right now. But as she unceremoniously dumped all the bags and the box on her office floor, she admitted it might have been nice to have company in the dark, empty house, even if it was the small furry kind.

Maybe next time, she promised herself, and set about flicking on a few lights, stripping off her damp coat and boots and starting a fire to chase away the chill. She was feeling warm and comfortably sloppy, having changed into her flannel lounge pants and oversized shirt, searching the cabinet for the cocoa, when the doorbell, followed by a sharp knocking, interrupted her.

Aria glanced at the clock. It was past ten. Uneasiness slithered over her. A visitor at this time of night was rarely a good thing. Giving up the hunt for the cocoa, she snapped on the outside light and glanced out the front window before unbolting the door. And froze in sheer surprise.

Cruz Déclan stood on her doorstep, the last person she'd expected to see here or ever again.

A hundred different questions shot through her head but the one clear thought she had was he looked terrible, hunched against the cold and snow, as if he'd driven a thousand miles without stopping to bring her the worst possible news. Instinct kicked in and she moved quickly to twist the locks and yank open the door.

"Aria…" The way he said her name, almost prayerfully, twisted her heart. "I'm sorry, I…it's late—"

"No, come in." She stepped aside and after a heartbeat's hesitation, he came in, waiting as she closed and bolted the door. They stood looking at each other, and for the life of her, all Aria could think was he seemed like a different man than the one who'd fought with her, kissed her and left her without a goodbye. She wondered if he'd slept in the time he'd been gone. It seemed more like he'd been fighting demons and the demons were winning.

"Give me this," she said, plucking at the sleeve of his leather duster. He silently complied and she slung it over a peg before leading him into the living room, near the fire. The way he followed, without a word of questioning or protest, bothered her, gave her the uneasy feeling she'd break something else in him if she said or did the wrong thing. Studying him for a moment, she tried to gauge his mood, but all she could think was he'd reached some limit of what he could tolerate, what he could cope with. With several days' beard, and in worn jeans and a weathered brown Henley, his hair rumpled, he'd lost his polish and that slightly arrogant air of command. It bothered her more than she wanted to admit.

"Cruz," she said softly, "what's wrong?"

"I didn't know where else to go. No—that's not right." He gave himself a sharp shake, pushed at the back of his neck with both hands. "I didn't want to go anywhere else. I can't deal with anyone else right now." Sitting down heavily on the couch, he dropped his head to his hands. "I can't seem to deal with anything."

She didn't hesitate but sat down next to him, putting her arm around him, stroking his hair, compelled to offer whatever comfort she could. Maybe it was none, but he didn't move away and the moment stretched into minutes before Aria finally said quietly, "You came back."

It wasn't a question, but there were questions in it. All kinds of questions about why he was here, of all the places he could have chosen to go, and what he wanted from her. But she left them unspoken because part of her was fiercely glad he had chosen to come to her.

The huffing sound he made was too bitter to be called a laugh. "I couldn't stay there." She waited, letting him decide how much he wanted to say. "Nothing is working. I don't know what's wrong. I feel like things are falling apart and I can't do a damned thing to stop it."

Aria had never felt more inadequate in her life and at the same time, more desperate to want to do something, the right something, to help him. "Maybe too much happened. The war and Jed and finding your brothers. All of that, and trying to pick up where you left off—that would make anyone feel crazy."

His head snapped up. "Not me. It doesn't happen to me."

"Why? What makes you invincible?"

"I don't let it happen." Jerking to his feet, Cruz paced back to the fireplace, his hands fisted as he pushed them against the stone mantel. Tension radiated off him, evident in the stiff way he held himself, as if the emotions in him were too tightly coiled and poised, quivering at the edge of bursting out.

"Can I get you something?" Aria asked then winced at how lame that sounded.

"You have anything stronger than water?"

"I've got a bottle of wine." Glad of the chance to do something useful she left and came back a few moments later with two glasses, silently handing him one. Cruz finished his in a matter of seconds, gripping the thin glass so tightly his knuckles shone white. She took a sip of hers, not really wanting it but needing the prop to keep her hands busy. Nodding at his empty glass, she asked tentatively, "Do you—"

"No, it just makes it worse."

"I wish I knew how to make it better."

"Yeah." He looked away. "Me, too."

"You can stay here," she offered. She heard herself and knew it was a mistake. And that trying to—wanting to—fix things for him was an even bigger mistake. But she could have stopped breathing easier than she could have kept herself from reaching out to him.

"Stay? And do what?"

The question frustrated her for some reason. "I don't know. Just—stay. What else do you want from me, Cruz?"

He went still, the emotion in his eyes so intense she swore she could feel the heat.

Then, without warning, the glass he held shattered.

Chapter Six

For a moment, it seemed unreal, something that couldn't have happened. His hand was still half-clenched, a rivulet of red running in a thin line down his wrist, glass scattered between them on the tile. It was seeing the blood that jolted Aria back to reality.

Setting her own glass on the mantel, she grasped his hand, ignoring his attempt to pull it back. A jagged line cut across his palm. "That looks bad."

"Don't worry about it," Cruz said in a voice that was strangely flat after his outburst.

"Fine, I won't, but I don't want you bleeding all over my floor," she said tartly. She didn't let herself think about anything further than the practicalities of tending to his cut. The emotion that caused him to shatter a glass just with the force of his fingers wasn't something she wanted to delve into very deeply right now. "I'll be right back."

She hurried to dig the first-aid kit out of the bathroom cabinet and grabbed a couple of towels on her way out. When she came back, Cruz stood in roughly the same place, staring dispassionately at his hand. The glass shards, though, had been neatly piled atop the mantel.

"You'll make my life easier if you sit down," she said, nodding at the couch. He surprised her by complying without a protest and she knelt down in front of him and tried to be gentle as she mopped up the blood and bandaged the cut. When she'd finished, she piled the towels and first-aid kit on the coffee table and looked over her handiwork one more time before starting to get up.

Cruz's fingers curved around her wrist, stopping her. "I'm sorry," he said quietly. "For everything."

"It's okay. Do you want another drink, coffee maybe?" Giving her voice the barest hint of teasing, she added, "I've got a mug that I'm pretty sure even you can't break."

It didn't even earn her a hint of a smile. He pulled his hand back. "Yeah, coffee. Fine."

If she expected anything, it was that he would wait in the living room for her. Instead, he followed her into the kitchen, leaning against the counter, silently watching her as she went through her coffee-making ritual and tried not to clue him in to how jumpy she felt having him there in what suddenly seemed like a very small space. It was hard not to be aware of him, his slightest movement; hard not to remember the look on his face when he broke the glass.

During the awkward minutes before the coffee was ready, Aria decided to brave a question, to get more out of him than the little he'd given her. "What happened in Phoenix?" she asked.

She thought he might not answer her, or would tell her to mind her own business. But finally, staring at a point over her shoulder, he said, "I'm not sure. I haven't been able to sleep. I can't work. I can't focus on anything for more than five minutes. I walk around half the time feeling like I want to break something—" he winced ruefully "—and the other half… I'm just lost. My last day there—" His mouth pulled into a hard line, his hands flexing against the counter edge.

"You don't have to go on," Aria said quickly, cursing herself for pushing him into telling her things he obviously would rather have left unsaid.

"My last day there, I was at a meeting and someone dropped a mug and I went for my gun," he said, going on as if she hadn't interrupted. "Then I had a fight with my mother—"

"About Jed?"

"I finally told her I'd met him. To say she didn't take it well is an understatement. After that, I decided I'd better get the hell out of there before I lost it completely." He put both hands at the crux of his shoulder and neck and leaned his head back for a moment, blowing out a breath, then at last looked at her. "Maybe you're right. Maybe I am going crazy."

"I didn't say that. But you are human and what I did say is that most anyone would feel overwhelmed by everything you've got going on right now." It was a waste of breath, she knew, but she tentatively suggested, "Have you thought about seeing a counselor? A lot of veterans—"

"No." He dismissed the idea sharply. "No, I just need to get away from it for a while."

"And coming here is getting away from it?"

That drew from him, for the first time that night, a ghost of a smile. "It seemed like it at the time."

Aria shook her head, not sure how to interpret that. The coffeemaker finished, giving her a reprieve, and after she'd handed him a mug, she turned and led the way back into the living room. For a while, they sat together on the couch, drinking coffee and listening to the hiss and spit of the fire and the soft ticking of the mantel clock. She thought of the first time they'd met and wondered if they were making a habit of this, meeting in the semi-darkness, making their midnight confessions, only to pretend in the light of day it never happened or that it didn't mean anything.

Out of nowhere, Cruz said, "I broke my clock at home." At Aria's confused look, he added, "It felt better for some reason. It took away some of the pressure to be somewhere and do something productive. Yeah—" his mouth quirked a little at the corner "—I know, that does sound crazy."

She didn't rise to the bait to agree. Instead she contemplated him for a moment and then got up, strode purposefully to the mantel, grabbed the clock, took it with her as she opened the front door, and then flung it as far as she could out into the snow. "I've always hated that thing," she said, coming back to flop down on the couch again. "It's the noisiest thing in here at night. I only put it there to begin with because my great aunt gave it to me and I felt guilty about not using it."

He stared at her and she looked back and then they both started laughing. His mirth had an edge, but it didn't matter, because at least she'd succeeded in distracting him, even for a short time.

Finally, with a roll of his shoulders, Cruz set his mug down. "I should go."

If she'd been wary of his mood before, it suddenly seemed even more dangerous. The tension shifted, to something that had been there all along, but that neither of them wanted to acknowledge. He was right; he should go before one of them did something they'd surely regret. But she was loath to let him leave, especially in his frame of mind. "Where are you going to go?"

"I don't know," Cruz said, frowning as if the question disconcerted him. "Josh invited me to stay with him and Eliana for the holidays. I don't think it's a good idea to show up there right now, though. I'll find a hotel."

She wanted to say it was ridiculous to try to get a room at this time of night, to repeat her offer for him to stay, but all that came out was, "It's late."

"I know that," Cruz said dryly.

"I mean, it's late and the snow's bad. And out-of-town guests are already arriving for Christmas. It'll be hard to find a room tonight."

"I can't stay here."

"It's not a problem, I have the room," Aria added, hearing herself fumble to get the words out fast. "And you probably shouldn't be alone right now—"

His smile was little more than a wry twist of his lips. "My urge to break things only applies to inanimate objects."

"That's not what I meant—"

"Trust me, I'm better off alone."

"I'm not afraid," she asserted, not quite truthfully but wanting to dispel the idea that she was frightened of him. Perhaps it wasn't him she was afraid of, but herself, and what she might do if he stayed.

"I am."

"Cruz, please." *And why did that sound like a plea?* "Be reasonable." Much later, reflecting back, she decided it was at that moment she made her mistake. And yet at the time it seemed innocent enough, just a gesture to reassure—a brush of her fingers on his forearm that was never intended to be more.

Cruz reacted as if she'd communicated all her fantasies about him in one simple touch. Reaching for her, he jerked her into his arms and covered her mouth with his. There was no slow, soft seduction about it, no invitation to consider where it might lead. It was demanding and passionate, incinerating doubt or hesitation. Whatever happened in Phoenix—or maybe it was everything else, the war, coming home, finding his family—seemed to have loosened the restraints he kept on his feelings. But instead of tightening the bonds again, he ripped them away.

Aria tried to rein in her own feelings, to stop herself from giving in to what she knew she'd regret later. But she'd lost the battle long before it ever began. He wouldn't let her think, barely let her breathe. His mouth moved over her jaw and the sensation of him lightly dragging his teeth over her throat then soothing the spot with his tongue had her leaning back, baring more skin for him.

Too fast. It was too fast—not fast enough. Too much—and she wanted more.

Sensation blurred into feverish attempts to touch, and taste and kiss, both of them made clumsy by some complicit need to hurry, to have everything all at once. She felt Cruz fumbling with the buttons of her shirt, and then with a frustrated growl, he used both hands to yank it open and push it off her shoulders.

When he palmed her breasts she heard herself moan his name. It was like hearing someone else. And then he replaced his hands with his mouth and she thought the aching need to get even closer to him would drive her crazy.

You shouldn't be doing this, the cool inner voice she rarely paid any heed urgently whispered.

I don't care.

His hands slid to her hips, rocking her against him, and the friction sparked like wildfire, threatening to burn her alive.

You're going to regret it.

What she regretted was not being able to touch him the way he touched her. The layers of clothing still between them irrationally irritated her and she tugged up his shirt, rewarding him with her lips and hands when he yanked it over his head and tossed it aside.

It doesn't matter. He needs me.

As if to lend strength to her inner argument with reason, Cruz whispered her name, a low, needy plea spoken against her mouth before he kissed her.

I want this.

She wanted him, more strongly that she'd ever wanted anyone before.

You're going to end up hurt again.

Shut up!

The voice of reason finally fell silent and Aria willingly, wantonly, let herself fall into a place ruled by dark sinful desires and the way Cruz could make her feel.

If this was insanity, Cruz couldn't stop it.

The sensory overload overwhelmed him. The texture of her skin under his hands and mouth, warm, smooth, the taste and smell as rich as cream and as heady as incense. The throaty sounds she made and the way she said his name, putting so much desire and need into that one syllable he almost lost himself then and there.

Hurtling toward the inevitable crash and burn, Cruz knew he should slow down, pull back, stop before he slammed into reality. But she was the only thing that seemed real to him now, the only thing that didn't make him feel powerless and uncertain. This was Aria, at once strong and yielding, giving as much as she took, inciting a primal need in him to make her his.

He leaned her back far enough to tug off her pants, baring her body to his greedy gaze. She didn't protest, didn't hesitate, but seemed as impatient as he was with the clothing that slowed them down. The wild, almost desperate look in her eyes wound the almost painful tension in him tighter, threatening to snap the fragile thread of what meager control he could lay claim to.

Waiting became impossible. He sat up and pulled her into his lap. She easily straddled his hips and, fisting her hands in his hair, she kissed him, driving him to the edge of losing his mind.

Her hands slid between them, pushing at the button of his jeans. Cruz leaned back enough to give her what she wanted, but when her fingers brushed against skin instead of fabric her intimate touch suddenly and sharply reminded him that what he was about to let happen wasn't right.

"Wait," he muttered.

"No."

"Aria—" Clumsily trying to keep up as she went back to kissing him senseless, he fumbled in his back pocket and finally pried out his wallet. For a few frantic seconds, he couldn't find what he desperately wanted right now. Finally, he located it, shoved in a long forgotten corner. He shifted away from her for a moment to put on protection. Then she took what she wanted, sliding down the length of him, gasping a breath as she joined them together.

Cruz couldn't pretend to have any grip on himself, so he let go completely, slipping his hands around her shoulders, holding her as she arched, her head thrown back, her hair spilling over his fingers. The rhythm built between them, hot and fast, and he let it control them. Kissing her everywhere he could reach, he held back during the final seconds until she peaked, crying out his name, shuddering in his arms, taking him with her in an explosion of feeling that in a single instant seemed to obliterate all the doubt, fear and confusion he'd brought with him tonight.

She fell against his chest, panting, and he held her, gently stroking his fingers through her hair as they both eased down from their shared high. He'd expected and welcomed that rush, the pure, feral sensation. What he hadn't expected was the feelings that came in its ebb. They crept up on him and he hardly recognized them because it had been so long since he'd felt tenderness, warmth, the need to be held; he couldn't remember the last time he felt them with a lover.

For a long time they sat there, entwined, until at last Aria, with a sigh, levered up and off him. Not bothering to reach for any clothes, she simply stood there, searching his face, as if she weren't quite sure what to expect from him. Cruz wasn't sure, either. The vulnerability in her eyes hurt him somehow, but he couldn't think of anything to say that didn't sound wrong or clichéd. So instead, he got to his feet, took her hand and by silent agreement, let her lead him to her bedroom.

Stripping off the rest of his clothes, he climbed into bed with her, gathering her into his arms and holding her close to his heart. In minutes, the warmth of her body, the idle stroking of her fingers against his chest and the soft sound of her breathing lulled him into the deepest sleep he'd had in months, free of nightmares, his only dreams memories of loving her.

If it was a dream, it was a good one. At least while she lingered in the limbo between sleep and wakefulness, Aria could enjoy the sensation of a warm, solid body spooned against hers, the light rasp of a days' old beard on her temple, Cruz's rhythmic breathing caressing her cheek. *Cruz...*

She shot to fully awake the instant her brain processed what her body already knew: she was in bed with Cruz Déclan, it was morning, and even in sleep, he held her close.

Two strong and contradictory urges hit her at once. The first tempted her to kiss him awake and rekindle the wildfire they'd let loose last night. The other counseled her to creep away now before he opened his eyes and forced her to confront the inevitable morning-after awkwardness, naked and without a serious caffeine fortification.

This time she listened to the more sensible voice. Moving cautiously, she inched away from him and out of bed. As if he sensed her loss, Cruz frowned, muttering something into the pillow. But he didn't wake and Aria, grabbing a robe, made her escape into the kitchen.

While she waited for the coffeemaker, she dropped into a chair, shoving her hands into her hair, rubbing at her temples. After all her promises to herself, she'd done it again, acted impulsively, threw herself headlong into a relationship that couldn't even be called that because it was destined to last only as long as Cruz was in Luna Hermosa. Considering the abrupt way he'd left the last time, she doubted that would be long.

She supposed she should regret everything. Yet she couldn't. He'd needed her. He'd chosen to come to her over anyone else and that touched her in a way she couldn't explain. No one had ever needed her like that. She'd been wanted, depended on, taken for granted, but never needed, never trusted as Cruz had trusted her so that he was willing to lay bare his insecurities and fears.

Despite herself, she felt a connection to him that even his leaving hadn't been able to break. And one night as his lover hadn't satisfied her desires, only intensified them.

The whole thing confused her and she had no clue what to do next.

"Is there enough to share?"

The deep sleep-roughened voice jolted Aria out of her thoughts. Cruz stood in the entryway. His only concession to dressing had been to pull on his jeans. Though she wanted to read that as a sign he felt comfortable with her and the intimacy of their situation, his expression gave her no hint to his thoughts or feelings.

"There's more than enough," she said, getting up to pour them both large mugs of coffee. She handed him his and, feeling uncomfortable standing there, sat back down again, gesturing him to a chair across from her.

Concentrating on his coffee, he didn't make any attempt at conversation for several minutes until finally he said, "I'm going to take Josh up on his offer."

"Okay, that's—good." He frowned and she backtracked. "Isn't it?"

"That remains to be seen." Rubbing at the back of his neck, he sighed and looked back at her. "If you want, while I'm here, I can give you a hand with the ranch plans. I'm not working on much else right now."

His offer stung. He'd retreated behind the pretense that there was nothing between them but a shared project, ignoring everything that had happened. *Sorry, but you'll have to do better because I'm not going to duck and run.* "You think that's a good idea after last night?" she said bluntly. "Or am I supposed to follow your example and pretend it never happened?"

"I never said that."

"You didn't say anything. Never mind," she said, waving him off. She forced herself to sound cool, uncaring. But she couldn't sit there any longer, fooling herself into thinking that she was something more than a one-night stand to him. She shoved back her chair and turned her back to him. "Let's just call it a one-time impulse. I mean, I'm sure that's all it meant to you. You were upset. I was—" *Stupid. Reckless. Not thinking.* No way could she tell him about her contradictory feelings. And she was pretty sure he wouldn't want to hear it anyway.

The scrape of his chair, soft footsteps, and then his hands, gentle on her shoulders, guided her to face him. He held her, compelling her to meet his dark gaze. "That's not all it meant." His fingers tightened for a moment and then he let her go. "I never wanted to make you feel that way. But at this point, I'm not sure of anything. Too much doesn't make sense. You deserve more, but I can't give you anything else right now."

It sounded like a version of every brush-off she'd ever heard. Yet she didn't doubt he was sincere. Whatever else Cruz was, she'd never questioned his honesty. He wasn't the kind of man who would placate her with easy lies and meaningless sentiments to avoid a confrontation.

It still hurt, though, with an intensity that caught her off guard.

"I don't want anything more," she said, forcing the words around the thickness in her throat. She stared at the floor, unable to look at him anymore. "This was a mistake."

"No." The force behind his denial brought her head up sharply. "It wasn't a mistake." He cut off her protest by bending quickly and kissing her, hard, fast and hot. When he let her go, he took a step back and she could clearly see his struggle, an echo of her own, between desire and reason. "It wasn't a mistake."

"Cruz—"

"But if I don't leave now, it's going to be."

Before she could respond, he whipped around and strode out of the kitchen, leaving her alone with the cold company of her regrets.

Chapter Seven

"You made it. And just in time for our present-opening insanity." Cort slung Cruz's coat on a rack and ushered him inside to a noisy, chaotic Christmas Eve family scene the likes of which Cruz had thought only existed in sappy holiday movies. "You may wish you'd brought earplugs. As you can see—and hear—the kids are wound up and out of control."

A little girl with big dark eyes and a mournful droop to her mouth was suddenly at Cort's side, tugging at his hand. "Daddy, Waffle is lost."

"I'm sure he's around here somewhere," Cort said, scooping her up. "Her stuffed rabbit," he added in an aside to Cruz. "You'll have to excuse us a minute while we find him. He's a special friend of Sophie's. Come on in. Everyone else is already here."

Cruz didn't follow his brother into the living room, but stayed at the entrance, an outsider looking in to where his brothers and their wives and children and two other couples he didn't recognize were laughing, passing gifts around, teasing and playing. A gigantic Christmas tree took up an entire corner, stretching almost to touch the fourteen-foot ceiling. Decorations, most of them looking homemade, bright ribbons and little lights in the shape of red chiles covered the tree until the limbs bowed, begging for mercy. Beneath the tree stacks and stacks of boxes and bags stretched out many feet beyond the Native American blanket that had been wrapped around the base of the tree.

The house smelled of spiced cider, cinnamon, chocolate and *piñón*. A huge fire blazed in an adobe fireplace across the room, casting a warm, inviting glow over everything. In the background, between excited children's squeals, laughter and adults trying to maintain some semblance of order, Cruz heard the strains of a Spanish rendition of "Greensleeves."

He stood a long moment staring, feeling like a whore in church. This was the last place he fit in. He wanted to turn and bolt. The child in him belonged alone or alone with his mother, with one small token gift, usually not wrapped, to exchange in a silent, unceremonious atmosphere that could have been on any day of the year.

Only one thought, or more specifically, the thought of one person, held him still. Aria. She wasn't family, but his brothers and sisters-in-law treated her as if she were and although he had no reason to assume it, he'd half expected her to be here. He hadn't seen her since that night they'd become lovers; hadn't even spoken to her, unsure of how he'd be received and what he'd feel. Scanning the room, he didn't see her, and very nearly listened to the voice in his head, urging him to get away from what felt so completely alien.

A hand on his arm stopped him. "It looks like Cort deserted you," Laurel said, her voice filled with genuine welcome. "But we're all so glad you came."

He turned to see her smiling up at him. That and the warmth in her eyes quelled his impulse to flee. She wore a long-skirted dress in a deep shade of red, the firelight picking out the gold in her hair, and he realized he hadn't noticed before how lovely a woman she was.

"Thanks," he said, annoyed at himself for the hesitant sound of it. Not wanting her to take his coolness personally, he added, "You look nice tonight."

Laurel laughed. "Thank you. But it won't last. The girls are already covered with chocolate and sticky candy. It's only a matter of minutes before that becomes my new jewelry. See why I hardly ever change out of my sweats?"

Cruz laughed, relaxing a little. "I'm sure you look great in those, too."

"May I get you a mug of hot cocoa or a brandy, or anything?"

"I don't—" He started, then stopped, nagged by the tension pulsing in his temples. Without Aria, his motivation to stay was pretty slim. "Actually, brandy sounds good right now."

"Coming up. Aria is in the kitchen, by the way, if you're looking for her."

Am I that obvious? Uncomfortable now for new reasons, Cruz nodded. The part of him that wanted to see her relented, giving way to doubt. Since that night they'd...what? Had sex? Made love? What had it been? Whatever it was, he hadn't stopped thinking of her body under his hands, hair tangled in his fingers, her mouth eager to taste and kiss, every moment etched in his memory in vivid detail.

Yet he hadn't called her. Well, that wasn't true, exactly. He'd picked up his cell phone dozens of times, but couldn't bring his fingers to punch in her number. *What's the matter with you, Déclan?* He'd repeatedly asked himself that question, consistently failing to find an answer. From that first night at the wedding reception he'd behaved like a stranger, someone he didn't recognize; bereft of his usual confidence and assertiveness, openly baring his vulnerabilities to her without a thought for the consequences.

Before he could regain any equilibrium, she emerged from the arched kitchen doorway carrying his brandy snifter and the sight of her knocked him sideways yet again.

She'd left her hair loose, the dark green dress she wore made of some supple material that clung to her curves, sharply reminding him of another night, when the only color she wore was skin.

She moved within polite distance, handing him his drink. "Hello. I really didn't expect to you to be here."

"To be honest, neither did I," he said, taking the brandy snifter from her, his fingers brushing hers. He took a slow sip, watching her all the while. "You look amazing."

"Thank you." The words came with a smile that didn't quite reach her eyes. "That's a nice thing to say." Any semblance of a smile vanished. "But a phone call some time in the last week would have been nicer."

"I don't know about nicer. Conventional, maybe. I thought we were something else."

"Is that your excuse?"

"Partly. Most of it is I didn't know what to say."

"Me, either," she admitted quietly. "So maybe it's better you didn't."

"Maybe."

Silence hung between them, weighty with things unspoken. He sensed in her the same reluctance to leave things unsettled and a shared uncertainty about the wisdom of pursuing them.

An excited squeal pierced the hum of conversations. Aria smiled, this time with genuine warmth, as she watched Sawyer and Maya's oldest son, Joey, bouncing up and down on a new tricycle. "I'm glad I didn't miss this," she said softly, almost to herself.

Cruz wished he could echo the sentiment, but the whole picture-perfect family thing was beginning to grate on him, like a deep ache under the skin that nothing would relieve.

"You, on the other hand, look like you'd rather be anywhere else," Aria said and Cruz shifted his attention back to find her studying him.

"I'm not used to this," he said, attempting to sound as if it didn't matter.

"You're used to it being just you and your mom?"

He nodded. "We didn't celebrate much of anything. We had a nice dinner, went to mass and she gave me a gift. That was about it."

"My Christmases were more like this because we always had so many kids in the house. This feels like home to me."

"I'm a little surprised you aren't with your family tonight," he said.

"Tomorrow," she promised. "Risa—my sister—is there now

and I wanted to give her some time alone with Dad. She hasn't had much of that in the last couple of years." When Cruz left that alone, not sure how to interpret it, she added, "I love my sister, but she can be a bit prickly. For some reason, she feels like she could never measure up to me or our parents. When she was younger, she was about as wild as Josh used to be, but lately she's thrown herself with a vengeance into all these different causes." Aria shook her head, offering him a rueful smile. "I'm sorry, you don't really want to hear all this."

"I don't mind," Cruz said, wondering if there would have been similar rivalries and bonds between him and his brothers, if they'd all grown up together, instead of now trying to patch themselves together into a family. Pushing the thought aside, he jerked his head towards the ongoing melee involving kids and packages. "Is this what you've got to look forward to tomorrow, too?"

"Not quite on this scale," Aria said with a smile. "Dad's only fostering a couple of boys right now, and Risa and I are sadly lacking in the significant other department. You're welcome to come along and see for yourself, though," she added, almost off-handedly, though she looked at him intently, waiting for his answer.

"Thanks, but I'm expected at the ranch in the morning, and then Cort and Sawyer talked me into having dinner with them and their grandparents." He didn't add he would prefer to spend the time alone.

"It doesn't sound to me like you're getting what you want for Christmas."

"Not exactly," he said. "How about you? Are you getting what you want?"

"Not exactly," she mimicked. Then she looked a little sheepish, avoiding his eyes.

"What?"

"Nothing, I was just thinking of a whim I almost indulged the other day." He raised a brow expectantly, challenging her to tell him, and with a self-conscious laugh, she gave in. "I nearly got myself a puppy."

"That doesn't sound too terribly decadent. Why didn't you?"

"Oh, I don't know. At the time it seemed impractical and a

little silly. But when I got home and the house was empty, I wished I had. Just to have something warm and living there besides me." She gave a little sharp shake. "That sounds a lot more depressing than it is."

As if embarrassed by her confession, she shifted to look back into the living room and Cruz followed her gaze to where Cort and his son, Tommy, were engrossed in a video game. When Tommy apparently won, Cort, grinning, slung an arm over Tommy's shoulder, ruffling his hair. Cruz turned away.

Gentle fingers brushed his hand, briefly curling against his. He looked at Aria but she only looked back, the understanding in her eyes exposing an old pain he thought he'd buried deeply enough to never have to acknowledge it again.

And suddenly he couldn't spend another moment there. "I'm going out for some air," he said abruptly. "Come with me."

"Well, gosh, how can I refuse an invitation like that?" she drawled, arms crossed against her chest.

Realizing how he'd sounded, Cruz tried to soften it. "I'd like for you to come with me. I'm just not feeling very social right now."

She contemplated him for a moment, then nodded. "I'll get my coat and meet you out back."

In the entryway where Cort had left his coat, Cruz found Rafe pacing back and forth, his son, Dakota, cradled against his chest. Rafe took one look at him and shifted the sleepy baby to his shoulder, freeing one hand to briefly grasp Cruz's arm. "You okay?"

"Fine. I've just got a headache," he said, grabbing his coat off the rack.

"It's crazy in there, isn't it? It can really get to you if you're not used to it."

"Yeah, I need a breather."

"No problem." Rafe's dark eyes spoke volumes and Cruz felt his brother's support was sincere and nonjudgmental even as he inwardly squirmed at the idea of anyone guessing the turmoil he was battling. "Do what you need to do."

"Thanks. I'll be back in a while."

"Take your time." Rafe's mouth quirked in a smile. "We haven't even started the Christmas carols yet."

"I wish you were kidding," Cruz muttered, deciding to circumvent the living room and escape through the kitchen. Unfortunately, his plan to go unnoticed was doomed to fail. Josh and Cort had moved there, standing at the counter snacking on the last scraps of broken gingerbread men.

"Making an escape?" Cort said lightly.

"I need some air," Cruz said, the pounding in his head increasing to a painful throb. It was all he could do not to snap.

Cort frowned. "You don't look so good. Are you okay?"

Resisting the impulse to blurt out, no, he wasn't okay, and hadn't been for weeks, Cruz answered tightly, "Fine, it's just a headache."

"I can't imagine why you'd have one of those," Josh said with a laugh. "With all the peace and quiet goin' on in there."

"I'm going for a walk. I'll be back in a while."

Eyeing him thoughtfully, Cort seemed to want to add something, but settled on a nod.

Josh waved him out. "Go ahead, we'll pretend we never saw you. Otherwise, Maya'll be tryin' to feed you some kinda weed tea."

"But we're here if you need anything," Cort said. "You know that, right?"

He knew it. They were there and that was the one thing he didn't know how to deal with.

Aria was standing on the patio, bundled in her fleecy coat and staring up at the brilliant display of stars, when Cruz appeared. Moonlight against snow lit his face, lending it a pallor she wasn't sure was a trick of the light or real.

He scarcely glanced at her, but strode straight past, headed for the open back land. She nearly stayed put, uneasy at his mood, and let him walk off whatever devils he seemed to be struggling with. Yet she couldn't. Instead, she double-timed her steps to stay at his side.

She sensed his agitation was more than simply feeling awkward in his role as newfound brother and son. Spending three years in overseas combat had obviously made some dents in his emotional armor, too. Remembering the night they'd made love, she thought back to what he'd told her then.

I haven't been able to sleep. I can't work. I can't focus on anything for more than five minutes. I walk around half the time feeling like I want to break something—and the other half... I'm just lost.

Seeing him like this wasn't helping her keep him at arm's length, either. Her instinct was to reach out, to help, to comfort. But keeping her silence was the better—safer—option, and so she focused on the cold, crisp air kissing her cheeks and nose. It was a gorgeous mountain night. A winter's fairy tale complete with a light dusting of snowflakes gently falling on an already thick blanket of white fluff. Towering pines, their bows laden and glistening with snow, made for a glowing canopy as they walked beneath the full moon.

She lost count of the minutes, startled when Cruz abruptly stopped and, without a word or warning, tugged her into his arms and covered her mouth with his. His kiss tasted of desperation and regret, passion and need.

When he pulled back, she searched his face but held her tongue. So much was there in his eyes, she didn't know where to start asking how she could help.

"Thank you."

"For what?"

"For being with me, leaving me alone. Understanding."

She didn't understand, not all of it. But the fact that he trusted her was enough. Lightly, she brushed her fingers against his cheek. "Are you all right?"

"Fine. Okay—" he winced at her skeptical look "—better."

"Cruz—"

"No, don't." He touched a finger to her lips. "I know what you're thinking—the other night. Let's not dissect it. It just happened. I don't want to explain it beyond that."

Maybe it was better they didn't, she thought, because delving too deeply might raise all kinds of questions and ghosts she wasn't prepared to confront.

He pulled her to him again, this time kissing her with a tenderness that melted her resolve and left her aching for more. She returned his gentle touch with slow, soft lingering kisses and time slipped away as they stood together in the still of the winter night.

Words didn't exist, only touch and sensation; inseparable caresses that spoke the language they needed to share their feelings. Lost, Aria scarcely noticed the faint music starting from inside the house.

"Guess what?" she told him lightly when he broke away to glance back. "It's time for carols."

Cruz rolled his eyes. "I don't sing."

"No singing required. I'm sure the kids will be happy to take control of that." Not looking convinced, he started back with her. "This isn't working for you, is it? The whole warm, fuzzy family thing," she added when he glanced at her questioningly.

"I don't know. Not now, anyway," he admitted, rubbing at the back of his neck. "It's too—much, of everything. They've all gone out of their way to include me, but I walked into the middle of this after years of being a secret. The only thing tying me to the rest of them is that I'm Garrett's son. They don't owe me anything."

"It's not about owing you. They're not that way. They want to know you. They want you to feel you're a part of the family."

"That might be too much to ask."

"Why?" He was talking about his brothers, but Aria had the impression he was putting up a wall with her, too. And it hurt. "How hard can it be to accept that they're your family and they want to be part of your life?"

He shifted away, his expression hardening. "Look, I wasn't raised in a big happy family like you were. My mother did the best she could by me, but I can't go from that to that—" he pointed to the house, aglow with the warmth emanating from inside "—overnight."

"No one's asking you to," she said, trying to put herself in his position, yet defensive of her friends, whom he seemingly wanted to dismiss out of his life with little thought or feeling. "But if you won't even give them a chance, you'll never know if it's possible or not."

She reached to open the kitchen door only to have Cruz's hand on her arm stop her mid-motion.

"I know you're trying to help," he said. "But I can't work through this tonight."

Or ever? she nearly added, yet held her tongue and nodded instead. She led him back inside to a place she wanted to be, but from where he wanted to run.

Cruz reluctantly stayed to listen to the children sing carols. When Aria sat on the opposite side of the room, he caught a glance exchanged between Maya and Jule. It only increased his sense of claustrophobia. Nothing went on in this family that everyone wasn't in on. If his ears burned every time they'd spoken his name, no doubt they'd be charcoal by now.

Forcing himself not to dwell on that idea, he tried to focus on the music. Laurel played piano and gradually even most of the adults began to chime in and sing rounds of familiar holiday songs. He had to admit the makeshift choir exuded genuine enthusiasm and held an innocent charm about it, distracting him for a time from dwelling on all the reasons he shouldn't have accepted tonight's invitation. But when they'd finished and the women began a soft, angelic chorus of "What Child is This?" something changed.

Watching Aria join with the rest of them, an unfamiliar sensation struck him that took a moment to register as longing. This was what he'd missed, all those years, what he could never have back, and what would likely never be his, no matter how his brothers tried to draw him into their lives. He could tell himself he didn't need or want it, he could resent being forced to confront it, but a part of him would always be that boy who had dreamed of Christmases like this, of being more than the bastard child who couldn't call anywhere home.

The song finally ended, and everyone drifted back together. Aria sat on the floor, sharing a Christmas cookie tea party with Angela and Sophie, Sophie happily clutching a battered-looking pink rabbit, and Cruz found himself next to Tommy, getting an impromptu lesson on battle strategies in some science fiction-themed video game.

It was a short time later when he noticed Maya come back into the room and say something to Sawyer that had his brother instantly on alert. Giving his wife a quick one-armed hug, he strode quickly toward the foyer where the coats had been stashed.

"Is everything okay?" Aria asked, looking up at her friend, drawing the attention of the others.

"It will be," Maya answered. She winced, her hands cradling her belly. "We're going to have the best Christmas present possible. Isabel has decided to make an early appearance."

There was a general flurry of activity then, with Cort helping Sawyer get Maya outside, and Aria and Eliana taking charge of the couple's two sons, trying to distract them from their parents' abrupt departure.

It was nearly nine, and Cruz decided then it would be possible to say his goodbyes now, leaving the rest of them to cope with sleepy children, cleaning up and the wait, however long that might be, for news on the baby.

Yet he stayed, after Rafe and Jule took their twins home and the other couples left, pitching in to help with the cleanup as Cort and Laurel started getting the younger kids ready for bed.

"Could you hold Nico for a minute?" Aria appeared at his elbow, transferring Sawyer's youngest son to his arms before Cruz could protest. "I'm going to see if Laurel needs help getting his bed ready."

After she left him, the toddler blinked up at him and then stuck his thumb in his mouth, plopping his head against Cruz's chest. He'd never held a child before and at first the feeling was strange; he didn't know what to do with his hands, his ineptitude in this arena glaringly obvious.

Nico, though, seemed perfectly comfortable, and after a few minutes, he gave a contented sigh, his eyes drifted closed and the tension in Cruz ebbed. He had an inkling of insight then, watching the slumbering little boy, of what family meant to his brothers. He had made up his mind he wouldn't be a father, but holding the little boy, the product of his parents' love, he could understand too well why his brothers, with their less-than-perfect childhoods, would want the lives they'd been denied growing up.

He sensed eyes on him and looked up at Aria, a few feet from him, catching her soft, almost tender, expression as she watched him and the sleeping child.

And for a fleeting but powerful moment, this was where he wanted to be.

Chapter Eight

She'd switched off the phone ringer, killed the lights and locked herself in, with only the fire and a stack of sappy movies for company. After all the emotional upheaval of Christmas, Aria promised herself she'd avoid a repeat on New Year's Eve. Turning down half a dozen invitations, offering excuses of some vague ailment, she'd managed to avoid all the festivities. Eliana, for one, hadn't believed her and had threatened to stop by to prove her suspicions, but Aria flatly told her she didn't want company. Of all the holidays, New Year's Eve was her least favorite. All that emphasis on new beginnings and fresh starts brought out the worst in her. This year, her only nod to the holiday was a resolution to ignore it.

Fortified with a plate of brownies, a glass of wine and her woolliest blanket, she curled up on the couch and popped in a movie, settling in with a determination to enjoy her solitude.

It lasted less than an hour.

At the first buzz of the doorbell, she considered ignoring it. But after a few moments, whoever had first leaned on the thing then resorted to pounding the knocker. Mentally running through the list of potential visitors and cussing the lot of them, Aria gave in to the insistent thumping and went to answer the summons.

For some reason, it didn't surprise her to find Cruz on her doorstep, although this time he'd come burdened with a large box covered with a blanket and a stuffed-looking bag. He was making a habit of this, showing up unexpectedly in places she was. This time, she wasn't sure she wanted to see him. It felt weird. They'd been lovers for only a brief time and having him here now felt too much like a repeat of that night, too much like temptation. She knew him well enough, though, to be certain that he wouldn't leave until he'd seen her. With a sigh, she relented.

"Are you all right?" he said the instant she opened the door.

The sharp, taut note of concern in his voice caught her by surprise. "I'm—fine. Why would you think—?"

"Eliana said you were sick." Without waiting for her invitation, he pushed his way inside. "I was worried it was something serious and if it was, you're so stubborn, you'd probably refuse to call anyone for help."

"The only thing wrong with me is an overdose of the holidays and Eliana knows it," she said, exasperated at her friend's none too subtle attempt at matchmaking. "I wasn't up to another party. So did you come all the way out here just to hear me admit that? Because I'm pretty sure you've already guessed it."

"I had an idea. But I wanted to be sure."

"And you brought those because—" She eyed the box and bag and then looked back up at him. "Should I ask?"

"These?" he asked. He looked a little embarrassed as if she caught him doing something sweet and thoughtful and her discovery made him uncomfortable. "It's a late Christmas present. I wasn't sure about the color so I had to give it my best guess."

Her curiosity piqued, Aria let him lead the way to the living room, where he carefully set the box down in front of the couch, dumped the bag on the floor and began pulling off his duster. "Go ahead," he said, gesturing toward the box.

"Cruz, you know you shouldn't have—"

"Don't give me the speech until after you've seen it. You may not feel like thanking me then."

"Now you've got me worried." She sat down on the couch. Carefully pulling away the blanket she looked inside and caught her breath in surprise. Inside was a puppy curled up on another blanket, a battered-looking teddy bear snuggled up beside it. "Oh, Cruz..."

Whether it was the brighter light or her soft exclamation, the puppy snuffled, stretched, yawned and slowly opened its eyes. The moment it caught sight of her and Cruz, it scrambled to its feet, wriggling all over, it's fuzzy, brown fur sticking up at odd angles, pink tongue lolling. Aria, unable to resist, picked it up for a better look. The puppy gave an excited yip and licked her nose. "Hello to you, too," she said, with a laugh.

At the same time, tears blurred her eyes. She remembered past gifts—jewelry, artwork, expensive dinners, armfuls of flowers— and none of them had been as personal. Cruz had chosen the gift because he understood it fulfilled a need, not simply a desire. Blinking hard, she turned to him, self-conscious at being unable to control her emotions but wanting him to know how much his gesture meant to her.

Cruz, after one searching glance at her face, abruptly dropped his gaze to the puppy. He scratched the little dog behind the ears and the puppy squirmed in delight. "Someone left him and his sister at Jule's clinic. He's obviously not a pure anything but—"

"He's perfect," Aria finished for him. She cuddled the puppy close, her cheek rubbing his warm fur. Reaching over a hand, she briefly curled her fingers over Cruz's, making him look at her. "Thank you. I was—" There was nothing she could put into words; nothing that came close to expressing her feelings. "This is just what I needed."

A ghost of a smile flitted over his mouth, but was quickly banished. "Jule says he's four or five months old and he's house-broken." Cruz eyed the puppy doubtfully. "You'll have to take her word for it. She also sent all this." He dragged the bag closer and offered it to her. She said it was packed with puppy food, dishes, toys and other paraphernalia. "It seemed to me like a lot for one little fuzzball, but she insisted."

"Let's see if I can find the basics for now." The puppy twisted in her arms and she let him down, giving him a few minutes to explore. Her hands free, she dug through the bag. She found food and water dishes and a container of dry food. "I think we'd better do this in the kitchen," she said, and both the puppy and Cruz followed her. Once the puppy was tucking into the food and water, Aria studied him, head to one side. "He needs a name. 'Hey you,' is only going to go so far."

"He looks like a Sully."

Aria looked up at Cruz. "Like a what?"

"A Sully."

She waited for more and when he didn't give it, she prodded, "Are you going to explain that?"

He rubbed at his neck, looking sheepish. "I guess, unless you're just going to take my word for it."

"Sorry, no."

"Remind me to keep my mouth shut next time," he muttered. "It's nothing very interesting. When I was a kid, I never had a pet. We moved around too much and my mom always said we didn't have the time or the space. But I wanted a dog and when I couldn't have one, I made up this picture in my head of what he'd look like. I called him Sully. I have no idea why. I'm sure I had some reason when I was ten, but I can't remember it. Sully looked like him—" he concluded, flicking a finger at the puppy.

"That's—"

"If you're going to say cute, please don't."

"Never. Sully's cute." She pointed at the puppy. "You're—"

Leaning back against the counter, Cruz crossed his arms over his chest, brow arched, his expression faintly amused. "Yes?"

Dangerous, especially when you do things like this. "Not cute."

That earned her a laugh. At the sound of it, she resolved to get another one out of him.

"You say the nicest things to me," Cruz said.

"You seem to like it, so I don't know which of us is worse. Okay, okay," she said as Sully danced around her legs, giving her the message he needed to go outside *now*. "You're lucky I've got a fence because it's definitely not walking weather."

Since Cruz had on jeans and boots, Aria let him take Sully outside and used the few minutes to straighten up the living room. When they came back inside, Cruz seemed content to watch her for a while as she played with Sully until the puppy, tired out, curled up on the blanket by the fire with his bear for a nap.

The distraction of the puppy gone, the awkwardness Aria expected at first now settled over them, heavy and significant. It didn't help to sit together on the couch where they'd made love and to see in his eyes that Cruz remembered as clearly as she did. Yet neither of them dared to say anything and when Cruz finally broke the silence, it was to ask a question that seemed safe compared to all the other questions neither of them had answers for.

"So why did you decide to hide out here tonight? Everyone was commenting on you missing the parties. Apparently, it's a first."

"You make me sound like a party girl and I'm not. I don't like New Year's. Apart from all the baggage that comes with it, I've decided it's cursed, at least for me."

"That seems a little—" his mouth twitched into a brief smile, turning it to a light tease "—dramatic."

"Okay, fine," she amended, "then it seems things go wrong and I figured if I stayed in this time, I could avoid another mini-disaster."

"It can't be all that bad."

"Oh, really? Let's see…" She started ticking off on her fingers. "Last year, my date left me stranded at a party at a stranger's house after he got caught with the host's girlfriend making out in the hot tub. The year before that, a man I'd been dating for nearly a year took me to dinner, made an eloquent speech that sounded like a prelude to a proposal—about how wonderful I was and how he appreciated me helping him find himself and supporting him through all those months of soul searching. Then he announced he was going to marry his secretary. And then there was the time I found out this nice, sweet guy who seemed so perfect in every way couldn't spend the holidays with me because he needed to be with his wife and kids." She paused for breath. "I could go on."

Cruz held up a hand to stop her. "And I could ask how a smart, beautiful woman keeps ending up with so many losers."

"Apparently I attract them and then don't have the sense to run in the other direction." She couldn't look at him, couldn't help thinking that she could add him to her list of mistakes.

"Maybe you're just too quick to get involved," he said quietly.

That brought her head up sharply and she eyed him hard. "I suppose you should know."

"I didn't mean it that way."

"I think you did."

"No, it's—" Blowing out a breath, he shook his head. "I'm sorry. But you have to admit, things happened too fast. I'd like to think it wasn't just pity on your part."

"It wasn't," she said flatly.

They held a staring contest for several moments that stretched and tightened the longer they went on. She could read the tension in his face and the unyielding set of his jaw and shoulders. Despite her irritation with him, she couldn't help feeling a twinge of guilt. Knowing everything he was going through, this— whatever it was he had with her—was only adding to the pile of things he was trying to cope with. Then again, she told herself she was only making excuses for him shutting her out and then more or less dumping her. But he had come here tonight, worried for her and bringing her a puppy and…and none of it made sense. So she gave up trying. "I started on a bottle of wine earlier. I'll get you a glass." She started to get up.

"No, don't," he said, pulling her back down with his words, half-demand, half-plea. She threw him a questioning look and he glanced away. "It's been too tempting lately to use that as a crutch to get through the night. I don't want to start something I can't stop later."

Oh, he could do this, soften her, make her forget why she shouldn't care. And she did care, cared like hell, and couldn't stop herself. "You're still having nightmares?"

"The only time I haven't in weeks was after—" He left it unsaid, the silence full of memories. "But at Christmas—"

"I know," she interrupted quickly, not wanting him to feel compelled to revisit an incident that had hurt him, left him ashamed at his lack of control.

He didn't seem to hear her. "I almost lost it again. Christmas Eve, when I had to leave. I could feel it about to explode. Everyone else knew it, too."

"Everyone understood. Your brothers don't think less of you because of it."

"How about you?"

"No, why would I?"

Cruz answered her with a derisive huff, shaking his head.

"You can't always control everything. It doesn't make you weak to admit it." Aria regretted saying it almost immediately. It sounded clichéd, dismissive of his struggles to refind himself. When he didn't answer, staring at the floor rather than at her, she finally asked, "How long are you staying?"

"I'm not sure. I'd like to say I'm ready to pick up where I left off, but I can't. But I want to get my life back, in one form or another. I can't hide out here forever." Shifting back, he raised his eyes to hers. "It feels strange not to be working. Like I've lost a limb."

"You really need a vacation."

For a moment, she mentally kicked herself for once again blurting out what sounded to her like the most insensitive thing possible. But Cruz gave a short laugh, rubbing his hand over his neck. "Apparently I do."

"If you want to work, then help me with the ranch project," she offered before she let herself agonize over the implications. "We can go back out to the site next week and start getting the final plans ready. I'd like to be able to start construction in the spring."

"I thought you didn't think that was a good idea."

"Spring construction is a great idea. Working together, probably not," she said honestly. "But it might do you some good. No pressure. Just give me a few opinions, give yourself something else to think about."

The way he studied her and the long moments it took him to answer nearly convinced her he was trying to think of a gentle way to tell her to forget it. She was about to forestall him when he said, "Okay, if you really want my help. I'll give it a couple of weeks."

"Fine." She let go the breath she didn't know she'd been holding. "That's settled then."

"If you want to call it that," Cruz said dryly.

"We agreed we weren't going to talk about anything more *personal,*" she reminded him.

"Talk," he emphasized, punctuating it with a slow appraisal of her body that suggested he had better things to do with his mouth.

She flushed. "Or act on. Are you sure you don't want a glass of wine, because I do. And stop smirking. It isn't funny."

"No, but you trying to avoid the subject is." He easily deflected the pillow she threw at him and propped it behind his head. "So what were you watching before I intruded on your solitude?"

"You didn't intrude. It's *Casablanca.* For the twenty-third time."

The amusement was definite this time. "Twenty-third? Is that a personal record?"

"It's one of my favorites, okay? Don't tell me when you were a kid you didn't have something you watched or listened to over and over again."

"I might have seen *Star Wars* a few times. Okay, fourteen times," he admitted, answering her skeptical look. "I was six, I thought it was cool."

Aria laughed. "I never took you for a *Star Wars* geek."

"I never took you for a hopeless romantic," he countered.

"Well, you've definitely got the hopeless part right. So do you want to stay? I've got popcorn. And if you're nice, I might even share my brownies."

He seemed to consider. "How nice?"

"For triple chocolate brownies, pretty nice."

"I might have to settle for popcorn," Cruz said. Reaching out, he laced his fingers with hers long enough to say, "I want to stay," before releasing her from his touch, but not his steady gaze.

"Then stay," she said softly.

For a moment, both brief and timeless, her invitation meant more than a shared evening between friends. She couldn't let it be more than that, though, and added quickly, "But you'll have to put up with my hopelessly romantic movie."

"I happen to like *Casablanca.*"

"Right," she said, rolling her eyes, "like I believe that. Lying won't get you brownies."

Cruz smiled, the first easy gesture she'd gotten from him all evening and despite herself, her pulse leaped. "I mean it. I'm not totally lacking in romance."

"That remains to be seen," she said over her shoulder, as she got up to get popcorn. "I'll give you points for Sully, though."

She distracted herself in the kitchen for a bit, returning about fifteen minutes later with a big bowl of popcorn, the rest of the brownies and two mugs of Mexican hot chocolate precariously balanced on a tray. He made room on the coffee table; she started the movie, and then dropped down on her end of the couch. They didn't talk much, but it was a comfortable quiet—she felt relaxed because he was. It was somewhere in the middle of the movie, with neither of them seemingly aware of it, that they ended up next to each other, Cruz's arm around her, she leaning into his side, her feet tucked up under her.

The new arrangement wasn't nearly as comfortable, at least to her peace of mind. He rubbed patterns against her shoulder, yet appeared focused on the movie. She spent the remainder of the movie wondering what he was up to, kept speculating through the start of the credits, until Cruz stretched, rolling his neck. Despite his outward appearance of being at ease, he winced at the motion.

"Are you okay?" she asked.

"Just tired. It's got to be close to midnight."

"I wouldn't know. My clock is still buried in the snow somewhere."

He laughed at that and Aria got up to flip on a local channel in time to see there were only minutes of the old year left. By tacit agreement, they waited out the time together, watching until the seconds ticked away and the celebrations began in earnest.

"Over at last," she murmured, stabbing the off button on the remote.

"And no mini-disasters." Very gently, he trailed his fingers over her face from temple to lips and then bending to her, lightly kissed her. "Happy New Year."

She briefly closed her eyes, against temptation, against reality rushing back in. When she opened them he was watching her, nothing in his face giving her any clue to what he felt, how she should react. "Cruz—"

He abruptly pushed to his feet. "I should be going. I don't want to be too late getting back to Josh and Eliana's."

Not daring this time to suggest he stay, Aria saw him to the door. "Thank you again for Sully," she said, trying for friendly and appreciative instead of the desperate and needy she felt. "You'll have to come and visit him once in a while."

This time he looked uncertain, so she reached up, her hand on his shoulder to steady herself, and kissed him. She meant it to be as brief a caress as he'd given her, but Cruz slipped his hand into her hair, held her in thrall at the first touch and kissed her back, long and with intent, tenderness woven with passion into a heady mix.

They were both breathing harder when he broke away. Aria felt bemused, as if she'd been transported far away and back in one jolt.

"I should…no." He stepped back. "I need to go. I'll see you in a couple of days."

Not trusting her voice, she nodded. Cruz hesitated a moment longer and then he turned and left her, and as Aria closed the door against the cold and darkness, she wondered why this kept happening. Why they kept coming back to each other when they both had reasons to believe it couldn't last.

Chapter Nine

It was barely morning, the sky paling at the edges where the first tentative light began spreading up from the horizon, but Cruz was already up and waiting for the coffee to finish brewing. He'd had another restless night, typical of the two months since he'd been back from overseas. It took hours sometimes to fall asleep, only to be wrenched awake by nightmares, followed by fitful dozing. Finally, he'd given up the pretense of resting to head straight for the strongest jolt of caffeine he could lay his hands on.

As usual, he was the first one in the kitchen. This morning, it underscored the feeling that had nagged him for days now—that after three weeks, he'd overstayed his welcome. It wasn't anything Josh or Eliana had said or done that gave him the sense they'd be happy to see the back of him. Just the opposite, in fact. They'd gone out of their way to make him feel comfortable, to encourage him to treat their house as home. But they were still newlyweds, the holidays were over and it was time he got out.

He should to back to Phoenix and stay, start getting his life back in order again. He'd been working sporadically over the past weeks, largely via e-mail and video conferencing, and had taken a few days to fly to Toronto, to finalize a contract on a new project his company had taken on. It wasn't enough; he was hardly pulling his weight, and that knowledge added to the ever-present tension riding under his skin.

Yet he hadn't made the decision to leave New Mexico. Things here felt unresolved and if he were honest, much of that had to do with Aria. The coffee finished, Cruz poured himself a large mug, pulled on a heavy jacket over his sweater and walked outside to stand on the porch in the cold, clear morning. The sun had topped the mountain peaks and it glittered on the snow, dazzling his eyes, so for a moment all he could see was emptiness, echoing the feeling in his chest.

Something still felt broken inside him and he wasn't ready to leave the sort of sanctuary he'd found here. At the same time, he was impatient with himself. He wanted to be healed and done with it, to be finished with this particular sickness, and to shake off the strange reluctance to confront the past and move beyond it.

He needed to push himself and he'd made up his mind to go through with a decision he'd come to sometime in the darkest part of the night. He didn't like it. But he wasn't going to move forward by standing still.

"Hey, you okay?" Josh came up behind him, pulling Cruz away from his thoughts. His brother looked as if he'd just tumbled out of bed and thrown on the first clothes that came to hand.

"Fine. I was just thinking."

"I try and avoid that myself as much as possible," Josh said. "And you picked a cold place to do it."

"It helps me clear my head." Cruz paused then said, "I'm leaving, probably later today. I appreciate the hospitality, but I've been here too long." When Josh started to protest, he held up a hand to stop him. "You and your wife need some time to yourselves and I need to settle things with Jed, make some decisions about how I feel about this whole family thing."

Josh studied him a moment. "I get the feelin' that means you've decided to move over to the ranch. You think that's a good idea? Don't take this the wrong way, but it seems to me, with everything you've got goin' on, it might make things worse."

"I'm not sure it's a good idea, either, but I need to do it." He said it firmly, as much to convince himself as his brother. "Jed's been pushing me, harder since Christmas, to spend some time there and hear his side. I've made it clear he's not going to change my mind about taking a share of the ranch, but he says it's not about that. He's decided I haven't gotten the straight story about him from anyone else. He's not going to quit until I give him his say."

"Probably not," Josh agreed. "But you don't have to do it livin' in the same house with him."

Not living in the same house, only staying for a few days, long enough to settle things between him and Jed, to the extent they could be settled. Maybe he didn't owe Jed the time, but he owed it to himself to confront head-on his feelings about his father and to decide what, if any, part Jed would have in his life. At least, that was the argument he gave Eliana when, after he and Josh had gone inside for breakfast, she echoed Josh's concerns about him staying with Jed.

At a glance from Josh, she didn't press, but she looked troubled and Cruz, already uneasy about his decision, changed the subject to something almost as unsettling. "Is Aria still coming out this morning?" he asked.

A few days ago, Eliana had passed along the message that Aria wanted to come out today and go over a few things concerning the children's ranch plans. He'd wondered why Aria hadn't called him directly and had come to the conclusion she was trying to avoid him after everything that had happened over the holidays. He wasn't sure how he felt about that. On the one hand, it seemed the right, sensible thing to do—to stop themselves from getting any more entangled emotionally then they already had. But a part of him felt her absence almost like grief, as if he'd lost something he didn't know the importance of until it was gone.

Eliana, getting up to refill her coffee cup, glanced back over her shoulder. "She's coming out later this morning. I thought she might have called you."

Cruz didn't answer, not sure what he could say that wouldn't lead to speculation on Eliana's part about where he and Aria stood.

"Cort's bringin' Sammy and Anna out for a ridin' lesson this morning," Josh said. "Why don't you come over to the ring and watch while we're waitin' for Aria. It might give you a better idea of what we're tryin' to do with this ranch, help with the plannin'."

"It might. I understand the concept, but seeing it in practice couldn't hurt." He suddenly wanted to go along, not because he thought it would make any real difference to his ideas for the ranch, but because it could give him some additional insight into Aria's passion for the project. It was important to her and that made it important to him to understand.

He asked them why he cared, why it mattered when he was making plans to leave, when the idea of staying in Luna Hermosa permanently was laughable. But his plans seemed nebulous and Phoenix had never felt less like home.

There were a dozen excuses he could give for his reluctance to reclaim his former life, except that if he was honest, the dominant reason was Aria. She wasn't a part of that life.

He didn't know whether she could be. All he was certain of was that here, in Luna Hermosa, they had opportunities, chances to start something that would be impossible if he returned to Phoenix. And he wasn't ready to leave and give those up.

"Are you sure that's a good idea?" Cort repeated Josh and Eliana almost word for word when Cruz admitted he was going to stay at Rancho Pintada for a short while. They were standing at the corral fence, on their own for the moment, while Josh, helped by Tommy, worked with Eliana's siblings, Sammy and Anna, and Eliana stood nearby, offering praise and encouragement. Something of Cruz's resignation at having to explain himself all over again must have shown in his face because Cort cut him off before he could start. "Sorry, that was out of line. It's not anybody's call but yours."

"It's okay," Cruz said. "It's just hard making a case in favor of it to everyone else when I'm having trouble justifying it to myself."

"Well, if it's any consolation, I'd have probably done the same thing in your place. When are you moving?"

"This afternoon. I talked to Jed this morning before coming over here. He's giving me Josh's old rooms," Cruz added, grimacing a little. "I think he's made up his mind this is going to be a lot more permanent than the week or so I'm planning on."

"You're moving to the ranch?"

Both Cruz and Cort turned at the sound of the voice—*her* voice—directly behind them. Distracted by the conversation with his brother and half watching the riding lesson, he hadn't heard Aria walk up until she was right next to him.

"Oh, hey, Aria, good to see you, too," Cort said, lightly teasing, an obvious attempt to deflect her attention away from the ranch question.

While Cruz appreciated Cort's effort to spare him yet another explanation of his reasons for accepting Garrett's offer, Aria was the one person he didn't mind telling because he was pretty sure she, of anyone, would understand and accept it without questioning his judgment or his sanity.

She flushed, glancing at him, before turning to Cort. "I didn't mean to interrupt, but don't change the subject on my account."

"It's fine," Cruz told his brother when Cort looked like he was going to protest. "I'm going to hear about it from everyone anyway so it might as well be sooner than later."

"So it's true?" Aria asked. "You're going to move out to the ranch?"

"Not exactly *move*. I'm only staying for a few days."

"That's a good idea."

"The only staying a couple of days?"

"No," she amended, "staying at all. I think it'll help you resolve things with Jed, one way or the other."

It so accurately reflected his own feeling about it that Cruz couldn't think of a comeback.

"If nothing else, you'll definitely get Jed's side of the story," Cort said with a grimace. "He'll make sure of that." He looked between Cruz and Aria, making Cruz a little uncomfortable at the scrutiny, and then glanced toward the corral. "I should go check on Tommy. He's still getting the hang of being a teacher."

"Oh, gee, Cort, that was subtle," Aria said, rolling her eyes as Cort started for the gate.

He threw her a grin over his shoulder. "Give me some advance warning next time and I'll do better."

Cruz sensed uncertainty in her now as she turned to watch the riding lessons, quiet with him as if she were trying to find the right things to say.

"Thanks for the support," he said, breaking the silence because it was better than speculating in his head what she might or might not be thinking. "You're the only one who didn't ask me if it was a good idea."

She smiled then, focusing again on him, and despite himself his pulse leaped and he felt like the teenage nerd who'd been asked to the dance by the prettiest girl in school. It was a stupid feeling, unfamiliar to a man used to women gravitating in his direction, but everything he felt around her seemed unfamiliar so he just added it to the growing list.

"I'm surprised Cort would ask," she said. "He's always trying to play peacemaker."

"He did ask, but then he took it back. So—" he gestured toward the group in the corral "—are we working or just watching today?"

"A little of both, I guess. Was the watching Josh's idea?"

Cruz nodded. "He thought I'd be of more help with the plans if I met Sammy and saw firsthand what you're trying to do here. Apparently I've been pegged as someone who builds things but never thinks about how they'll be used or by whom."

"I seriously doubt that," Aria said, laughing. "But I'll admit knowing Sammy and a lot of the other kids has made this much more personal for me. Take Sammy, for example. It wasn't that long ago that Eliana and her family were worried about the state stepping in because social services didn't think they could take care of him properly. But since he's started taking riding lessons with Josh and gone to a few weeks of summer camp at the temporary ranch, he's been better at school and he's got a lot more self-confidence. I think even you'd be impressed with what we can accomplish with this project, once it's up and running."

"What makes you think I'm not already impressed?"

"After all those big, flashy projects you've worked on all over the world? I've got the feeling it would take a lot more than a small-town project like this to impress you."

"I might surprise you," Cruz said quietly. "Projects like these have their own appeal."

She eyed him skeptically, but didn't argue, settling for a non-committal murmur that could have meant anything. He didn't get time to pursue it, though, because with the lessons apparently over, everyone appeared to converge on them at once, talking and laughing. Sammy tried to monopolize Aria's attention by telling her all about his ride and beaming when she warmly praised his riding skills.

They'd started back to where they'd all parked, after having decided to go to Josh and Eliana's house to warm up and give Aria and Cruz time to work on the plans. Halfway there, Aria stopped and stooped down, partly turning away from the rest of the group. Thinking she'd dropped something, Cruz was about to offer to help, when she straightened, hands casually behind her back, a mischievous smile tugging at her mouth.

"Is something wrong?" Cruz asked, not sure how to interpret that expression.

"Oh, no," she said airily. "I just owe Cort something, for earlier." Running forward a few steps, she hauled off and zinged a snowball at Cort, hitting him square in the back.

Cort whipped around in time to get another one in the chest. "You know this means war," he warned, already grabbing up a handful of snow.

"You'll lose. I'm still faster than you." Aria ducked his throw, flinging another frozen missile at him that cuffed his shin.

"Bad shot, Dad," Tommy called.

"You could help!"

"Maybe you'd better, Tommy," Josh added. "Your dad's never been all that good at—"

Cort's next snowball clipped Josh's shoulder and launched an all-out melee, with the kids and Eliana gleefully joining in.

Watching from the sidelines, Cruz felt oddly detached. He

couldn't remember, even as a kid and certainly not as an adult, abandoning all decorum and letting loose, for the sheer fun of it. And once again that ache of longing revisited him, the prick of jealousy and regret that he'd lost his chance to ever be part of a family like this. He started to turn away, to walk into the cold, to try and outpace his feelings.

He'd only taken a few steps before Aria snagged his arm. "You aren't getting off that easily. I need you—"

Suddenly, she dodged behind him to avoid an incoming snowball flung at her by Sammy. The lump of snow smacked Cruz instead. For a moment, Sammy stared at him, wide-eyed, as if he expected to be chewed out for bombarding a stranger.

But saying to hell with decorum, Cruz twisted, scooped his arm around Aria's waist and swung her in front of him. "I think you meant to hit her," he said, flashing a grin at Sammy.

"Yeah!" Sammy laughed and tossed a small plop of snow at Aria, who gave an exaggerated squeal and protested, "Hey, no fair! You guys are gonna regret this."

She managed to wriggle out of Cruz's hold and immediately snatched up a fistful of snow and landed a good blow on Cruz's chest. Sammy, who apparently decided Cruz made a good partner as well as a big and willing shield, ran over next to him and became his ally in fending off the attacks from Aria and, after a few minutes, everyone else.

Finally, breathless and covered in snow, they all agreed on a truce and a serious hot chocolate break at Josh and Eliana's.

"Need a ride?" Aria offered Cruz, as they neared her SUV.

"If you promise to keep your snowballs to yourself."

"I notice you said snowballs, not hands."

He returned her wicked little smile. "Did you now?"

"I wanna go with you, too, Aria!" Sammy begged.

"Sammy, I don't think—" Eliana started to say, but Cruz interrupted.

"It's okay." He held out a hand to Sammy, very aware of Aria's smile. "Partners stick together, right?"

Sammy happily clambered into Aria's SUV and chattered non-stop during the five-minute drive back to the house. Not used to kids and half expecting even those few minutes to be awkward, Cruz found it wasn't all that hard to win Sammy's approval simply by giving the little boy his full attention and throwing in a question every now and then. By the time Aria pulled into the driveway, Cruz had learned Sammy was nine and in second grade and his favorite color was yellow, along with the names of all his siblings and all the kinds of cookies his step-mom made for him. And that Josh had given him a horse named Sara for his birthday and he liked riding her better than anything.

Letting Sammy race ahead of them into the house, Cruz followed with Aria. "You've made a new friend," she commented.

"He's a nice kid," Cruz said. "I can see why you'd want to help him." He thought of all the projects he'd worked on in his career, the monuments to wealth and prosperity, and how he'd never known how, or if, they'd benefit the people who used them. And he compared that to her work, smaller and not as significant in terms of design and size, but with personal meaning to her because they were environmentally friendly or they helped kids like Sammy. They were worlds apart, in lifestyle and work and what family meant, but lately, he'd found himself more comfortable in her world and increasingly reluctant to go back to his.

Aria nudged his arm. "You still with me?"

Shaken out of his thoughts, Cruz realized they'd reached the porch and everyone else was already inside. "Sorry, I was… thinking."

"Maybe you shouldn't do it so much. It looks painful."

He smiled a little. "Sometimes it is."

"We should get in there before all the marshmallows are gone," she said. But she didn't move. Instead she stood there, watching him, a thoughtful look in her eyes that left him feeling exposed, certain she'd somehow read his mind. "When are you moving?"

"This afternoon. I want to get this over with."

"Need some help? I left Sully with my dad today so I've got the time."

"Are you volunteering to carry my suitcases?"

"No." She reached out and laced her fingers with his. "I could be persuaded to hold your hand, though."

Cruz tightened his hand around hers and gently pulled her a few inches closer. "Do you think I need a protector?"

She closed the gap between them even farther, so close now, their bodies brushed and he could feel her warmth and smell the now familiar scent of her perfume. "How about a friend?"

"Friend?" He drew out the word, considering it. "Is that what we are, friends?"

"Sometimes," she said, so softly he almost missed it.

"Sometimes," he agreed even as he closed that small sliver of a gap between them and did what he'd wanted since she'd shown up this morning. He kissed her, long and slowly to start, deepening it at her invitation until it became something wild and almost frantic and a warning sounded at the back of his head telling him they shouldn't be doing this on his brother's front porch.

They broke off the kiss, almost at the same moment. She stayed in his arms for several heartbeats, her forehead leaned against his shoulder as she tried to catch her breath.

"We're definitely not getting any marshmallows," she said finally, and if her laugh was a little shaky, he pretended not to notice.

"Maybe we can at least get a cup of coffee," he said, and then let her lead him into the warmth and light of the big kitchen, no longer feeling a stranger, watching from the outside, because she was with him.

Chapter Ten

A sense of uneasiness nagged at Aria as she followed Cruz through the gates of Rancho Pintada. She kept reminding herself she'd told him this was a good idea; that she believed him when he said it would help him reconcile with his feelings about Jed and his past. The closer they got to the big ranch house, though, the more her confidence this would work out for the best ebbed.

Jed was hardly warm and empathetic, and in some ways Cruz was fragile right now, on uncertain ground when it came to sorting out his emotions. The two of them together, without the buffer of his brothers, could be a disaster.

She could tell she wasn't the only one having second thoughts when Cruz came over to open her door for her after she'd parked behind him. He offered her his hand as she slid out, holding her a moment with the pressure of his palm against hers and his straightforward gaze.

"I'm glad you're here," he said quietly. He smiled a little. "I'm pretty sure this makes me a coward, but I wasn't looking forward to walking in there alone."

"Then I'm one, too because I'm not looking forward to walking in there at all. Jed Garrett's not one of my favorite people. Actually," she mused, "I don't think he's anybody's favorite person. Just the opposite." Cruz's brow rose and she flushed. "Sorry, I know he's your father but—"

Cruz brushed aside her apology. "It's okay. He's only my father in that he contributed the sperm. I'm not expecting this is going to lead to a long and lasting relationship. If I was just doing it to get him off my back about having his say, then this would be a bad idea. I need to do this for me. I need to settle things, one way or the other."

And once it was and he'd made his peace with it, and decided how close he wanted to be to his brothers, he'd be gone. Back to Phoenix and beyond, and out of her life for good. She knew that, but the longer he stayed, the harder it was to accept it.

A gentle stroke against her cheek brought her eyes back to his. "You were the one telling me what a good idea this was. That frown of yours isn't instilling me with confidence."

"I was just thinking of Del," she lied, deliberately ignoring the prickling of her conscience reminding her that she and Cruz, if nothing else, had been honest with each other. "Jed might be a bastard to everyone, but Del *gushes*. I can handle him being rude and confrontational a lot better than I can her gushing."

Cruz laughed and started them walking toward the house. "And now I really want to be here."

No, he didn't and she didn't, either, but there wasn't any turning back now. The housekeeper met them at the door and showed them into the large great room where Jed and Del were waiting. Aria kept her polite smile pasted in place as both Jed and Del looked at her as if she were a disreputable stray cat Cruz had dragged along with him.

"Well, now, this is a surprise," Del said. She flicked a nervous glance at Jed. "I knew Cruz was helpin' you with our little project, Aria, but I didn't realize you were such friends."

"Aria had a few details on the ranch plans she wanted to talk to me about and since I was already packed, I asked her to meet me here," Cruz said smoothly. "I hope it's not a problem." He gave Del a polished smile and Del flushed a little, reaching up to finger the hair at her nape.

"Of course not," Del hurried to assure him. She looked from him to Aria, slipping into the role of gracious hostess. "Why don't you stay for dinner? Then the both of you can tell me all about how the plans are comin'."

"This isn't one of your tea parties," Jed grumbled. He swept all three of them with a glower, his eyes settling hard on Aria. "I wasn't plannin' on company tonight."

Refusing to let him intimidate her, Aria opened her mouth to say something she'd regret later, to tell Jed she'd rather have Rafe's bison as dinner companions, but Del interrupted.

"Now, don't mind him," she said, prodding Jed in the shoulder and earning herself a deeper scowl. "We'd love to have you stay, especially seein' as you're such a special friend of Cruz's."

Aria barely stopped herself from rolling her eyes. She risked a glance at Cruz, expecting to see signs of barely controlled irritation. Instead, he caught her quick look, the corner of his mouth twitching in amusement. Aria had to look away to keep from laughing and thoroughly offending Del and angering Jed more than he already was.

Jed grunted something under his breath, glaring at his wife, who pretended not to see.

"That's very nice of you," Aria began, fully intending to turn down the invitation. Helping Cruz get settled in was one thing; sitting through a dinner with Del and Jed was above and beyond her offer to him.

"Thanks, that'll give us more time to go over these plans," Cruz interjected before she could get the words out.

"Well, that's settled then," Del said, beaming. "Now I'll just show you to your room and you all can get your work out of the way and then we'll have us a nice dinner together."

It was a frustrating fifteen minutes before Del finally left them alone in Josh's old rooms. Aria turned to Cruz, not sure whether to be annoyed with him or flattered that he wanted her at his side through what was most likely going to be an awkward evening.

"I know," he said, holding up his hands. "I'm sorry. I shouldn't have spoken for you. There's no reason for you to stay. I'll give them the time-honored excuse of a headache and you can—"

"Cruz—stop." It was almost funny, the way he was hurrying out the apologies and the quick fixes—almost. "I don't mind. I'll stay."

He frowned. "Like I said, it's okay. I spent over three years trying to avoid real land mines. I think I can manage these particular ones."

"I'm sure you can." Throwing aside her aggravation, she came up to him, brushed his hand with hers. "I'm just trying to even up the odds. Without me, it's two against one."

He didn't say anything for several long moments. Aria wondered if he was trying to come up with the best way to tell her to mind her own business, let him handle things, go home. Instead, he finally gave a huff of laughter, and shaking his head, said gruffly, "I don't understand why you keep sticking with me."

"That's okay," she admitted softly. "Neither do I."

Dinner, at least, could have been worse. The conversation was stilted and banal, confined mostly to Del's chatter about the ranch project, various fund-raising efforts and the latest gossip around town, and Cruz's and Aria's brief answers about how the plans were progressing. It was afterward, when Del—in what was obviously a prearranged plan to leave Cruz alone with Jed—insisted Aria give her an opinion on some item Del planned to donate to a silent auction fund-raiser for the ranch project, that Jed took control.

Aria hadn't wanted to go, he could see that, but he didn't want to make a habit of leaning on her emotionally; he'd done it enough already and it was starting to feel like an addiction, one he couldn't afford to feed if he was ever going to get his head straight again.

"I was beginnin' to think you'd made up your mind not to come," Jed said, dropping into the largest of the heavy leather chairs in the oversized den, gesturing Cruz to a seat alongside. Fishing into a box at his elbow, he pulled out a cigar and lit it, taking a deep puff of the smoke before fixing his attention on Cruz again. "You've been spendin' a lot of time with your brothers. Too much, I guess."

"I thought that was the point of you getting me here," Cruz said dryly. "A little family reunion."

"Maybe it was. But I doubt any of my other boys have had a good word for me."

"Were you expecting them to?"

Jed's harsh bark of laughter struck a discordant note in the room. "Hell, no. No reason to start now." He let his gaze roam the big room, with its abundance of leather and wood, and the enormous fireplace, its flames crackling and snapping against the winter cold. "I'd like to see one of you boys take over this place one day. It's too damn big for two people."

"It won't be me." Cruz said it bluntly, not wanting to leave any room for speculation on Jed's part, though he'd said it often enough. "I'm not a family man and I don't have the least interest in becoming a rancher. You should be giving this speech to Rafe or Josh, not me."

"It's by rights part yours."

"So you keep telling me. But, like I've said, that didn't seem to occur to you until a few months ago. I can't see that it matters much now. If the only reason you wanted me here was to try and convince me to change my mind, you're wasting your time."

After looking hard at him a few moments, Jed fixed his stare on the fire, taking another long pull of his cigar. "I've said it before, I can't change what's past. But I can make this right."

"You can't ever make it right for my mother."

"That just happened," Jed said gruffly. "It never meant anything and Maria knew it. She knew I was gonna marry Teresa and I wasn't gonna back out of it for her."

Cruz gritted his teeth against a surge of bitter anger—years of it, held inside because his father, the man he'd most wanted to vent it against, had never had a face or a name. "She didn't know it. She loved you. All those years she said she hated you, but she could never make things work with anyone else. I think a part of her still loves you, though I sure as hell don't know why. At least she did love someone, which is apparently more than I could say for you."

"There are a lot of things you don't know, boy." He sounded

tired, still searching the flames as if trying to catch a glimpse of past ghosts.

A completely alien sensation visited Cruz, so at odds with what he knew and had decided about Jed Garrett that he didn't trust it. "Who was she?" he asked abruptly, acting on an instinct that told him this might be the only time he'd get a straight answer to the question.

"Rafe's mother. Halona." Jed pronounced the name softly, almost reverently. "We were both married and Teresa was expectin' Sawyer, but I didn't give a damn. Maybe, if I'd known her boy was mine, things would've been different. But she took that secret to her grave. She told her mother and the old lady told Rafe, but Halona never told me. Guess she had her reasons."

Cruz didn't want to hear it—that Jed had, once in his life, actually cared for one woman among the many he'd used and discarded. It marred the image he'd come to believe of a cold-hearted, selfish bastard who'd married for money, abused and abandoned his children, and now tried to justify it by forcing a legacy on those of his sons who least wanted it.

"Did you ever tell Rafe?" he finally asked.

"No sense in that. He'd have called me a liar and it doesn't make a damn bit of difference to anything."

"No, it doesn't." Loving Halona hadn't changed Jed, except that it gave him a reason for adopting her son after she and her husband were killed, for keeping Rafe even after he'd abandoned Cruz, Sawyer and Cort. It didn't lessen his feelings, either, of bitterness, anger and, somewhere deep inside, that remnant of hurt, a relic of his childhood that he'd never been able to completely banish. But then he doubted anything Jed could say or do ever would.

"You're right," he repeated quietly, "it doesn't make a difference at all."

"For heaven's sake, Cruz, it's been over a month. What can you possibly be doing there?"

Holding in a sigh, Cruz scrubbed a hand over his face. There didn't seem to be any answer to his mother's question that wouldn't create more hurt and anger on her part than was already there. It was the first time he'd talked to her since he'd settled in at the ranch and he wondered if he'd subconsciously been putting off calling her for just this reason.

"There are some things I haven't settled yet with my brothers," he said, trying to sound reassuring, matter-of-fact. "And I've been working on a project here that's taken more time than I expected. I'll be back there soon."

"You've been saying that for weeks now and giving me the same excuses," Maria said. "What are you hoping to accomplish by staying? All this talk about settling things. They're strangers, all of them. Do you really expect they're ever going to truly consider you part of their family?"

Her words cut him because he didn't know. But he'd come to the realization that at least where his brothers were concerned, part of him wanted that—to belong, without reservation. Admitting that to his mother, though, would only add fuel to her fears that she would eventually lose her prominence in his life to others she couldn't help but resent. "I don't know what I expect," he said, not quite truthfully, "but I need time to figure it out. Like I said, I'll be back soon. We can talk more then."

He cut the connection a few moments later and stared at the cell phone in his hand as if it would suddenly provide him with answers. What he wanted to do right now, over anything else, was to call Aria, yet he felt like he needed an excuse, something more than just, *I need to hear your voice.*

That was the truth, and had been, almost from the first. Except lately, he could amend that to, *I need you.* He didn't know when it had happened and while he would have liked to write it off as simple emotional dependence during a time when he was at his most vulnerable, it wasn't that simple.

She'd suggested weeks ago he see a counselor, but she'd done more for him than anyone else ever could. Since he'd moved out of Josh's place, she'd encouraged him in his slow transition back into the work he loved, as well as keeping him involved helping her with the children's ranch project, and he'd found it better therapy than anything else he'd tried. Despite staying at the ranch and the tensions with Jed, his nightmares had been less frequent and he'd had fewer times when he felt as if things were falling apart.

Surprisingly, although he had no interest in Rancho Pintada itself, he found he liked this little corner of New Mexico. The open country, the mountains and the feeling of space soothed the rough patches of nerves, left him feeling unfettered by stress and the pressure to perform. Yet that was Aria, too. She never pushed, never left him worrying about what she thought about him or pressed him to live up to expectations he didn't know he could ever achieve. Luna Hermosa would never be more than a temporary refuge, but with Aria it felt more like home.

It wasn't, though, not really, not yet—if ever—and more and more lately he'd felt himself drawn back into his old life in Phoenix, restless to return to a hands-on running of his company instead of relying on long-distance e-mails and phone calls. He'd talked with Aria about it and she said she understood, had told him he needed to regain what he'd lost in his years overseas, that it was good he was ready to move forward. They'd finished the plans for the children's ranch a few days ago and so, she had pointed out, there was nothing holding him there.

The problem was while part of him agreed and urged him to leave, part of him—newer and untested—wanted to stay.

He couldn't justify it by saying he needed more time with his family. Jed had stopped pushing him to accept a share of the ranch and they'd shifted to being uneasy with each other, Cruz still uncertain how much more of a relationship he wanted with his father. His brothers he had no doubts about. They'd started to form bonds that would continue to strengthen whether he stayed or returned permanently to Phoenix.

It was Aria. He didn't want to leave Aria.

Rubbing his thumb over the smooth face of his phone, he thought about the e-mail he'd gotten from Derek that morning, detailing a new project. He smiled a little, flipped open the cell and punched in her number.

"I'm glad it's you," she said and he smiled, hearing Sully yipping in the background. "Somebody here wants attention and apparently I'm not providing it fast enough."

"I'm not going to help matters any. I was hoping to get some of your attention, too."

"Is something wrong?"

"I know you'll find this hard to believe, but there are times when I'm not trying to cope with some crisis or another."

"So something is wrong."

Cruz laughed. "No, I'd like your opinion on something. My company has a chance to bid on a project in San Francisco, but the client is interested in some alternative energy elements. I thought since you're the expert on green designs, you might be interested in doing some consulting work on this. I could come by, show you the proposal, if you've got some time today."

"How about I come there instead?" she said without hesitation. "Long story, but I need to drop a package by for Rafe anyway. I shouldn't be more than an hour or so."

True to her word, it was less than an hour and he was meeting her at the front door, avoiding the explanations to Jed or Del by leading her directly to the far end of the house, where he'd been spending a lot of his time.

"Does Jule know about your clandestine visits to her husband?" he teased lightly as Aria immediately flopped down onto the couch in the small office adjacent to his temporary bedroom.

She laid her head back against the cushions, eyeing him through half-closed lids. "I hope not this time. Jule's birthday is next week. I have a friend in Taos who designs jewelry and Rafe asked me for help in getting a special piece made." Her eyes drooped shut all the way and she made a contented murmur. "It's so warm in here. This project of yours better be really interesting or I might just go for a nap instead."

A glance at his watch told Cruz it was scarcely eleven, and yet she had the look of a woman at the end of a long, busy day. Concerned, he sat down next to her and reached over to brush a wayward curl from her cheek. "Has Sully been keeping you up?"

"What? Oh—no." Aria lifted her head, rubbing at her eyes like a sleepy child. "I'm sorry. I've been dragging the last couple of days. Too much going on, I guess."

"Then maybe this was a bad idea."

"No, it's fine. I'd like to take a look at the drawings, at least."

Not quite convinced it was fine, but not wanting to push, Cruz retrieved his laptop and showed her Derek's e-mail, containing the specifications for the bid. When she'd finished reading, Aria settled back again, lips pursed, nodding.

"It's an interesting concept," she said. "If you really want the help, I have a few ideas that could work."

Cruz got up to return the laptop to the desk and glanced back at her over his shoulder. "I can set you up as a consultant on the project. Are you sure this isn't going to interfere with everything else you've got going on? I've seen your workload."

"I'm busy but I can always fit in another project. And with the plans done there's not much else we can do with the ranch right now," she said, waving off his concerns. "We won't be able to break ground until spring. And that's only if the fund-raising goes well."

"Hasn't it been?"

"Pretty well," she hedged. "It's always a worry because even if we get enough to build, there's no guarantee right now we'll have enough to operate it. But I've been trying to confine my worrying to one thing at a time, and right now, that's getting the buildings up."

"Now who needs a vacation?" Cruz said. He sat down beside her again and after a moment, slid his hands over her shoulders and shifted her on the couch and started massaging the tight muscle. She felt good, her body becoming soft and pliant as she relaxed under his gentle kneading. Her yielding had the opposite effect on him. There was nothing soft or pliant about the way he felt when she was this close. Touching her woke the urge—the need—to move closer, to put his hands other places, making his rhythm falter.

He gave up massaging and pulled her against him, into his arms, for a moment pressing his face into the curve of her neck, against the soft mass of her hair. "I'm going back to Phoenix."

She stiffened, not moving away, but he could feel the sudden tension ripple through her. "Soon?"

"In a day or two," he said. "I need to get back to work full time. Derek has been doing his job and most of mine long enough. And

I need to spend some time with my mother." When she didn't respond, Cruz let her go. She turned to face him and he nearly took it all back. He'd hurt her and it felt like the worst thing in the world. Her eyes glimmered with unshed tears, her mouth a tremulous line. "Aria, we talked about this. You said—"

"Yes, I know. Don't remind me." She briefly pushed her palms against her eyes, taking a deep breath, and when she looked back up at him, she made a good show of being in control again. "It's okay. I knew this was going to happen. Like you said, it's not as if we didn't talk about it. I guess I'd convinced myself it would be later than sooner."

"Come with me."

The words came out suddenly, startling them both. And yet once spoken, it felt like what he'd meant to say all along.

"I do want your help on this project, but this is a good chance for us to spend some time together." She kept staring at him and he plunged ahead. "It seems stupid at this point to pretend we can forget everything that's happened and I don't want to. We keep saying it's not going to work, but we keep coming back to each other. Maybe we should stay this time and see where it leads."

He could almost hear her thinking it over and when the silence had stretched thin, he was pretty sure she was going to tell him to forget it, that whatever it was between them was over before it really got started.

"I'll go," she said at last.

Expecting rejection, it took him several moments to realize she'd said yes. "I can meet you in Phoenix." His blank expression seemed to amuse her and she smiled. "I always think it's a good idea to get as much of a hands-on feel for a project as possible."

"The project is in San Francisco," he reminded her. "We can go over the plans in Phoenix, but you may have to fly to California with me eventually to take a look."

Moving a little closer, she kissed him—a soft, sensual caress of her mouth on his. "I wasn't talking about that project," she murmured, and suddenly, instead of an obstacle, the trip back to Phoenix became full of possibilities.

Chapter Eleven

Aria was a bundle of nerves before the plane landed in Phoenix around dusk. And when a driver with a private car met her instead of Cruz, she wondered where Cruz was. He'd gone back two days earlier and she'd assumed he'd be there to pick her up.

Not that she hadn't traveled some, but entering Cruz's world, his life, especially after he'd mentioned a few things they might do in Scottsdale—spa, golf, tennis—as though she did those things every day, concerned her. Luna Hermosa didn't have a golf course or tennis court and the nearest "spa" was a mountain hot springs near Taos she'd never had the time to visit.

To her the idea of spending time in what many would consider luxury pursuits was uncomfortable. To him, it was obviously a way of life. So, as she climbed into the big black car that had been sent for her, she drew in a deep breath and sucked up her resolve. It could be fun after all, she supposed. Of course it could.

Carlos, the driver, wasn't a help in explaining why Cruz hadn't met her personally, other than telling her Mr. Déclan had asked him to pick her up. He took her to a high-rise building in downtown

Phoenix, parked, helped her out of the car and walked her inside to the elevator. When the door opened, he rolled her luggage bag inside, pressed the button marked "penthouse" and nodded a goodbye as the heavy doors pressed shut in front of his face.

When Cruz had talked about the apartment he hadn't seen in over two years, this was nothing like she'd imagined. She'd anticipated it to be smaller, spare, Spartan even. This place made her feel as if she were visiting a stranger, a man far removed from her world.

The elevator opened to a huge living area lined with floor-to-ceiling windows all around. The setting sun lent a coppery glow to the sophisticated room. Below, city lights hinted at nightlife and busy restaurants. The room was dimly lit and decorated in an elegant, masculine style. Soft music, jazz, helped to create an atmosphere that should have been relaxing, and might have helped soothe her nerves a bit if the man she'd come to see had been there.

"Hello? Cruz?" When no one answered, she was sorely tempted to turn, jab the elevator button and get out. She'd been dumped here alone, with no explanation and was expected to—what? Hang out until he decided to show up? Frustrated, she rolled her bag out of the way and walked over to the window to stare out at the hustle and bustle below.

A *ding* sounded behind her and the elevator door opened. Cruz, laden with an armload of rolled-up drawings and a briefcase, strode into the room, looking a little windblown and harried, but that didn't detract from how handsome a figure he cut in a dark designer suit, tailored perfectly to flatter his broad shoulders and trim waist. He tossed off the suit coat, dropped his drawings and briefcase on the floor and was pulling her into his arms before she could decide whether she wanted to complain, protest, or just kiss the hell out of him.

"I'm sorry I couldn't meet your plane," he said. "I had an unexpected client show up right when I was about to leave for the airport. He's Japanese and his English is sketchy at best. He was only going to be in Phoenix for the day, so I couldn't miss meeting with him." Not letting her answer, he slanted his mouth against hers in a long, deep kiss.

Giving up on protests, she pushed her fingers into his hair and savored the feel of him, breathing in the scent of his spicy cologne. Despite the kiss, the sense of unreality strengthened. This was a different man than she'd known in Luna Hermosa; his mouth and the things it could do to her were familiar, but the suit and the penthouse and the whole weird sense she'd walked into a different world had changed him into someone she scarcely recognized.

She suspected he could be as cold and hard-driving as any ambitious businessman, but she wondered how deeply imbedded that part of him was. To be as successful as he was, especially coming from nothing, no doubt he'd made some tough decisions along the way. Yet it was hard to reconcile the image of a driven man, arrogant, ruthless even, with the damaged, vulnerable man who'd brought her a puppy and trusted her, of all the people he could have confided in, with his insecurities and uncertainties.

"I don't blame you for being angry with me," he murmured, brushing a last, lingering kiss near her ear. "I promise, I'll do my best to make it up to you."

"I'm not angry," she assured him. "Just a little confused there for a while. I didn't know you had a driver and he isn't exactly talkative."

"We're still getting used to each other. He's a relative of my mother's who recently moved here from Guadalajara. I don't make a habit of using a driver, but I thought this might be a good way to give him a chance to make a living here. He's got five kids to feed."

"That's nice of you."

He shrugged, flashing a smile that belied his serious professional demeanor. "Mom didn't give me much of a choice."

"Ah, I see." She couldn't help but smile back. "Well, you're a good son."

Cruz backed away from her enough to loosen his tie and toss it onto a chair. He unbuttoned his shirt and pulled it out of the waistband of his slacks. "She would beg to differ with you on that at the moment," he said, turning to head for the kitchen. "Would you like a drink?"

She followed him into a large, modern kitchen of mostly stainless steel and deep sea green granite. "Wow, this is beautiful," she said brushing her fingers across the cool, stone bar countertop. Beautiful, but like everything else in the penthouse, impersonal, the design calculated to convey a specific image, not a personality.

"Thanks." He pulled an expensive-looking bottle of Vouvray out of a wine cooler and pulled out the cork. "I do enough business here to take the place off my taxes, so I have to let the style speak to my architectural bent."

"That makes sense," she said, accepting a glass of wine, while she wondered what her own modest house, the décor chosen because it was comfortable and pleased her, said about her bent, architectural or otherwise.

He lifted his glass to hers and looked deeply into her eyes. "To you. I want this time to be all about you."

"I'm here to work on the San Francisco project, remember? I don't want you to interrupt your schedule for me."

Setting his glass down and taking hers to place next to his, he gathered her back into his arms. "We'll work half days on that. And then we're going to play. This is our time and we're going to make the most of it."

"You know, this is not the way you sold this trip back in New Mexico," she said, trying in vain to keep her head and not completely succumb to the temptation he was dangling in front of her. "What are you up to?"

"Well, for starters, we have dinner reservations in Scottsdale at the Biltmore. Are you hungry?"

"Yes, but the Biltmore, come on Cruz, you know me well enough to know a green chili burger suits me just fine."

He nodded, taking her hand and leading her down an oversized hallway. "I know, but there's a reason I want to take you there."

She followed, loving the simple satisfaction of her hand resting in his palm, the only thing simple about this whole situation. "And that is?"

"The hotel was designed by Frank Lloyd Wright. It's an architectural wonder that I thought you might enjoy seeing, if you haven't already."

"No…" The feeling of being in the middle of a particularly vivid dream grew stronger. With his return to Phoenix, Cruz appeared to have regained an identity she scarcely recognized and wasn't sure she liked. While there probably wasn't a woman alive who wouldn't call her crazy for questioning the attraction of a sexy, successful, wealthy man, ready and willing to fulfill a few of her more sinful fantasies, that wasn't the man she'd shared confidences with in a darkened room. That man didn't have any vulnerabilities; he wanted her, but he didn't need her, and that made him no different than the other sexy, successful men who'd come her way.

"The frown doesn't bode well," he said, his voice caressing her ear, and she realized with a start they were standing at the doorway of a bedroom. "If you're not comfortable with staying here—"

"It's not that…" She hesitated. "Well, actually, it is that. But not for the reasons you're probably thinking."

"This isn't my bedroom."

"Too bad," she returned bluntly.

His eyes widened slightly and he momentarily seemed lost for words. She might have found it amusing if it wasn't important for her to make him understand.

"When you asked me to come with you, you said you wanted us to spend time together. I didn't think that meant living a fantasy life for a couple of days. You should have told me—"

"What? That my ideas of spending time together are different than yours?"

"That you were someone different than the man I met in Luna Hermosa."

That caught him off guard and he stared at her before blowing out a long breath, scrubbing a hand against the back of his neck. "I'm not."

"Cruz, look at this—" She gestured around them. "Everything I know about you, it isn't this. I can't imagine you calling this home."

"I don't," he said flatly. "It's a place to live and do business. I told you, I've never called anywhere home. This is no exception."

That made it worse. More and more, she was wishing that for

once, she'd listened to the voice of reason and stayed home, not let herself be seduced by the hope that maybe, with Cruz, things would turn out differently.

"Aria…" He reached out and gently traced his fingers over her face. "Give us a chance. For a few days, at least. Who knows…?" Leaning in, he brushed her mouth with his. "You might actually enjoy a little decadence and vice."

"Maybe," she agreed softly. If she could think of it as just that, a few days in a fool's paradise and then—and then home without him, packing a whole bag full of new regrets. But for now, she could pretend. Moving closer, she slipped her hands to his shoulders, murmuring against his throat, "It depends on the vice."

His smile suggested all sort of possibilities. "Let's start with dinner and then decide."

An hour later, in a new midnight blue Porsche, they pulled up to the valet waiting in front of the Biltmore. Cruz had treated himself to the car after his return from his tour of duty. It was an extravagance, but with the clients he served, it was also almost a business necessity to drive something that spoke of success.

"Hey, Fernando, how's it going?" he asked the valet as he handed him his keys.

"Good, Mr. Déclan, really busy tonight."

"Better busy than bored, right?" Cruz asked as he took Aria's hand after Fernando opened the door and helped her out.

"Have a wonderful evening," Fernando said with a nod.

Cruz bent and touched a kiss to Aria's hand. "We intend to."

"Okay, I'm feeling pretty decadent," she murmured as they walked through the breezeway into the lobby of the elegant hotel. "And definitely underdressed."

Slanting an appreciative look over the sleek long-sleeved black dress she'd chosen, he shook his head, smiling a little. "You're beautiful. You always are."

That earned him a return smile, even if it was touched with skepticism. "Careful, or I might start to believe you."

"I see I'm going to have my work cut out convincing you," he said, touching his hand to her waist as he led her through the lobby into the restaurant. He didn't see how she could possibly doubt it or be unaware of the heads she turned.

But then he also didn't understand her mood since she'd arrived. He anticipated her visit as an opportunity to escape, for a few days at least, the dramas in Luna Hermosa. He'd meant it when he said he wanted to see where whatever was between them would lead and he'd thought she wanted that, too.

She seemed hesitant, though, awkward about his lifestyle, and it was the last thing he wanted. Yet in a way, he could empathize, because it was how he'd felt in her world and around his family, an outsider floundering his way through, not knowing what pitfalls awaited him.

The insight strengthened his resolve to put her at ease, give them both a few days of respite from the emotional traumas of the past weeks.

"This whole place is gorgeous," Aria commented, glancing around them. "I've never seen anything like it."

"That's why I wanted to bring you here. After dinner we can go for a walk on the grounds," he suggested. "The lighting is beautiful at night."

As they were seated, he dedicated himself to keeping the conversation light and amusing, describing some of the history and the construction of the resort for her, and relating a few stories of his travels. Aria seemed genuinely interested, asking dozens of questions, looking impossibly lovely every time she laughed.

He was momentarily caught off guard when she changed the direction of the conversation to something far more personal.

"So, hasn't it been difficult to readjust to life back here, work, the daily routine? I've tried to imagine what it must be like for you, but it's hard. I've never lived so far away from home for so long."

Her question struck a sensitive nerve, and at first Cruz hesitated to reveal his true feelings. But with Aria, he couldn't hide, nor did he want to. "Yes. It's been more than difficult. I'm not comfortable here anymore, but I don't know exactly what to do about that. Traveling to Luna Hermosa has actually been a good thing for me—" he paused, emotions from the war, from learning about his father, from meeting and growing close to Aria sweeping over him "—in a lot of ways."

She smiled. "I'm glad about that." She reached across the table and laid her palm atop his hand. "Things will fall into place for you again," she said softly. "When the time is right."

Somehow her caring, her simple answer, comforted him and Cruz relaxed again. "For now, I'll take that on faith."

They both fell silent for a moment, then moved into an easy exchange of professional opinions on the San Francisco project and others they'd worked on, and he found himself as fascinated with the way her mind worked as he was the way her dress clung to her every curve.

"Dessert?" he finally asked.

"Tempting, but I couldn't, thanks."

"Then how about that walk?"

She smiled and this time, it was easy and natural. "Sounds perfect."

Cruz led her outside into the cool evening air. Even though it was the dead of winter elsewhere, it was warm enough in Arizona to be outdoors with only light jackets. They strolled past huge fire pits where people relaxed, sipping warm brandies and cool ports.

"I see why you like this place," she said, leaning into his side, her hands tucked around his arm.

"Not too sinful for you?"

"I could get used to it." There was a pause, a sigh. "Which probably isn't a good thing."

"I don't know about that," he said. Stopping, he shaped the curve of her face with the lightest of touches, savoring the tactile pleasure of her skin kissing his fingertips. "From where I stand, it seems like a very good thing."

"Cruz…"

His name came out on a breath of both longing and uncertainty, a potent mix that roused in him both a heady desire and an aching tenderness. He could remember all the things that stood between them, all the reasons why he didn't want a relationship fraught with meanings he'd yet to define. But he deliberately forgot them now, and instead of stepping back, he kissed her.

She yielded even as she took and her open willingness ignited what had been smoldering desire the moment he had first stepped inside his apartment and seen her across the room. He deepened his kiss and she met him equally, pushing her hands up his back where he slid his down hers. She moaned softly at the intimate press of their bodies, the sound finding an answering echo in him.

What began as a whisper of desire was rapidly becoming too strong and urgent to contain, and he knew he had to regain some control before they did something they both might regret right here in the backyard of the Biltmore. She didn't make it easy, wrapping her ankle around his, pulling him as close as possible, letting him know she wanted exactly what he wanted, regardless of where they were.

He almost—almost—let go of the frayed restraints, saying to hell with decorum and safety and a piece of his sanity. He could, knowing she would do the same and damn the consequences. He couldn't, because it would be much more than just sex and neither of them would walk away unscathed.

Jerking back a step, he let her go, breathing hard as they stared at each other.

It was Aria who finally broke the silence, in a voice that came out ragged. "We keep doing this. We don't *think*. We just …" Her hand came up in entreaty or a gesture of futility, both emotions written on her face.

"Yeah…" He hooked his hands behind his neck to keep from reaching for her again. "We do."

"It scares me," she said, so quietly he almost missed it.

Easily giving up the fight against what he wanted, Cruz pulled her close again, cradling her against his heart. "Me, too, sweetheart," he whispered into her hair. "Me, too."

Morning came too early for Aria after a restless night, disturbed by her private war between unresolved desires and that nagging voice of reason. She kept telling reason to shut up and let her enjoy the attention and the pampering, but also it was relentless, reminding her at every turn not only how different her and Cruz's lives were, but that he would never be content in Luna

Hermosa and she would never be at home anywhere else. He must have sensed her doubts when, last night, despite their moment of shared desire in the hotel garden, Cruz had left her at the entry to his guest room with only a kiss good-night and a wish for sweet dreams.

After a busy and productive morning at Cruz's office, he insisted on taking her to a desert spa, set in the shadow of rugged red rocky hills.

A tall, thin blonde Cruz introduced as Minelle greeted them. Her sharp blue eyes took quick measure of Aria before she turned a brilliant smile on Cruz. "I've missed seeing you. It's been a long time."

He smiled easily back, but it was devoid of real warmth and his hand stayed at Aria's waist in a subtle show of possession. "I've missed the hot spring. I think we'll try that first. Both of us could use some relaxation after the last few weeks."

Looking as if she wanted to pursue the subject of Cruz's absence, Minelle hesitated, then motioned Aria to follow her. "This way. We'll see Cruz out at the pools."

After showing her to a private dressing room and telling her to call when she was ready, Minelle left her to change. Aria swiftly exchanged her clothes for the bikini she'd brought, but after taking stock of herself in the mirrors surrounding her, she wondered what on earth had possessed her to bring a bikini instead of something more sensible.

She laughed at that. There wasn't anything sensible about the things she did around Cruz Déclan. Why start now?

Quickly grabbing up the robe that had been left for her, she took a breath and stepped outside to where Minelle was waiting to lead her to an outdoor pool. There were a number of similar pools of varying sizes and shapes, fountains and tiled walkways, intermingled between oases of rippling blue waters. They approached a cluster of walled-in circular structures made of adobe and rough-hewn wood. Minelle stopped to pull out a key. "Cruz reserved a private pool for you."

Of course he did. At this point, she wouldn't have been surprised if he'd reserved the whole place for them, intent as he seemed to be on indulging her at every turn.

He was already there, stretched out in the pool. The enticing view he presented made her forget feeling self-conscious. She gave herself over to the delicious sensation of slipping into the soft heat of the water while knowing his eyes never left her.

"Oh," she murmured, embarrassed that it came out more of a pleasured moan, "this is amazing."

Cruz, with a fingertip, followed the line of her bikini from her shoulder to the hollow between her breasts. "You're right, it is." She cocked a brow and he tried for innocence and failed. "Oh, you meant the water."

"Isn't that why we're here?"

He replaced his finger with his mouth, lightly tasting the side of her neck. "Something like that."

Her attempt at a clever comeback didn't get past the "mmm" stage. He was right. There were a lot more amazing things between them than the water. "Okay, you win. I'm definitely enjoying the decadence." She lightly kissed him, lingering long enough for it to become a sensual caress. "Thank you, for everything."

"It's the other way around. I'm the one who should be thanking you."

"For what? Unless I've missed something, you're the one fulfilling the fantasies here."

"I could argue with that," he said, and although they'd been lovers, the intensity in his eyes made her blush. "I meant thank you for agreeing to come here to begin with. I know you've had doubts, but I think this has been good for us. I know it's been good for me."

Aria wanted to agree and nearly did. But she was certain whatever good was coming out of this wouldn't last. For her, this trip and the time with him had only emphasized the difficulties, even the impossibilities, of them ever being more than temporary lovers. Instead of an outright untruth, she settled for nothing, a lie of omission. She leaned into him, sliding her hand around his nape and kissing him, intimately and from her heart.

He responded in kind and this time, there was nothing of the fierce, almost desperate passion between them, but a sweet, aching tenderness that brought tears to her eyes.

When Cruz shifted her into his lap, her mind fell silent with the resurgence of desire that came from the slick wetness of his skin under her hands and mouth, and the hardness of his body under hers. She couldn't think beyond how good it felt. Wrapping her legs around his waist, rocking against him, she reveled in the groan she elicited, wanting to push him to the edge, to give them both what they wanted.

One hand tangled in her hair, he reached around to flick open the tie of her top, letting it fall to her waist. The combination of the water and bare skin coming together nearly drove her wild.

Caught up in each other, neither of them heard the lock or the turn of the gate.

"Well, now," a woman's voice drawled. "I see why I wasn't invited today."

Chapter Twelve

It was the last way he'd wanted to introduce Aria to his mother: Aria in his arms, nearly naked, and Minelle watching the results of her escorting Maria Déclan into her son's private pool area, a glint of satisfaction in her smile. Cruz could cheerfully have wrung the woman's neck.

Unfortunately, the sight didn't dissuade his mother in the least. Maria walked poolside to take a seat on a lounge chair, scraped Aria with a glance and then fixed her attention on Cruz. "I went by your office and they told me you were taking the after-noon off and coming to the spa with your...*friend* from Luna Hermosa." She gave Aria a condescending once-over. "My son usually brings me to the spa, but he's been distracted and has avoided me ever since he got back home. Now I know why."

Guilt pricked him because there was some truth to his mother's complaint. It wasn't strong enough, though, to rid him of the overriding desire to leave Aria to recover her dignity and firmly escort his mother back to her car. Gritting his teeth, he pulled Aria's swimsuit top up, refastened it for her and briefly touched her cheek, apologizing with his eyes for the decidedly uncomfortable encounter to come. The side of her mouth quirked up in a bare, wry smile and then she slid off his lap, accepting his hand out of the pool.

"Mama, this is Aria Charez," Cruz said, making the introductions. "She's the architect from Luna Hermosa I told you about. Aria, this is my mother, Maria."

He wouldn't have blamed Aria if she'd acknowledged his mother and made a quick escape. But she acted as if she were meeting Maria in a formal setting, fully dressed and prepared, instead of having just been caught by her lover's mother in an intimate embrace, wearing a wet, revealing swimsuit. He couldn't remember admiring a woman more when Aria, poised and graceful, offered Maria her hand.

"I'm happy to meet you, Ms. Déclan," she said. "Cruz has told me so much about you."

"I can't say the same," Maria returned coldly. "But I'm also glad to meet the woman who has tempted my son away from home for so many weeks."

Cruz clamped down hard on his temper. "Mama, be nice. I've been going to Luna Hermosa for several reasons and you know it." The smile Aria had pasted on for his mother's benefit faltered and he inwardly winced at what sounded dismissive of their relationship. Taking Aria's hand, he squeezed lightly, relieved at the answering press of her fingers. "But I confess, Aria's become the most important of those reasons."

Maria's mouth tightened and she said nothing, although it was clear his involvement with Aria, a woman tying Cruz to the place that was Maria's version of hell on earth, was one more betrayal in her eyes.

"We were nearly finished here," he lied, trying to salvage what he could out of the situation, "so what do you say we all go grab dinner and get better acquainted. You can have a drink with Minelle while we change."

There was a pause, long enough that Cruz expected his mother would refuse, and then Maria gave a sharp nod.

When she'd left them, he shifted to face Aria. "Don't let her get to you. She hasn't forgiven me for agreeing to meet Jed and unfortunately, you're just one more reminder of where I've been the past few weeks."

"It's all right, I understand," she said as they started walking back to the dressing rooms, hand-in-hand. "The idea of Jed back in her life, even if it's just secondhand through you, has got to be upsetting. And then you meeting him, and finding your brothers and now me, after you'd been gone three years—all of that's got to be very threatening to her."

"Part of it's my fault. I haven't confided in her about any of this, at least beyond the bare minimum. She's not used to having to make her own guesses about what's going on with me and what comes next."

They stopped to turn into separate dressing rooms. Facing each other, she searched his eyes before asking quietly, "And what does come next?"

Cruz brushed his knuckles gently down the side of her cheek. Shaking his head, he said, "I don't have a clue."

Dinner on the patio at the exclusive resort was every bit as spectacular as dinner the night before had been. The atmosphere was completely different, though. It was all southwestern elegance with huge adobe buildings, giant potted palms, soft lanterns and colored lights illuminating ponds with fountains. Bright pink, orange and red bougainvilleas lined the walkways and the soft strains of Spanish guitar were in the air.

But all of the beauty and opulence did nothing to ease the tension Aria felt as the three of them toasted with an expensive champagne Maria had chosen.

"To new beginnings," Cruz said, lifting his glass.

Aria smiled, repeating softly, "To new beginnings."

Maria held her glass slightly away, adding, *"A la familia y a la prosperidad."*

Family and prosperity, Aria heard the underlying message, that she was a threat to both in Maria's mind. In one way, she could understand. From what little she knew, Cruz had been Maria's only family since she'd left Luna Hermosa and after so many years of struggling, she was now enjoying the security having a successful and devoted son could provide.

Nonetheless, it bothered Aria—she hadn't dared say anything to Cruz, knowing how defensive he was of his mother—that Maria had, all those years, kept secret that he had brothers. Maria's hatred of Jed was one thing, though as far as Aria could see, nurturing it over thirty-five years had accomplished nothing, and only prolonged the pain for Maria, twisting it into bitterness. Denying Cruz the chance to know his brothers—or even his father's name—was something else. This decision made out of vindictiveness against Jed that had damaged Cruz. In seeking to punish Jed, Maria had punished her son.

"Aria may help in increasing our prosperity," he was saying, drawing Aria back into the conversation. "Part of the reason she's here is to work with me on a project that involves green building. She is an expert in green design and so much progress was made in that area while I was overseas, I'm behind the trends."

"I'm returning a favor," Aria told him with a smile, adding for Maria's benefit, "Cruz is lending his expertise to a ranch I'm designing in Luna Hermosa for children with special needs. He's been a big help in resolving some problems I've had."

"A ranch?" Maria set her glass down. "What do you know about building ranch houses?"

"The engineering principles are the same," Cruz said with a slight edge to his voice. "And it never hurts to learn something new. Aria is using green building techniques on the ranch, too, so I'm picking up more about that from the design."

An uncomfortable silence fell over the group and Aria was relieved when the waiter brought the first course. "These salads are beautiful," she commented, trying to find a topic that Maria didn't object to. "Even the Morentes' restaurants don't have this elegant a presentation."

Maria stopped mid-bite at the mention of the name and Aria immediately wished she had duct tape for her mouth. Apart from Jed, Teresa Morente was probably the last person Maria wanted to be reminded of.

"I'm so sorry," she said hurriedly. "I should have thought—"

Cruz touched his hand to hers. "Don't worry. That was another lifetime, wasn't it?" He looked pointedly at Maria.

Maria sipped her champagne, avoiding his eyes. "Perhaps. For you."

Oh, boy, Aria inwardly winced.

Cruz let the drama slide, as evidently he often did, and turned to Aria. "As you were saying, the food is really good here. Wait until you taste the bison steak you ordered. The mushroom sauce is amazing."

"I'm looking forward to it. Bison is a favorite of mine."

"Maybe we should see who their supplier is," Cruz said with a small smile. "We might be able to get Rafe more business."

That he would bring his brother up so casually in front of his mother surprised Aria and she darted at glance at Maria, anticipating his comment would cause a new fuss.

But Maria instead frowned a little. "I thought he would have gone back to the reservation by now, to his family," she said with unexpected empathy in her voice.

Cruz and Aria exchanged a look. "Mama, he is with his family," he said with some hesitation.

"I meant his tribe. I know Teresa and Jed adopted him after his parents were killed, but I thought Rafe would have gone back to his birth family the first chance he had."

If things could get more difficult, Aria didn't know how. Obviously, Maria didn't know Rafe was Jed's biological son. She tried not to stare at Cruz, wondering if he'd explain or attempt to circumvent the dangerous pitfall with vagueness.

"Rafe stayed. He's expanded the ranch to include bison." Cruz toyed with his drink for a moment, let go a sigh. "He recently found out he's Jed's son. He's my half brother, the same as Cort, Sawyer and Josh."

Maria blanched. "That's not possible," she whispered. "Rafe and Sawyer are almost the same age. He was married to Teresa…"

"Jed had an affair with Rafe's mother. Rafe only found out last year."

Shaking her head, her expression stricken, Maria muttered something in Spanish too low for the others to hear. Aria had a good idea whatever it was involved damning Jed Garrett to a particularly vile place in hell.

Cruz briefly touched his mother's arm. "I think most would agree with you, but unfortunately, the devil is my father and I have to find a way to make peace with that." He paused then added quietly, "And so do you."

Aria's heart went out to both of them, but Cruz in particular. She could imagine the pain he shared with Maria, had shared all those years. She'd been blessed with parents who had been consistently and unconditionally loving to her and Risa and countless foster children. Cruz had never known any family but a mother who'd considered past wrongs old companions that she was unable or unwilling to abandon.

Before they'd finished their salads, the main dish came, a welcome distraction. It looked delicious, but something about her meal—maybe the advertised mushroom sauce—made her stomach give a sickening flip. She dismissed it as stress, brought on by the emotional ups and downs of the past few days, and tried to disguise her sudden lack of appetite.

The rest of the meal, Cruz did his best to keep the conversation light and as far away from Luna Hermosa as possible. Aria followed his cue and, ignoring her stomach, did her best to support him, to try and divert Maria from dwelling on past and present resentments.

As the evening wore down, though, so did her tolerance for Maria and her determination to remain foremost in Cruz's life. She admired Cruz for being a dedicated and responsible son, but at the same time, she doubted his sense of duty to Maria would ever let him expand his idea of family to include his brothers or Aria. It was startling how much that hurt. Yet hadn't she known from the start that Cruz and she were on opposite sides when it came to their vision of the future?

She skipped dessert and insisted on taking a taxi back to Cruz's apartment so he could drive his mother home. Cruz refused but she persisted, pleading queasiness and a strong desire to get out of her high heels and fall into bed.

Finally he gave in, writing down the lock code to his penthouse for her. Her stomach churning, she lay down in the back of the taxi for the hour's ride back to his apartment. By the time she got there her stomach had settled, but she felt strangely exhausted. So she caught the elevator to the top floor, punched in the code and went straight to her room to collapse into bed.

She awoke sometime later to the dip of the mattress and a large hand smoothing the hair from her cheek. In the darkness, Cruz was a shadow, but she knew his touch by heart.

"Oh, hi," she said, rubbing at her eyes. "Did you just get in?" She reached for the bedside lamp but he stopped her, his hand sliding from her face down the side of her arm to lace her fingers with his. The darkness, her inability to see his expression, was disconcerting, but Cruz, for some reason, seemed to want it that way.

"How are you feeling?"

"Better, thanks. I think that sauce was a bit rich for my peasant tastes, that's all."

Cruz bent and brushed a kiss to her forehead. "I was worried. I figured it was tension. Neither the conversation or the company was exactly relaxing."

"It's okay," she said, giving his hand a small squeeze. "This is hard on your mom."

There was a brief silence. She could feel him watching her, almost hear him weighing what he wanted to say. "You're amazing, you know that?"

A little confused, she asked, "What did I do to deserve the compliment?"

"My mother went out of her way to make you uncomfortable and yet you didn't resort to the obvious comebacks. I'm sure there were times you wanted to."

This time she was grateful for the concealing night, hiding her flush because although they hadn't talked about it, from that remark, she was pretty sure Cruz knew the less-than-complimentary thoughts she'd been having about Maria. "Anyone would have done the same, knowing what your mom has been through," she said aloud.

"No, they wouldn't. Trust me. I know from experience."

Oh, and there was a topic—Cruz's past relationships—that

she didn't want to get close to. Freeing her hand, she sat up and flicked on the light before he could stop her. He winced and she could see lines drawn around his eyes and mouth by too many troubling thoughts. "You must be exhausted," she said and without waiting for his permission, pushed his jacket off his shoulders.

He accommodated her, shrugging out of it, pulling off his tie, half unbuttoning his shirt, and then he reached for her, gathering her close in his arms. "I'm fine," he murmured into her hair.

"Sure you are." Gently disengaging herself and sliding over to make room, she patted the bed. "Lie down with me. Just let me hold you."

"This is the first time anyone's ever asked me to come to bed for that," he said, his half smile wry.

"Well, then you're way overdue." She waited, while he kicked off his shoes and stretched out beside her, settling in close, his head pillowed on her shoulder. Now and again, she swept a kiss over his hair, letting her fingers follow in a light massaging movement.

He felt so strong here in her arms and yet she knew parts of him were vulnerable. His experiences overseas had hurt him emotionally and psychically, and the effects still haunted him, the recent upheaval of meeting his family and Maria's sense of betrayal only adding to the burden already there. She longed to take it all away, all the pain and frustrations. But now she realized some of those wounds were old, remnants of his childhood, and buried deep in places she wasn't sure she could ever reach.

He had ties to his mother, his work and his way of life that were unlikely to be broken by what she could offer. She was committed, to her home, her family and friends and her dream of the children's ranch.

So it was good, the sensible voice of reason reminded her, that she'd come here where seeing the firsthand reality of his life, his priorities, his duties, forced her out of her fantasies, unraveled the dreams she'd tentatively begun to spin of a future with him.

Her heart wouldn't let it go, though, and continued to search for that place between here and there where their lives could intersect, until sometime during the small hours of the night, she dozed off, her thoughts escaping into a vision of them in the secluded pool, beneath the warm sun, holding each other, encircled by a wall she imagined would shelter them from tomorrow.

When she awoke to a kiss, she thought for a sleepy, fleeting moment she was still in the dream. Finding herself wrapped in Cruz's arms, she smiled into the darkness.

"You slept," he murmured against her lips.

"Passed out is more like it. You, too. What woke you?"

He pressed his lips to hers again, parting them to deepen the kiss, then he pulled back a little to answer in a voice husky with longing, "Wanting you."

"I want you, too," she said, and the urgency sprung up between them, yet tempered this time for her by the lingering bittersweet taste of her dreams.

As though her words unleashed him, he shifted over her. At the same time, she stretched her arms back up over her head, palms up, in a gesture that beckoned him to link his hands with hers, and he didn't resist. Even as he completed the motion, though, he was telling her, in a voice heavy with desire, "I don't want you to regret this."

"I won't. I couldn't. I need you."

With that he lowered himself to hold and kiss her with all of the passion he'd tried to bury, to deny. She clung to him, tugging the shirt from his pants and sliding her hands up under it to stroke sleek skin and hard muscle. He began to move against her, his clothes and hers unwelcome obstructions to the closeness they both craved.

They undressed each other, hurriedly, with no care for where their clothes ended up, and the heated touch of skin to skin made them bolder, greedier for each nuance of sensation. She pulled him closer, her mouth hungry for his, relishing his taste, his masculine, spicy scent, the strength of his body enveloping her.

She wanted him, with a need that consumed her, felt like it would never be satisfied. Cruz, though, seemed determined this time to stretch out each moment and make it last a small lifetime; intent on touching and tasting every inch of her body with the aim of obliterating every thought in her head and replacing them with feeling, pure and unquestioning.

It wasn't enough. It would never be enough. It was so strong, so overwhelming, she feared she would never want anything else, that everything else would measure as a poor second to what Cruz made her feel.

Patience fraying, she pushed her hips against his, and he met her, pressing his hard passion against her soft warmth, yet still holding back enough to drive her wild.

"Cruz ..." His name came out on a breath, both needy and frustrated and he answered with a low laugh.

"We have the rest of the night," he said, his mouth sliding downward from the curve of her neck to tease at her breasts.

"That's not going to be enough."

He paused to look at her then and even the darkness she could feel the intensity. "No, it isn't."

"Since that first night—" Her fingers traced his face, memorizing each plane and curve. "Every time I see you , every time you touch me, I want this. I need this—with you. Only you."

"I need you," he said, and the fierceness of emotion in his voice made it a vow. "There's never been anyone else, not like this."

"Then love, me, just love me," she almost begged him, no longer caring that he knew how weak she was when it came to him, no longer certain if she meant for tonight or forever.

Kissing her deeply, he shifted away far enough to slip protection between them before abandoning any pretense of control and sliding into her. The intimate joining stole her breath, had her arching to take him deeper, to make him a part of her so nothing mattered but them together.

She wouldn't think about tomorrow, or beyond the next moment. This, this closeness was all she wanted or needed, this ancient rhythm that felt new because it was them.

Their music grew louder, passion escalating the private dance as she wrapped her legs around his waist and held him as though she could never let him go. He moved further into her, their bodies damp with exertion, soft moans and cries becoming the air between them.

It came too soon for her, the blaze of release for both of them, and when it was over and she was lying in his arms, listening to his breath and heartbeat slow, then the tears came and she closed her eyes against them, wanting to believe, for a little while longer, that in the light, her heart wouldn't break.

Morning came, too early, it seemed, when Cruz's nuzzling woke her. But a glance at the nightstand clock told her it was nearly ten thirty, too late for any longer in his arms if she planned to follow through on her promise to herself to leave today.

"This feels incredibly sinful," she murmured, exerting every bit of willpower she had not to succumb to his slow, sensual caresses. "I can't remember the last time I stayed in bed this late."

"It's okay," he assured her, lightly nipping at her earlobe then laving the spot with his tongue. "We have a light day today. We'll stop by my office, go over a few things, and then we're free to play."

Oh no, she couldn't do this. Not again. The incredible night they'd had played over in her mind's eye. But in harsh morning light, she couldn't pretend any more. She'd caved into her yearning for him last night, knowing today she would have to leave him. It was selfish perhaps, but in the wee hours all she had wanted was him, his love, their passion, one more memory.

Before she said goodbye.

She eased out of his arms, avoiding his eyes. "I'm going to take a shower, okay?" Confronting him with her decision wasn't going to happen without clothes and caffeine.

"Sure. I'll do the same and then I can make you some breakfast," he said following her out of bed. Her back was to him but he turned her around and searched her eyes. "You okay? You seem—distant. Do you regret last night?"

"No, no regrets," she told him. "Last night was…unforgettable." Taking his face between her palms, she reached up and brushed her lips with hers. "I just have a lot on my mind. We'll talk at breakfast, okay?"

"All right," he said slowly, looking unconvinced. "But I'm already not sure I like where this is going."

Not able to offer any reassurance, she lightly kissed him, swallowing against a surge of emotion. "I won't be long," she said, quickly heading for the bathroom.

When he'd gone back to his bedroom she hurried to shower, dress and pack. She had to do this quickly or she'd be right back in his bed with him continuing in a dream bound for disaster. No matter how incredible, how tender, loving and perfect their union in bed was, it wasn't enough. And more of the same would only complicate, not resolve things.

By the time she got to the kitchen he had coffee, eggs and toast ready for her. Smiling, he set their plates out, but she found she could scarcely eat a bite. Even the smell of coffee, usually one of her favorite aromas, was knotting her stomach.

"I can't believe you're not hungry," he said, indicating her barely touched meal. "Especially after last night," and his smile suggested every intimacy they'd shared.

"My stomach is still a little queasy. Thanks so much for making this." She briefly closed her eyes, wishing this wasn't so hard. "I'm sorry."

Reaching across the table, Cruz lifted her chin with his fingertips. "Hey, no apologies, okay? I can make you something else, if it sounds good."

"No, it's not that." She drew in a deep breath, forcing herself to say it. "I'm going home. Today."

He stared at her a moment, his expression frozen. Then he leaned back in his seat. "If this is about yesterday—"

"It's not about yesterday or any other day I've been here. This trip has been wonderful. I've loved being with you and I enjoyed all of the things we did. And last night was—" she felt her voice tripping over itself "—perfect." Pausing to grip her composure closer around herself, she measured her next words. "But being here has also shown me what kind of world you live in."

"As opposed to what?"

"As opposed to mine. Our lives are so different, it's almost funny. I can't expect you to change, I wouldn't want you to give all this up, or cause any more problems with your mother."

"I know she's been difficult," he said, and Aria could almost hear his internal wrestling between his loyalty to his mother and wanting her to feel he understood her reservations. "She'll come around, in time."

"I think we both know time won't solve it. Any of it." Pressing her palms against her forehead, she struggled to find the words, any words, that would make it all easier, stop it from being so painful. "I can't believe I let myself do this again." She had, too, jumped in heart first to the deepest place possible with him, without thinking, letting her feckless feelings take charge. "You have this and I can't leave my life and my work in Luna Hermosa. If I let this go any further I know you could seriously hurt me and I just don't have it in me to be able to go through that one more time."

"And you're so sure I'm going to hurt you?" Looking at him, she was caught off guard at the bared pain in his eyes.

"No—" she said hoarsely. "No, it—it's not you, it's…this." She gestured helplessly around them. "It's everything."

"I don't want you to go. I don't want you to give up on us so easily." His tone held an edge she hadn't heard before. "You're the only person I can trust completely with what I feel. I need you. Especially now." Pushing to his feet, he put his back to her, rubbing a hand over his neck, abruptly spinning around to rivet his gaze on her. "More than anything, I want you. I want to be with you. I don't know how this is going to work, but I want the chance to try."

She wanted to believe it was that simple. That if they wanted, need, cared enough, that somehow the walls between them would crumble. She'd never felt closer to a man than she did to him. From that first night, it might have been meant to be.

But that was just romantic nonsense. Experience had taught her there were no happily ever afters. Love came down to practicalities and trust. He might trust her and she'd no doubts he sincerely wanted to make them work. Reality was they couldn't work while he wanted one thing and she another, and there was no middle ground between the two.

"I want to. But I can't." Overpowering her self-control, never more than tenuous to start, tears slid down her face. "I can't take the chance."

"On me? Are you sure about that? Because I think you're afraid to take a chance on you. I'm not saying it would be easy or that we wouldn't have to make compromises. But you've apparently been in this pattern of failed relationships for so long that I think you don't know a good one when you see it."

Aria felt as if he'd hit her. "I know exactly what I see. You just won't admit that there's more wrong between us than right." She couldn't do this anymore. Couldn't hear any more, argue, fight a battle that she desperately wanted to lose. Getting to her feet, she faced his hurt and anger and asked quietly, "Could you call me a taxi? Please?"

"I can," he said and in his voice the pain was layered with a stubborn determination. "But there's no need. I'm going with you."

He was there then, at her side and when he touched her, she wouldn't be able to stop him, to resist falling into his arms and back into the dream.

"No, Cruz. You're not." She stepped back. "Please, don't. It'll only hurt us both more than it already has."

But that, she thought, couldn't be true, because surely nothing could compare to the wrench of leaving him, this time for good.

Chapter Thirteen

The tiny baby cuddled in her arms snuffled a little, yawned and opened her eyes. Aria felt like crying.

She swallowed hard, blinking against the sudden blurring tears. What was the matter with her, that she couldn't hold a baby without getting choked up? Since she'd gotten back from Phoenix a week ago she'd had these moments, weepy and pathetic, and she blamed it on her decision to go in the first place.

"Aria, are you all right?" Maya came back into the living room, carrying the two mugs of tea she'd gone to fetch. "Here, give me that little girl," she said, sitting down next to Aria and reaching for her daughter, "and drink your tea. You look like you need it."

Great, caught in the act. "I'm fine." Aria gulped her tea, scalded her tongue and tried to look fine, figuring from the skeptical arch of Maya's brow she was doing a miserable job. Hoping to distract her friend from asking questions, or—worse— deciding for herself what was wrong, she lightly stroked Isabel's silky fluff of dark hair. "She's beautiful. It's hard to believe she's already six weeks old."

Maya smiled. "You mean after the drama of being born on Christmas Eve? I think she was trying to outdo her brother Joey, who was delivered by his dad in the back of an ambulance during a storm. Speaking of drama …" Shifting Isabel to her lap, Maya studied Aria for a moment. "Feel free to tell me to mind my own business, but I'm guessing something is wrong between you and Cruz."

"I'm not sure there was anything to go wrong to begin with," Aria said, trying to deflect Maya's probing.

"That's not the way it looked to everyone else. He spent more time with you than anyone. On New Year's Eve, when Eliana told him you weren't feeling well, he couldn't get to you fast enough. And then the trip to Phoenix… You have to admit, it looks like a lot of something is going on."

"Phoenix was business." Aria couldn't say it without flushing at the barefaced lie. "Okay, it wasn't business and maybe there was something between us, but not anymore." And that was a lie, too, but she had to find some way to make it the truth. "We're too different. He has his life there and mine is here, and believe me, there isn't much common ground. It would never have worked." Her voice caught at the end and she cursed not being able to keep her feelings out of it, knowing Maya and her finely tuned emotional radar would pick up on everything she wasn't saying. "I'm sorry, I'm tired. I think I picked up some bug in Arizona and that's not helping. It was a long week in Phoenix, and I came back to a pile of work that I'm still trying to catch up on."

"Yes…that could be it." The way Maya looked at her made Aria uncomfortable. Maya glanced at Isabel, gently caressing her daughter's cheek, a small smile touching her mouth.

Oh, no, don't even go there, Aria silently warned her. Even the thought of *that*—she couldn't bring herself to think of the word— was ridiculous. She and Cruz had used protection and… A jolt of fear pulsed through her, stopping her dead. No. She wasn't going to consider the possibility because there wasn't a possibility. It was impossible, just like her and Cruz being permanent was impossible. Not even she could mess things up that badly.

Apparently, her credit in Heaven wasn't completely maxed

out because before she was forced to completely change the subject—which would confirm to Maya that her suspicions about Aria and Cruz were right—Sawyer did it for her by coming home, Nico on one hip and Joey hanging off his hand. Peace and relative quiet gave way to a noisy flurry of activity as both boys made for Maya, Joey chattering nonstop about "buff'los" and horses and lots of cats.

"I think Rafe's decided Joey's a born rancher," Sawyer said to Aria, over Joey's excited retelling of his horseback ride to see the bison. "Joey would be over there every day if we'd let him."

"Apparently Joey wasn't the only one riding out to see the buffalos," Maya said, shaking her head at Sawyer. "Sawyer and Rafe don't see any problem in taking a three-year-old and a toddler out riding," she told Aria. "I swear they'd have Isabel and the twins out there if they thought they could get away with it."

Sawyer laughed, kissed his wife and scooped up his baby daughter, snuggling her in the crook of his arm. "I bet she'd love it."

"Hey, hey," Joey said, patting Aria's arm to get her attention. "Uncle Rafe has cats."

"He does?" Aria smiled at his enthusiastic nodding. "I didn't know that."

"In his barn. They was little, but now they're big. I want one. You can have one. There's lots."

"I'm sure there are, but I already have a puppy. I don't know if he'd like having a cat for a friend."

"Can I see your puppy? I want a puppy. And a buff'lo."

"Well, that might be fun, but where would they all sleep? Buffalos are pretty big."

Joey thought it over for a moment then said, "They can sleep in Nico's bed."

Hearing his name, Nico looked up from running one of his toy cars over Maya's knee, and scrunched up his face at his brother as if he understood Joey's solution to oust him from his bed in favor of a menagerie of critters. Everyone laughed.

Aria spent a few more minutes talking with Sawyer and Maya, and admiring Joey's and Nico's collection of cars, trucks and tractors. She was at the point of saying her goodbyes when the door chime interrupted. Sawyer went to get it, returning a few moments later, but not alone.

Cruz was with him and with no check in his stride, he came straight to her as she stood up to face him. "I was looking for you. We need to talk."

There was an awkward silence when no one seemed to know what to say, but Cruz ignored it. A sense of relief loosed the tension that had been gripping him since Aria left him behind in Phoenix with a finality that said whatever they'd started was over. Maybe he'd imagined it because it was what he wanted to see, but he could have sworn he'd seen a brief flare of hope in her eyes when he'd come into the room. He was counting on it because that would mean no matter what she'd said, she wasn't ready to give up on them, either.

"I know some boys who could use a snack," Maya said, getting to her feet and picking up Nico. She and Sawyer exchanged a meaningful glance. "Could you give me a hand?"

Left alone with her, Cruz resisted the desire to pull Aria into his arms and use the communication of touch they were so good at to tell her how much he'd missed her.

"How did you find me?" she asked.

"I made some calls and Jule told me you'd come here to see Maya. I would have called you first, but I didn't want to give you the opportunity to tell me to get lost." The barest trace of a smile flitted across her mouth and, encouraged, he added, "I thought I'd have a better chance face-to-face."

"Why did you come back?"

"I would have thought that was obvious," Cruz said. "I told you in Phoenix I was coming with you. It just took me a few days to get things wrapped up so I could get away. But after handling my company for the three years I was in Iraq, my staff easily manages things when I'm traveling."

She shook her head sharply, turning away from him. "I thought we'd agreed that we weren't going to work."

"You agreed."

"Cruz—"

"No, don't." Gently he turned her to look at him and on her face saw a mix of uncertainty and pain. "Don't give me the speech again about how different we are, or how we could never find any middle ground. Those are just excuses because you're so sure this is going to turn out like every other time."

"And you're going to offer me guarantees it won't?" she shot back at him.

"No, but I can promise I won't lie to you and I won't walk out because it gets hard or complicated."

"It's already complicated, and it's hard because we don't want the same things. You want honesty? Well, here it is—I want something permanent, I want a life in one place, a family, and I'm not willing to compromise on those things. Not anymore. I've tried that and ended up picking up the pieces too many times. With you it would mean—" Cutting herself short, she briefly closed her eyes, drawing in a shaky breath. "I can't do it again."

"I can't let you go." He reached for her, her protest smothered by his mouth on hers. There was no pretense about this; it was blatant, pure passion, intimate and deep and she gave, without hesitation, as much as she took. He finally broke it off when both of them were breathless, but he kept her close and she held to him tightly, whether to make sure he stayed or because she was steeling herself to let him go, he couldn't tell.

"Let's get out of here," he said against her ear. "Have dinner with me."

"*Dinner?*" Her short laugh had a ragged edge to it. "After that, you want to have dinner?"

"Not really," he admitted. "But I think we'd be more likely to make it through a conversation without it ending like this if we weren't alone."

Aria fingered the edge of his duster, looking troubled, divided on what she wanted to do. Then she seemed to make up her mind and lifted her eyes straight to his. "Okay, dinner. But I'm not making you any promises beyond that."

"Fair enough. All I want is a chance to talk."

She didn't tell him no, yet Cruz had the impression she wanted to. Instead of putting him off, though, it made him more determined. They said their goodbyes to Sawyer and Maya, and then he followed her back into town, to Morente's. Cruz had been to Sawyer and Cort's grandparents' restaurant a few times in his visits to Luna Hermosa, and because of his brothers, had become familiar with a lot of the staff. He wasn't surprised when the manager, Nova Vargas, greeted Aria as a friend, him warmly and eyed the two of them with a lively curiosity as she personally showed them to a table.

"You're getting married in two weeks, why are you here?" Aria asked Nova.

"Because I'm such a terrific manager, there's nothing left to do," Nova said with a mischievous grin. "At least that's what I keep telling Alex. Actually, we're keeping the wedding short and simple. I'm more interested in the party afterward. So we'll see you there, both of you," she said, including Cruz with a knowing smile.

"Ah…we aren't—"

"Three weddings in a row without a date and you'll never hear the end of it. Besides, you two won't want to miss seeing the scandal of Cort walking me down the aisle. See you Saturday." With a wink, she turned and left them to the attentions of the waitress.

After they'd ordered, Aria rubbed at her temple and slanted him a look, her smile rueful. "Sorry about that. That's just Nova. Don't feel like you have any obligation to go. I'll never hear the end of it, anyway."

"It sounds like it might be entertaining. Although I'm missing how Cort walking her down the aisle counts as scandalous."

She relaxed a little and Cruz congratulated himself on distracting her from her embarrassment over Nova's deciding they were a couple. "That's because you don't know their history. Cort and Nova used to be lovers and Alex Trejos is one of Cort's best friends."

"Okay, that's a little weird."

Aria smiled. "I guess, if you don't know them. Cort and Nova were never serious, but they've stayed friends since high school, and Cort's partly the reason she and Alex are together. Once Cort figured out they'd starting seeing each other, he went out of his way to encourage it. So now he's pulling double duty at the wedding. He's Alex's best man, too."

Cruz took her hand, lacing his fingers with hers. "Maybe we should go together. For Cort's sake." When she stared at him in confusion, he said, "If people have us to speculate about, maybe they'll leave him alone."

"Oh, that's lame," she said, laughing as she freed her hand and reached for the glass of seltzer water the waitress brought. "You're going to have to come up with a better excuse than that."

"How about I just want to be with you?"

Immediately, she sobered and put down her glass. "That sounds wonderful, but be realistic. It's hardly enough to qualify as a basis for a relationship."

"Do you want to be with me?" he asked bluntly, tired of all the details getting in the way of what really mattered.

"Cruz, I—"

"Do you?"

"Yes. But it doesn't change anything. Do you honestly believe that we'll ever be able compromise on the big things? We're used to completely different lifestyles. I'm here and you're everywhere. I want marriage and children, and you aren't sure if you even want close ties with your brothers."

"I didn't say it would be easy."

"I can't see that it would be anything but short-term," Aria said, refusing to back down. "And frankly, I'm tired of short-term. I've done that too many times. If I thought we had a chance…"

"We can make our chances." He wasn't going to back down, either, not when it was this important to him. "You're right, we've got a lot of ground to cover before we get to the middle and I can't give you any guarantees. All I can say is I think we've got something special and if we give up on it now, we're going to regret it like hell. I know I will."

Staring at the table in front of her, she ran her finger up and down her glass, drawing patterns in the wetness. Cruz hesitated to push her any more than he already had. Either she went into this willingly, wanting it as much as he did, or he had to be ready to cut his losses and walk away now, before it got any more painful.

"We keep doing everything backward," she said at last, so quietly he almost missed it.

He nearly asked her what she meant, but he thought about it a moment and realized she was right. They'd become confidants before they knew each other, lovers before they were friends, partners before they'd learned how to trust one another.

"It's probably a little late to start over and do it in the right order," he said, offering her a rueful smile when she looked up at him.

"Probably," she agreed. With a sigh, she finished off her seltzer water, setting the glass back down with a decisive snap. "We can't fix the past. And we can't realistically hope for a future. But for now we can be friends, can't we? So, will you go with me?"

"To the wedding? As a *friend?*"

She nodded. "But I'm giving you fair warning. I hate Valentine's Day."

Cruz considered her invitation. He wasn't wild about being called a friend, but at least she hadn't slammed the door completely on him. "I would ask what Valentine's Day has done to you, but I'm afraid I'd get a repeat of the New Year's Eve answer. Apparently whatever it was has caused you to misplace your sense of romance."

"It was more like it was knocked out of me," she said darkly.

"Then I'll have to see what I can do to help you find it."

"Is that a yes?"

"If you mean the wedding, how could I refuse such a charming invitation?"

Even in the low light, he could see her flush. He smiled and she yielded, her brisk, almost sharp manner softening. She was more at ease, as she laughed at herself and her grudge against holidays. "If you had any sense, you would. Wedding, Valentine's Day, being one of the top ten topics of gossip—that's a combination for disaster where I'm concerned. You're doomed."

He leaned over, slid his hand into her hair and lightly kissed her, lingering until he felt her pulse quicken under his fingertips. "I'll take my chances."

* * *

The next two weeks passed in a flurry of work. Cruz had gone back to Phoenix to see his mother and to work and Aria had buried herself in the San Francisco project and in tweaking details on the design for the children's ranch.

She could hardly believe Valentine's Day was already here. And happily, as Valentine's Days went, it was turning out to be one of the best, so much so that Aria was almost ready to call a truce in her one-woman boycott against all things hearts and cupids.

The wedding, as Nova had promised, had been short and simple, yet at the same time both romantic and moving. The party at Morente's afterward was a typical Nova affair—on the wild and loud side of fun.

Hours into the reception, as she waited for Cruz to return from getting them drinks, Aria reflected that inviting him had been one of her better impulses. Between the choices of fending off comments about why she was dateless again and being envied and whispered about because she'd shown up on the arm of the long-lost fifth Garrett brother, she much preferred the latter. It was a definite bonus that Cruz happened to be one of the sexiest men on the planet, and that he was giving a terrific impression he was all hers.

She admitted she liked it—the stir they caused showing up together and the speculation his attentiveness caused. It added an extra excitement to the evening, letting everyone guess, smiling in reply to their not-so-subtle questions about her and Cruz's relationship.

"I hope you're thinking about me," a deep voice intoned, brushing her ear. Cruz sat down beside her in the dimly lit corner they'd commandeered a few minutes earlier, both of them wanting a break from the crowd.

The combination of the warm whisper of breath and the rough-edged voice against her sensitive skin sent a shiver through her. "Why's that?"

With a deliberate casualness he picked up his wineglass and

leaned back a little in his chair, a small half smile playing with the corner of his mouth. "Because you looked…satisfied."

"Arrogant," she challenged him, but without heat.

"Ah, so you were thinking about me."

"Maybe."

"Care to share?" He straightened and shifted the slightest bit closer, not touching except in the way his eyes moved over her, renewing memories of the times they'd done so much more than touched.

"I was thinking how glad I am we came together," she said. She ran her finger around the edge of her own glass then lightly licked at the tip, tasting the intoxication. "See, we can be friends." The gap between them narrowed to heat and she whispered the last of it into his ear, "But I still like the way your pants fit."

"I'm glad you're enjoying yourself," Cruz said, the cool politeness of his tone betrayed by the undisguised lust in his face.

"Oh, I am. This is the best time I've had at a wedding in years," she assured him and meant it. Suddenly she wanted to be in his arms. It was in a roomful of people after all. What harm could there be? "Dance with me?"

He raised a brow, smiling a little. "My pleasure."

She stood up to encourage him, too quickly it seemed, because for a moment her blood rushed south and the room gave a sickening spin. Before she'd realized he'd moved, Cruz was at her side, his arm around her waist, steadying her.

"Are you all right?"

She grasped his hand until the feeling ebbed. "I'm fine. It's nothing."

Cruz's skeptical frown clearly said he didn't believe her. He swept her with a glance then gave a quick scan of the room. "Sit down," he told her, starting to guide her to a chair. "I'll find Sawyer."

"No, please, don't," she said. The last thing she wanted was Cruz convincing Sawyer that she needed a paramedic. Sawyer, she knew, would insist on checking her over, and there would be an embarrassing fuss over nothing. "I'm fine, really. I think I could use a sugar boost, though. Would you mind getting me a soda? I need to—" She gestured toward the restrooms in the opposite corner.

"I'll go with you."

"I'm pretty sure I can manage this on my own. Please—" She put a hand to his chest to stop him from following her anyway. "Just the soda, okay?"

He didn't like it, but she didn't give him another chance to argue with her. She managed to make it to the restroom without anyone stopping her, and by some miracle it was empty. Wetting a paper towel and pressing the coolness to her nape, she stood over the sink, closing her eyes, taking long, deep breaths. The light-headedness was gone but she still felt weird, off balance, edgy in a way that had nothing to do with her earlier desire to be alone with Cruz.

She started to give herself the usual excuses—she was tired, coming down with something, stressed over work and not knowing where she was going with Cruz—when her conversation with Maya earlier in the week haunted her.

Herself, using those same excuses with Maya, and Maya studying her, saying *Yes, that could be it,* then glancing to the baby in her lap.

A numbness—the kind of blankness that comes after a shock—settled over her. Mechanically she balled up the paper towel and tossed it away and then slowly walked back out into the throng.

She was grateful to Cruz for not asking any questions, for accepting her distraction as a sign of her not feeling well and, less than an hour later, offering to take her home. He saw her safely inside her house and hesitated, obviously debating whether to insist he stay to watch over her. Something in her face must have warned him she wouldn't agree, not tonight.

"I'll call you tomorrow before I come by, to see if you need anything," he said instead. Very gently he smoothed the hair back from her temple, tracing his fingertips down her cheek, then brushed a kiss over her mouth. "Get some sleep."

She nodded, not trusting herself to say anything, and waited by the door, watching him leave, staring at the empty darkness for several minutes before jerking on her coat, grabbing up her purse and keys and heading out to her SUV.

There was a grocery store at the edge of town, open until eleven, and she quickly found what she needed, managing to avoid running into anyone she knew in the few minutes it took her to make her purchase.

Back home again she took her time, leaving the small box sitting on the bathroom sink while she took care of Sully, changed her clothes and stripped off her makeup and found a dozen other things to do until, calling herself a coward, she made herself take the test.

Then she waited and all the while she told herself she was being ridiculous, paranoid because of what she imagined Maya was hinting. It just wasn't possible. She couldn't be pregnant.

She kept repeating it like a mantra while she waited for the test results, pacing restlessly, watching the clock. At the exact minute, she retrieved the wand and, holding her breath, looked at the result.

Chapter Fourteen

She stared at the test result, willing it to change.

This can't be. This can't happen. Not now. Not with Cruz.

Immediately she felt sick, though she doubted it had much to do with her being pregnant. This nausea stemmed from fear—no, fear was too mild a description. This was sheer panic.

Dropping down on the closed toilet seat, she buried her face in her hands. Of all her bad decisions, messed-up relationships, this had to be the worst. Cruz had made it clear he didn't want a family now—if ever. She wanted a family, but not like this. Nowhere in her dreams or plans had there been anything about single parenthood.

Why couldn't things have been different with him? He was the one man she'd been with whom she respected and admired enough to imagine as a father to her child. He had all the qualities of a good parent that counted in her estimation: intelligence, honesty, sensitivity, reliability, a capacity for devotion. But none of those traits could make him want to *be* a husband or father.

He'd said he wanted to try with her. Try what? He hadn't made any definite commitment. She knew he believed they had "something special," but what did that mean? Unfortunately, she doubted he would feel the same once he learned he was going to be a father.

How could she tell him?

Getting to her feet, she looked at her image in the mirror, the pale, drawn face, dark circles under her eyes, her hair a tangled mess. She grimaced at her reflection. "What are you going to do, girl?"

No answers magically appeared, only more questions. Shoving her hair back into a loose braid, she splashed cold water on her face and then took herself into the living room where Sully lay fast asleep on his puppy pillow. She bent to stroke his ears. "Funny. You've been helping prepare me for being a mommy, haven't you little guy?" With a snuffle, Sully half opened his eyes, rolled over and obligingly offered his belly for a good scratch. "You're easy, though, aren't you? You're fine with just me and I won't have to worry about midnight feedings or day care or your college education."

She crouched next to the puppy, absently rubbing his belly, considering her options.

Of course, she had to tell Cruz. Yet envisioning the resulting scene did nothing for her queasiness. Knowing Cruz, he would blame himself, insist on staying with her, probably marrying her, in part because that's the kind of man he was, but more certainly because he would do anything not to be the kind of man his father was.

And none of that was good. Duty, obligation, guilt and pride were all bad reasons to start a marriage and she wasn't about to use any of those to make him stay with her.

At the same time, she was afraid. Raising a child alone was an incredibly daunting proposition. She knew single mothers struggling to manage work, child care, finances and emotional needs. Many of them were amazing women she held in near awe. But she didn't want to be one of them. She wanted a willing partner to share her life, her love and their children. Wanted, but wasn't necessarily going to have in Cruz.

Yet despite her fears, all the reservations and regrets, she knew, if nothing else, she was going to have this baby, raise him or her with or without Cruz in her life. For her, at least, that wasn't a choice. The rest of it… She blew out a hard breath and got to her feet.

Going into the kitchen, she brewed a cup of chamomile tea to help her sleep, all the while worrying about how to tell Cruz. He had a right to know. She had to tell him—when? *Soon,* her conscience insisted. Except then it would be beyond her control; Cruz would take charge, and they would be at odds over what was best. There would be no time to sort out what they meant to each other because there would be too many other issues in the way. On top of it all, there would be all the ramifications of having to tell her family and his, and his mother—*aye, aye, aye, I don't even want to go there.*

The tea wove its spell and she yawned, a drugging tiredness settling heavily over her. Sleep, that was all she wanted now. She crawled into bed, curled up under the thick layer of blankets, anticipating the dark hours when there were no decisions to make, no prickly dilemmas to surmount. Oblivion came slowly, though, and lying alone there in the big bed, she splayed her palm on her flat belly. A little life was already growing beneath her hand. Miraculous, amazing, scary all at once. And beautiful. Was it a boy or a girl? Would he or she have Cruz's eyes or hers—or theirs? Would their baby be quiet and calm or feisty and talkative?

Dozens of questions drifted through her thoughts, eventually lulling her into a sleep woven with visions of a sweet brown-eyed baby girl with thick chestnut hair, and a rambunctious little boy with Cruz's smile.

"This is exactly what she needs," Cruz told the salesgirl at the Taos ski shop. "She's been a little under the weather lately. I'll get her skies and bindings now then bring her in a little later to size her for boots."

Cruz had been working in his makeshift office in Josh's old quarters at the ranch since Valentine's Day. He couldn't leave Luna Hermosa until he knew Aria was okay. For the past few days he'd tried to get Aria out of her house, but she'd steadily refused him, or to even let him stop by, claiming she had too much work to do and pleading the vague illness that seemed to be lingering long past Phoenix. She needed to relax, get out, have some fun, get away from her drafting board and out into the sunshine.

"Nice gift," the salesgirl said with envy. "My boyfriend won't even buy me a cup of cocoa at the ski lodge." She led him to the women's section of the store. "What color are her eyes?"

Envisioning the times he'd drowned in those eyes, he said, "Brown, dark brown."

"Perfect. She'll love this." Flicking through a rack of vests, jackets and sweaters, the girl pulled out a ski sweater in rich shades of dark turquoise and brown. "Isn't it awesome?"

"She would look amazing in this."

"Great! What size is she?"

Uncertain, he critically eyed the choices, selecting a medium, and then letting the girl package up his purchases. Satisfied with his plan for the day, he locked Aria's new skis next to his atop his rented SUV, pulled out of the parking lot and punched in her number. "Hey, how are you?"

"Um, okay," came the less than enthusiastic greeting. "You?"

"Great," he said, refusing to let her deter him with any more nebulous excuses. "Have you been outside today? The weather's terrific."

He waited through a long stretch of silence and then she hesitantly said, "Well, no, not yet. I've been home working on the San Francisco project."

"Good. Then you won't feel guilty if I tell you you should take the rest of the day off."

"Cruz, I can't—"

"I'll see you in an hour or so." Before she could object, he flicked off his phone and, smiling to himself, looked forward to making the drive to Luna Hermosa in the shortest time possible.

Aria stared at the phone. Quickly she redialed Cruz's number but got only his voice message. Damn him—his timing was rotten. Less than five minutes before he'd called, she'd lost her breakfast and the last thing she felt like doing now was having a confrontation with him. Then again, she should have known he wasn't going to buy her lame excuses forever.

Grabbing a brush, she smoothed her hair into some semblance of order, quickly changed out of her ratty sweatshirt into a newer fleece shirt. But the old faded jeans she wasn't going to give up. They were loose from years of wear and washing, and her stomach needed that comfort at the moment. Makeup? *Forget it,* she thought, getting away from the mirror as fast as possible.

What did he want to do today that had him so disgustingly cheerful? Shouldn't he be working on the San Francisco project too? Their deadline was just around the corner and they both had plenty of loose strings to tie up. She didn't want to see him. Not now; not like this. Hiding her pregnancy was hard enough when she felt well, but this morning, feeling and looking like roadkill, how could she look him in the eye and say everything was fine?

The ensuing hour felt like months, and she paced, gave up until the door chime woke Sully from his puppy dream. He rushed to the door, miniature guard dog on the job, barking with the protective ferocity of a dog three times his size.

"Okay, mister tough guy, you can back off," she said, picking him up. "It's only Cruz. You know—the Good Samaritan who rescued you?" Taking a deep breath, she planted a kiss on Sully's fuzzy head.

Reluctantly Aria opened the door to Cruz's smile. He was carrying a bag and the completely irrelevant thought wandered through her head that he always brought something to surprise her. "What are you up to this time?" she asked as he tossed his coat on the rack and stomped the snow off of his boots onto her entry mat.

"You'll see in a minute. But first, I want to have a look at this little guy," he said, dropping the bag and reaching for Sully, who was practically bouncing with excitement.

As he scratched the puppy's head, Aria's imagination pictured him with a baby in his arms, and in her mind's eye he was pleased, proud, wearing a loving expression that was raised to her when she came to his side. The image felt so real it made her want to throw herself into his arms and tell him she was pregnant. At the same time, it couldn't be real and that made her want to run.

Coward, she chided herself.

He turned his attention from Sully to her, cupping her face to kiss her, then handing her the bag. "Go ahead, open it. I want to see if you like it."

Curiosity won out for a moment, and she reached in and pulled out the most beautiful sweater she'd ever seen. "Oh, it's gorgeous." Fingering the silky soft garment, she smiled a little at his determination to please her and then the thought came to her that within a couple of months, she wouldn't be able to wear it.

Something must have shown in her face, because Cruz said softly, "If you don't like it, it's okay. We can return it when we get your boots."

"Boots? What boots?"

"The ski boots that will go with those," he answered, taking her by the hand to gesture out the window at the skis atop his SUV.

"You want to go skiing?"

"I know this is a surprise. I don't even know if you ski. But if you don't, this is the perfect day to learn. We'll take it easy and if nothing else, the lodge has great hot chocolate and a big fire."

She needed a defense against this, against him, and his way of making her feel they could do this, run away from life whenever they wanted, ignoring the necessity of coming back. "I do ski, but I haven't in years. Work, other things, are always in the way." *Other things, especially right now.*

"Those excuses aren't going to work today. You've been cooped up here for days. I guarantee, a few hours on the slopes, and you'll feel yourself again."

"If only…"

"If only what?"

"If only it were that easy."

"Trust me," he said softly, dragging his knuckles down her cheek. "It is that easy, if you'll let it be."

She couldn't. And it was her fault he didn't know it, adding guilt to the weighty mix of fear and uncertainty she was already struggling with. Putting the sweater back into the bag, she handed it back to him. "Thank you, but I can't keep this. And I can't go with you today."

His expression shuttered and for a moment, he studied her with an intentness that made her feel as if he could see through her. "Am I going to get an explanation?" he finally asked.

"I've told you, I'm—"

"Working, busy. Yeah," he drawled, "I've heard all that. How about an honest answer?" Her hesitation and the flush she couldn't control spoke before she could. He held up a hand, warding off whatever she might have said. "Guess not." Grabbing his coat, he shouldered into it before picking up the bag.

"Cruz, don't leave like this."

"I'm not seeing a lot of options here," he said shortly. Relenting a fraction, he gently brushed a strand of hair from her temple. "Whatever it is, you can tell me."

"I—" *want to, need to, wish so much I could and know that it was the right thing* "—can't. Not now. I'm sorry—"

"No apologies. This was a mistake on my part."

"It wasn't," she insisted, standing in the doorway when he stepped outside. "It's not you."

"Well, maybe another day." With a touch of his mouth to hers, he turned and strode to his SUV without so much as a glance back.

She watched him drive away, numb to the cold that couldn't compare to the chill in her heart, his words reverberating in her head.

This was a mistake on my part.

A shiver ran through her and she realized her palm was resting on her belly.

By early evening, after attempting to work on a drawing for the San Francisco project, but unable to focus enough to get any work done she realized she had to talk to someone or she was going to lose her mind. But who? Mentally, Aria ran through her list of friends and family, pausing when her dad's understanding smile came to mind. Deciding he was the one person she could confide in, she hurried to get her coat and boots, leaving her drafting table a mess.

He answered the door, his face creasing with familiar worry lines when he saw her there, unannounced and unexpected. But he didn't ask, letting her tell him, in words and feelings that tumbled out of her after being held inside, unshared, too long.

"You know what to do," he said when she'd finished. "Tell him, and the sooner the better."

"It's not that simple. I almost wish he'd go back to Phoenix so I didn't have to hear him tell me he doesn't want this baby. Or worse, accuse me of deliberately trying to trap him."

"I think that's you talking, not him," her father gently chided. "From what you've told me about Cruz, he'd be more likely to blame himself. Be honest with yourself, Aria, do you really think he's that kind of man?"

"No," she admitted, "he's not. He's the kind of man I always imagined I'd fall in love with. But I am being honest when I say he isn't ready for a family. He may never be. He's having difficulty coming to terms with having brothers. And then there's the whole mess with Jed. I can only imagine his reaction if he knew he was also going to be a father."

Joseph stroked his chin, contemplating her a moment. "Well, I can't judge what he may or may not do because I don't know him. But I have to ask if you're being fair to him. Or are you letting your other bad experiences make up your mind before you even give him a chance?"

"I can't envision him ever finding a place for a family in the life he lives. We're so different. We want completely opposite things. Besides there's the issues with his mother. Plus, I can't move from here and there's nothing here for him. I just don't see how it could ever work, even if he was willing to help me raise this baby."

"Beyond all those superficial things—"

"You wouldn't call them superficial if you'd met his mother," she replied darkly.

"How does he feel about you?"

Her father's softly spoken question caught her off guard. She'd agonized over how Cruz would react to a child and their opposing lifestyles and desires, never once considering his feelings for her. "I...don't know."

"Maybe you should answer that question before you make any decisions about this," Joseph said. He paused, looking off into the distance a moment and Aria imagined he was thinking of her mother. "When a man loves a woman, he can change his life overnight."

"I don't want him to do that, to change everything for me."

"But he might want to do exactly that. You'll never know what he really wants until you tell him about the baby."

Aria thought a minute before answering. "He's done so many things to show he cares. And he's been the one all along pushing me to give us a chance."

"So? Doesn't that count for something?"

Her defenses rising, Aria pushed off the couch to pace to the fire, staring into the low flames. "Yes, but I can't count on that being enough." *But I want it to be, I want it to be everything.* "I just want what you and Mom had. Is that too much to ask?"

Her father stood and embraced her, his arms protecting her as they had so many times when she was a little girl. "That's what I want for you, too. Your mother and I had a wonderful life together and even now, after she's been gone so long, I still love her. But you have to accept that with Cruz it might be a little late for that, honey. You have to deal with what has happened and the way things are now, regardless of the way you wanted things to be."

Aria knew her dad was right, but it was hard to accept. She'd always idealized her parents' loving, caring relationship, had always promised herself she'd settle for nothing less. Could she have that with Cruz? She'd never know unless she told him the truth.

"I wish I could have it to do over again," she said against her father's shirtfront, feeling as vulnerable as the child she no longer was.

"And what would you do differently?" he asked.

And the only answer she could give was the truth. "Nothing. I wouldn't change anything."

Stepping back and taking her hands in his, her father smiled. "Maybe it's time you let Cruz know that."

Chapter Fifteen

On the way to Taos to return Aria's gifts, Cruz abruptly stopped and turned the SUV around, back in the direction of Luna Hermosa. He didn't understand what was happening to her, to him, to them, to the universe in general, but he was at the point where he felt like banging his head against a tree.

For the first time in a long while—maybe ever—he wanted to talk with someone, a friend who would listen and might provide an insight into why he kept pursuing a relationship that seemed destined to go no further than it already had, why he wanted a woman who took one step toward him only to run a mile back. If he were honest, it wasn't insight he needed so much as confirmation of what he'd suspected for a while now—that he'd walked blindly into something he had no experience with, wasn't prepared for, and couldn't have anticipated, and that it was too late to extricate himself without inflicting a wound that would never heal.

He considered his friends in Phoenix, and immediately rejected calling any of them. Most were more colleagues than confidants, and this was too personal. Apart from that, they didn't know Aria. But his brothers did...

The thought was disconcerting and at the same time, strangely reassuring. Despite his stubbornness in accepting the family bond, it was there and for the first time, welcomed.

He considered each of them. Rafe or Josh would most likely be around this time of day, although he remembered Sawyer saying something about Josh going to Denver to pick up a piece of furniture for his mother. He felt awkward tracking Rafe down on the ranch to ask for a shoulder, but then again, if he never put his family ties to the test, he would never know if they were the real thing or tenuous.

Inside the gates to Rancho Pintada, he followed the narrowing road to Rafe and Jule's house. When he pulled into the drive he found Jule loading baby paraphernalia into her truck. He parked his car and walked over to her. The twins wiggled restlessly in their car seats, their big, dark eyes finding him.

"Hey, stranger, what a nice surprise," she said, giving him a warm hug. "What brings you our way?"

"I was wondering if Rafe was around. I wanted to talk to him."

"Rafe is with the herd. I need to go help him this afternoon because Josh got delayed in Denver. There's been so much snow this winter we're having to do a lot more supplemental feeding with the herds. They can't get down to the grass."

"I never considered the heavy snowfall in ranching terms," he admitted.

Jule snapped the car seats closed as Cruz stood glancing from baby to baby. "Why would you?" she asked.

"I suppose I wouldn't. But I can't help feeling a bit guilty about being happy with the snow this morning because all it meant to me was a great ski day."

"Hey, no worries," she said, smiling. "That's what it means to most people up here. Only cattle ranchers—or in Rafe's case, bison ranchers—see too much snow as something to dread."

Jule's understanding eased Cruz's mind and he focused again on the infants in front of him. He remembered Christmas Eve and having Nico, a sturdy toddler, in his arms, and how that had been daunting at first; he couldn't imagine cradling anything as small as these babies.

"Which one is which?" he asked Jule.

She laughed. "Sometimes I can't tell, either, so I have to dress them in clothes that identify them. The one in the yellow snowsuit is Catalina. The one in the purple is Dakota. Dakota's in a fussy mood today. He's clinging to Mommy. Normally he's all Daddy's boy, but not today. I think he's teething."

"Is he?" He hesitated at how it would sound then said, "I have to say, of all my brothers, I have the hardest time seeing Rafe as a father. I don't mean that like it sounds—"

"But he isn't exactly the daddy sort?" Jule finished. "It's okay, you're not the only one who thought that. All I can say is that from the moment they were born, he's been terrific with them. Not that it didn't take some time for him to be convinced they wouldn't break every time he picked them up, especially since they were both so small. But now he's more of a mother hen than I am. And don't you dare ever tell him I said that, because I'll deny it to the death."

"They're beautiful," he murmured. "Rafe's a lucky man to have you and these two great kids."

"Well, thank you. We feel pretty lucky, too."

When the babies were locked in securely, Jule turned her attention back to him. "Are you all right? You seem a little down."

Cruz walked her to the driver's side and opened the door for her. "I've got a lot on my mind, that's all. I thought maybe I'd talk to Rafe, but if he's busy I'll make it another day. It sounds like he's buried in work."

"He is, but then there's never a day when he isn't. That's the life here." She climbed into the driver's seat. "But you can go to the big barn and talk to him while he's getting the feed together."

"I can do better than that. I'll help him. As it turns out, I'm free today."

"Great. I might see you there a little later, after I drop off the munchkins."

"Thanks, Jule."

She stopped just short of turning the key in the truck's ignition. "For what?"

"For being a friend—"

"Hey, we're family remember?" Closing her door, she rolled down the window. "Talk to Rafe about whatever's on you mind. He might not be the warm, fuzzy type, and he's not much of a talker, but he's the best listener of the bunch and when he does say something, he's usually right on target."

"I'll keep that in mind, thanks." He turned to go back to his SUV, but she called after him.

"And Cruz, know that I'm always here for you, too. We all are, okay? You're stuck with us for better or for worse. Don't forget that whenever you need anything."

She left him, with a smile and a wave, and a renewed sense that here, in the unlikeliest of places, he was beginning to recover an elusive and missing piece of himself.

He found Rafe in the big barn hard at work doing something that involved mixing grains and some powdered mixture. "You slumming today?" Rafe asked when he turned at the crunch of hay beneath Cruz's boots. Brushing his palms down his jeans, Rafe offered a hand.

Cruz shook it and smiled. "I hardly call this slumming. You're running a huge organization here."

"Yeah, but my boots are covered in cow dung."

"Nothing wrong with that. Work is work."

"Well, I wouldn't trade it, but it's not exactly what you're used to. So, what brings you out here?"

Feeling uncomfortable and almost wishing he hadn't, again, made one of those impulsive decisions that threatened to backfire on him, Cruz considered what to tell his brother. "I heard you needed a hand and I had some time."

"Right." Rafe leaned back against a pole, his dark eyes narrowed. "You expect me to believe that?"

"Not really," Cruz said, shaking his head at the lameness of his excuse. "I'm just buying myself some time. I haven't gotten used to believing someone would care to listen to my angst."

"Took me a while myself. What is it? Something with the old

man?" Rafe paused, eyeing his brother closely. "No, it's not that, is it? Must be a woman. Aria?"

Cruz gave a huff of humorless laughter. "Jule said you were a quick study."

"Doesn't take a lot of brains to figure that. Only a woman can give a man your kind of look. You know—" he gestured in Cruz's direction "—the one that says you've been hit hard, fast and from behind."

"She's driving me crazy."

Rafe let out a derisive snort. "What else is new? That's what they do best. Jule and I are good now. But I'll tell you, I just about rode one of my bulls off a cliff a few times before we got married."

"I know the feeling." He paced a few steps away, back again, seeking an outlet for the tension wound hard inside. "I thought we had the start of something good. It felt—right. It still does. But she—" Blowing out a breath, he shook his head. "She's lying to me. I don't know what it is, but she keeps shutting me out. I know I should walk away. I don't need to be kicked in the head too many times to get that message. I just—can't."

"You sound like Jule with me. I was the stubborn one. I couldn't let her love me."

Knowing with a certainty the strong bond between Rafe and Jule, Cruz raised a skeptical brow. "That's hard to believe."

"Maybe, now. But then…I didn't think I deserved her."

"That's crazy," Cruz said bluntly, thinking about all he'd heard that Rafe had done with Rancho Pintada to increase its size, productivity and profits.

"People are crazy. You never know what's motivating them."

"I thought I knew with Aria. We've always been straight with each other. Until now."

Rafe fell silent a long minute, forehead furrowed as he considered the situation. "From what I know, Aria's not been real lucky when it comes to relationships. Maybe she's worried you won't stick around. Don't take this wrong, but you haven't given any of us the idea you plan on staying any longer than you have to."

There was truth in that, at least a partial truth. His ready answer would be he'd never had the opportunity to grow accustomed to settling in one place for very long after a lifetime on the move.

"When I was a kid, I used to imagine what it would be like to have more family than my mother, a whole family," he confessed. "Now that I've got one, I'm not quite sure what to do with it."

Rafe nodded, picking up his shovel again to shuffle some grains into a large bin. "It takes some getting used to. The question is, do you want that with Aria?"

"I don't know," Cruz said, giving the only honest answer. Until now, he hadn't seriously considered the idea of love, marriage, children, because it had been for him something other people did…people who had grown up with roots and an example of stability. Yet he began to see that as an excuse. Even though none of them had strayed from Luna Hermosa, his brothers—Rafe in particular—had been raised in fractured and less-than-loving homes and had overcome the handicap, allowing themselves to love and be loved.

"You might want to figure that out," Rafe said. "If you're sure that's what she wants, then you need to know what you want. I'm not much on giving advice, but don't do something you're not ready for. It's a big drop into those waters. But for the rest of us, it was the best dive we ever took."

His brother was right, and it was time, long past in fact, that he faced his feelings, daunting as that might be, and decided what exactly he wanted with Aria and the rest of his life. He had, before the war, before finding his family, been sure of what he wanted. Until his brother's wedding night, when he stepped into his father's house for the first time in his life and laid eyes on the woman who hadn't left his heart or mind for a single moment since.

Stripping off his ski parka, he tossed it on a stall gate. "Why don't you let me do that? From what Jule said, you've got more than enough to do today, and I'm pretty sure I can handle this. You'd be doing me a favor. Working is a good distraction."

Rafe swiped his forearm over his brow. "Can't say I would mind the help. It's pretty rough around here right now with all this damned snow."

"Good. Then we'll both be making the best of a bad day."

* * *

The door chime woke Aria, who was curled in a corner of her couch, from a light doze. She glanced to the mantel, to the clock that wasn't there, made an exasperated huff and grabbed her cell phone, flipping it open to check the time. Ten o'clock. Only one person would be on her doorstep at this hour of the night. She should have known he wouldn't keep his distance. Cruz was nothing if not single-minded when it came to something he wanted. Shoving her feet into fuzzy slippers, she steeled herself for another confrontation that couldn't possibly end well.

"It's freezing," she said, shivering as she hastily ushered him inside. She looked him up and down, trying to make sense of the dust and bits of hay on his parka and boots. "You look like you spent the afternoon in a barn. I thought you were heading for the ski slope."

"My plans changed."

"I'll make a pot of coffee and you can tell me about it." She surprised herself at how natural the offer felt, how frighteningly simple it was to overlook the way they'd parted this morning.

"Thanks, I won't turn it down. I wasn't sure you'd even open the door," he said, following her to the kitchen.

Guilt slammed her and she faced him, certain it was written on her face. "Cruz, I'm not angry with you. That's not what this is about."

"I know. You don't need to defend yourself. Let's have some coffee and talk."

"Do you mind decaf? It's kind of late." She hoped he wouldn't remember her drinking strong coffee at all hours. But now she had to be careful about caffeine.

"Decaf is fine. Sorry it's so late. I'll get the mugs."

Their easy partnership in the small and homey task was disarming. Even after the tensions of the morning, tonight it felt as if they'd been married for years. After their minor spat earlier, it seemed that all was forgiven, all forgotten for the pleasure of spending the waning moments of the day together.

When the fragrant rich aroma told her the coffee was ready she took the pot to the table, where he'd already set out the mugs, honey and milk. For a few moments they sat in silence, Aria taking comfort in the familiar ritual of doctoring her brew.

"So you couldn't stay away?" she asked finally, keeping her tone light, gently teasing.

"I'm a masochist."

"I believe it."

"I would, too," Cruz said. The tenor of his voice, somber, with a thin edge of anger, was a warning that the easiness between them couldn't last. "Except I believe there's more to this than you're telling me."

Aria's pulse leaped. She lowered her eyes to her coffee mug, hiding a stab of panic. He couldn't possibly know the truth. Could he? "Why would you think that?"

"Because I know that no matter what you say, you want to be with me as much as I want to be with you. And not just as a 'friend.'" Reaching between them, he took her hand. "Look at me and tell me it's not true."

Slowly, reluctantly, she raised her chin to meet his steady gaze. "I can't."

"Then I think I at least deserve a reason for why you've backed off from me so suddenly. I have a guess as to why, but I want to hear it from you first."

No, you don't. The truth is the last thing you want to hear, believe me.

Her conscience, though, restive since she'd learned about the baby, began rebelling in earnest. *Tell him. You have to tell him.*

She would, but she didn't have to do it today. She needed time to think, to plan, to get used to the idea of becoming a parent herself before she had to cope with all the emotional trauma Cruz learning the truth would inflict.

"I don't know what you want me to say," she told him. "We've been over this. Can't we just agree it isn't going to work and stick to being friends?"

"No," he said flatly. He let go of her hand and sat back in his chair. "I hardly think that's possible now, particularly when I don't agree."

"Maybe not, but I don't want us to be enemies."

"Nor do I. I want what we had, and more. I think you do, too. A lot more."

"Yes, I do. I've already told you that. But not like this."

Cruz made a frustrated gesture. "Like what? You're expecting me to accept something I don't understand and you won't explain."

You have to tell him. "I know who you are and what you want out of life." *Coward.* "You should go and get it." *The longer you keep secrets from him, the more he's going to hate you when he finds out.* "And let me stay here and live the life I want to live."

"Maybe you don't know what I want," he said quietly.

What is he saying? "I think you've made it pretty clear with the choices you've made."

"Choices change."

She waited, nerves spiked with anticipation, for him to elaborate. She'd reached the point of shaking it out of him when he caught her gaze head-on.

"I know you're afraid I'm going to hurt you. That whatever we have is temporary. I haven't given you a reason to believe otherwise. I've never been in a committed relationship, nor did I ever really intend to be." He paused and his eyes darkened with an emotion she didn't dare try to interpret. "Until I met you."

"Cruz, don't…" She nearly begged him. "Not now."

As if she hadn't spoken, he kept talking, kept saying things that made every moment she held her own secrets more painful. "I'm the first to admit I'm not very good at relationships. But I know one thing, most of my life, people have been hiding things from me, things that would have changed my life. I got into the habit of not trusting anyone, even my mother, to be straight with me. But I'm tired of living with secrets and lies. I want what we had from the start, honesty. I want to trust in us, that we can make this work."

Without knowing it, he had made everything worse. "I—I don't know what to say," she managed to say, ashamed at the lie.

"The truth," Cruz said. "If you've made up your mind we can't be together, tell me now because I am committed to you. I didn't plan it, I wasn't sure I even wanted it, but it happened and it's not going away. If it's not what you want, then say it and I'll be out of your life, for good." He rubbed at his temple, the motion jerky. "I can't do this back-and-forth with you anymore. I need to know."

The pain surged so strongly she couldn't have answered him even if she had known what to say, and Aria closed her eyes against it. She should tell the hardest lie and send him out of her life. It was better than turning his offer of commitment into an unwanted obligation by telling him the truth.

She felt him watching her, anticipating, uncertain of her response, and yet she couldn't think of anything that wouldn't destroy them both. She didn't want to hurt him; didn't want to lose him. But most of all she didn't want to hold him for the wrong reasons.

When she continued to feed the silence, Cruz pushed away from the table and knelt by her chair, drawing her into his arms. Leaning into him, she let her tears soak his sweater, as he rocked her gently, making soothing strokes along her back.

"It's okay," he said softly. "I don't need an answer now."

"You deserve one," she whispered. She was tired, so tired. His willingness to understand made it all the harder to be strong, to push past the fear and get an answer to a question she desperately needed to ask: would he accept her and the baby out of caring—maybe love—instead of cold duty and responsibility?

Could what they had be everything?

Chapter Sixteen

Maya shut the door to the exam room at the Wellness Clinic. She turned to where Aria waited, sitting on the exam table, after her consultation with Dr. Gonzales. "Congratulations, you're going to have a baby." Smiling, she walked over to her friend and laid a gentle hand on her arm. "But we both already knew that, didn't we?"

"I think you guessed before I knew," Aria said, her answering smile a pale imitation. After putting it off for days, she'd finally come to Dr. Gonzales for confirmation of the obvious, even though it meant Maya, who worked hand-in-hand with Sancia Gonzales, would find out.

"You don't seem exactly elated. I assume Cruz is the father and that you and he didn't plan this."

"Yes and hardly. We were using protection. Obviously it didn't work."

Maya handed over her shirt and jeans. "He doesn't know yet, does he?"

Guilt was like an old companion now, sitting in the corner,

nodding agreement every time someone reminded her that she'd failed, yet again, to do the right thing. Answering with a curt shake of her head, she avoided Maya's eyes as she shrugged into her shirt and jeans and slid off the table.

"Let's go to my office and have some tea," Maya offered. "I'm sure Sancia has told you that you and your baby are doing fine. But there are a couple of things we should talk about."

"If you're going to tell me I need to tell Cruz, I'll spare you the effort," Aria said bluntly. "Dad's already given me that talk and neither of you can do a better job than my conscience."

"What kind of tea do you like? I have a special herbal brew that most people find relaxing."

Aria gave a short laugh, the brittle sound of it grating on her own ears. "That's right, ignore me. And I know all about your *special brews*. Sawyer's warned the whole town about them."

"Sometimes I think Sawyer believes I'm practicing some form of witchcraft," Maya said, leading Aria to a small, cozy office at the back of the clinic. She waved her to a seat on the couch as she put a pot of water on to boil.

"Well, if you've got some potion that will solve all my problems, I don't care how bad it tastes.

"I'm not sure what I can tell you, beyond what you've probably already guessed," Aria hedged. She'd been over this, so many times, with her dad and in her head, it was becoming a mantra, repeating itself over and over through every thought.

Maya glanced up from pouring out two cups of tea. "If you're worried I'll tell Sawyer—"

"No, it's not that," Aria said as her friend sat down beside her. "It's just that I'm feeling bad enough over this whole thing, I'm not sure talking about it with anyone else but Cruz is going to help."

"But you haven't. So, where do things stand between you two now?"

"Honestly, it's pretty miserable. We've been together quite a bit lately because I'm working with him on a project in San Francisco and you know he's been helping me get ready for the groundbreaking on the children's ranch."

"At least you have work in common," Maya said. "It's got to be nice to be able to share what you love doing."

"Well, it would be if we didn't have this elephant in the room. It's my fault. Cruz knows I'm keeping something from him, he just doesn't know what. He tried to be patient and understanding at first, but then he wanted a commitment and I couldn't tell him yes, and he finally got fed up."

The unforgiving memories of that night stalked her, when Cruz had offered her a future and she had left him waiting again, too long this time. After several days of her silence on the subject and his practically pleading for an answer, he'd abruptly changed tactics, treating her with a cold professionalism. They now pretty much confined themselves to discussions of building materials and possible groundbreaking dates.

"You can't really blame him, can you?" Maya asked.

"No. I don't. How can I? He was more patient with me than most men would be. Especially given that his mother kept so many things from him. He hates secrets and now I'm keeping the biggest one of all from him."

Looking troubled, Maya began, "Aria—"

"Don't say it." Aria held up her hand to stop the inevitable. "I know, and I will tell him. I'm just not ready to deal with the consequences."

"And those would be—"

"Him staying." At her friend's slight start of surprise, Aria gave a rueful smile. "It doesn't make sense, unless you know Cruz like I do. He'll stay because he'll feel obligated and he'll try to convince me to marry him, for the sake of the baby. I can't do that. I've seen too many children suffer because one or both of their parents didn't want them."

For a few long moments Maya sipped her tea and contemplated Aria over the rim of her cup to the point Aria had to stop herself from squirming. When she finally did comment, it was the last thing Aria expected. "Do you really think that little of him?"

"I—of course not," Aria retorted, more sharply than she intended. "He's a terrific guy. I've never met anyone as honest and open about his feelings as he is, and I know I could always count on him to—" She was abruptly stopped by Maya's knowing smile. "Okay, you set me up for that one."

"Guilty. You just seem awfully determined to throw up obstacles when it's obvious you care about him."

"I do," Aria said softly. "I think he cares for me, too, and I know part of him wants that commitment. But he's also made it clear he's not a family man, and may never be."

"Never is a long time," Maya pointed out. "It seems to me that Cruz might be ready to have what he didn't have growing up."

"Brothers are one thing. A baby—" Pushing her hands into her hair, Aria shook her head. "I'm not ready for that, and I want a family of my own."

Maya reached over and touched Aria's hand. "I can't make up your mind for you, but unless you plan to hide from him, it won't be long before he figures out for himself you're pregnant. If that happens, you've got no chance of salvaging his trust."

All this time she'd been lying to him—lies of omission, but lies nonetheless. Aria doubted that once she did tell him, there would be any trust left to salvage.

"I just need a little more time," she said, not sure if she was appealing to Maya or trying to convince herself.

Her voice mail picked up and, for the tenth time, told him Aria wasn't available and to leave a message. Cruz jabbed hard to cut the connection and tossed his cell phone on the seat beside him. Where the hell was she?

She'd missed their meeting about the groundbreaking on the children's ranch and he'd been trying for over an hour to locate her, getting only her voice mail at both her home and cell. It wasn't like her to forget a meeting, and definitely without at least a call of explanation. More uneasy than he cared to admit, he'd resorted to driving the route from Rancho Pintada to her house, and then downtown, looking for her SUV.

Instead, when he was on the verge of calling everyone he knew in town to help locate her, he spotted her, hugging her coat to her, her woolen hat pulled low over her brow to shield her face from a blustery snow, about to go into the diner.

Stopping in the middle of the street, he rolled down his window and called her name. She turned, looked up from under her hat, started and gave him a look as if she'd been caught red-handed at some crime.

"Wait there, I'm going to park," he told her.

Cruz bit down hard on a surge of irritation. He didn't have a clue about what she was doing and why anymore, but he did know whatever was up with her, he was tired of it. It had started in Phoenix and he wished like hell he'd never asked her to come along, even more that he had taken her at her word and not come back to Luna Hermosa with the need to fix what had obviously been broken.

She was standing just inside the doorway, hatless now, waiting for him, her eyes wary as he pushed his way inside. "I've been looking everywhere for you," he grumbled, turning his sense of relief at finding her safe and whole into gruffness.

"Why?" she asked, looking confused. "Is something wrong?"

"We had a breakfast meeting scheduled today, at the ranch," he prompted. "We were supposed to go over the groundbreaking schedule."

Staring blankly for a moment, she then put a hand to her mouth, her expression stricken. "I'm so sorry. I thought we had rescheduled that."

"Well, that's news to me. What were you doing in town?"

"I—um, I had a chance for a last-minute hair appointment at Nellie's up the street first thing this morning and I took it. Hair emergency, you know?" she added with a nervous laugh.

He eyed her hair suspiciously. "I don't see any change."

"Well, that's a man for you. Hey, I haven't had breakfast yet. You hungry? We could go over the groundbreaking plans here."

"I had breakfast at the ranch," he said shortly. Her overly bright smile wavered and fell, and he inwardly sighed. Maybe she deserved to be treated coolly, but he had difficulty keeping it up. "I'll have coffee."

A sign at the entrance to the dining room read Seat Yourself, so they headed to the back where it was quieter to find a table. "I guess they still haven't found a replacement who can keep this job for more than a week. Nova's a hard act to follow. She used to waitress here, before Cort wooed her over to Morente's," she added as way of explanation.

"I see," he said, getting the distinct impression Aria was buying time with small talk, steeling herself for getting through a simple meal with him. *Fine. Then we'll make this short and not sweet.*

After they'd ordered, he forestalled any more meaningless chitchat on her part and went straight to the point. "We can break ground on the ranch as soon as the ground thaws. Do you have a crew lined up?"

"Yes." Fidgeting with her spoon, she avoided his eyes. "Mostly volunteers, fortunately. Our budget is tight enough, we need all the free labor we can muster." The waitress put a large glass of orange juice in front of her and she took a large drink, almost guzzling it.

"No coffee?" He'd never seen her drink anything but the strongest coffee she could get her hands on in the morning. The change touched of a spark of worry in him. "Are you still not feeling well?"

"I had a cup at home."

"Only one?

"I'm trying to be a little more health-conscious, that's all."

The explanation had him instinctively doubting her, but he couldn't define why. Nothing of what she did lately made sense to him. Brushing it off, he returned to the only safe subject between them at the moment. "We're still in agreement about the foundation, right?"

"Concrete slab."

"Right."

Her food came, at this point a welcome interruption, and Cruz left her to wolf down an enormous pile of scrambled eggs and toast while he largely ignored his coffee and worked at reining in all the things he really wanted to say to her. Anger, frustration, regret, they were all there, crowding for first place in his feelings, and yet overriding them all was an emotion he couldn't recognize at first until he realized it was closely akin to grief. He was losing her, or maybe she'd never really been with him to begin with, but it felt like a vital part of him had been ripped out, leaving a gaping emptiness that couldn't be filled because it belonged to her.

She couldn't see it, or she didn't want to, and that made the loss all the worse.

"On the San Francisco project—" He started abruptly, trying to distance himself from the feeling, knowing it was in vain.

She looked up from her last bite of scrambled eggs, "Yes? Is something wrong?"

"No, but I need to visit the site in person. I'm going in a couple of days. I have to check in with my office in Phoenix and pick up a few things, then I'm heading out to California for one, maybe two days. They're having problems with some of the support beams and I can't take a chance not looking at it for myself." He paused, reluctant to even hint at what was foremost on his mind. But they'd had an agreement and he, at least, was bound to honor it as a professional, regardless of what she decided. "When you started on the project, you mentioned you would like to see if firsthand. Are you still interested?"

Shifting in her seat, Aria looked straight at him for the first time that morning. "Yes, I'm very interested in the structure there."

He heard the slightest hesitation in her voice and he held up a hand, certain what was coming and determined not to hear it. "Never mind. You don't want to go. That's fine. I'll be rushed as it is, so it's probably better you don't."

"I'd like to go," she said quietly and he almost believed her. "But now, though…you're right, it's probably better I don't."

It was as simple and final as that.

They didn't want the same things, didn't feel the same way, and she wasn't going to reveal what had changed her. He cared for her, far more deeply than he would ever admit, but he wasn't going to keep torturing himself with what could or might have been.

Pushing to his feet, he tossed a twenty on the table and pulled on his coat. "I'll fax you a copy of my report from San Francisco, in case you have any input on what I find."

He didn't wait for her reply. It no longer mattered. Turning, he left her and headed out into the cold, gray morning.

* * *

Aria watched him walk away and inside her something crumbled and broke: her last defenses against her own feelings. He'd become the most important thing in her life, but she'd broken their bond, lost his trust.

I just need a little more time.

But there was no more time.

"You're still here."

A familiar voice and a gentle hand on her shoulder had her looking up and she discovered Maya standing next to her. She cleared her throat, swallowing against that seemingly permanent lump, and tried to smile. "Hey, how'd you get away from your patients?"

Maya came around and took the seat Cruz had left. "I left one in the waiting room, actually. I've only got a few minutes, but I wanted to try to catch you."

"What's wrong?" Aria asked.

"Sawyer just called and told me Rafe is going to have to move his entire herd to lower ground. Apparently the snow's so bad he's having trouble keeping them fed. If he doesn't do it soon, he could lose the lot of him. He needs all the volunteers he can get."

"You aren't going are you?"

"Don't look so worried," Maya said with a laugh. "Sawyer's yet to get me on a horse. Josh is back and Cort's coming up from Albuquerque and he's bringing Laurel and Tommy. Sawyer asked me to ask you if you could go along. You've done roundups before. They can use all the free hands they can get."

"Yes, of course. I'd love to help." Then she reconsidered. "The baby? I don't want to take any chances."

"Sancia agrees it won't be a problem this early in your pregnancy. Just take it easy and leave the wrangling to the others. You can ride alongside. You've done this so many times before. I don't have to tell you it's an easy pace and the terrain is mostly flat." Maya offered an encouraging smile. "It'll be good for you to get out in the cold, brisk air. You have warm clothes, don't you?"

Aria nodded as she thought it over a minute. It would be wonderful to get out and spend the day riding. It was cold, but she had plenty of winter gear and layers to wear. The ground was frozen, so the snow wouldn't be slippery. Riding at an easy pace would relax her. And riding with friends would double the benefit. She could, at least for a day, have a reprieve from agonizing over Cruz and the decisions she still had to make about her baby.

"So, what do you think?" Maya asked.

Aria smiled and for the first time in days it didn't feel forced. "Count me in."

Chapter Seventeen

The first faint touch of sun was staining the low-lying clouds, barely lightening their heavy gray thickness, when Aria pulled her SUV to a stop near the big house at Rancho Pintada. Morning, cold and sharp, had come with the threat of more snow and she hoped they'd be able to make headway today without a new storm making an already difficult situation worse.

There were already several vehicles and horse trailers parked along the drive; she recognized Cort's Jeep and Sawyer's truck, and a few others, friends who'd come to help with the roundup. Despite the weather and the long hours of riding ahead, she welcomed the chance to get away from brooding over Cruz. She'd thought too much about their last meeting and how, while she struggled to keep her emotions in check, he seemed to have no trouble maintaining a veneer of cool professionalism, as if all those things he'd said to her, all the passion and the intimacy, had never existed.

At least today, she wouldn't have to pretend it didn't hurt. He'd said he was going back to Phoenix and then on to San Francisco and she doubted whether he'd return to Luna Hermosa anytime soon.

Sawyer opened the door for her and the guilt bit down hard. From his easy greeting, it was obvious Maya had kept her promise and not told her husband that his oldest brother was going to be a father.

"We're getting ready to saddle up in a few minutes," Sawyer told her, leading her inside, "but you've got time to grab a cup of coffee." The door chime interrupted him and he gestured her toward the great room as he turned to answer it. "I've somehow ended up on door patrol. Coffee's that way."

Aria started inside, unfastening her heavy coat against the luxuriant warmth, but she'd only made it a few paces into the room when her step faltered. Ahead of her, Cruz stood in a group that included his brothers, Laurel, Tommy and Jule. She seriously considered turning around, except most everyone had noticed her and standing there staring or turning tail now would only make things worse. Forcing herself to smile, she went up to them, doing her best to act as if Cruz being there were nothing to her.

She felt him watching her as she greeted the others, his only acknowledgment to her a short nod. The curtness of it and the hard set of his expression slapped her as sharply as a physical blow. Instinctively she flinched away, swinging her attention to Josh to avoid looking at Cruz. "Where's your wife?"

"Home. She's not real comfortable ridin' alone, yet so I wasn't gonna win this one. I tried shamin' her into it, tellin' her Cruz was gonna show her up," Josh added with a grin at this brother, "but she wouldn't go for it. She and Maya are lookin' after the kids."

The end of Josh's sentence got lost as Aria stared at Cruz, frankly astonished. "You're going?"

"Is there a problem?" he returned coolly, his raised brow challenging her to answer honestly.

She couldn't. "No, I just didn't expect …" Her words ran out and she stopped, tried to regain her balance. "You said you didn't ride."

"He'll be fine," Cort answered for Cruz. "We've given him a couple of lessons."

"Yeah, he only fell off once," Tommy added.

"You had to remind me," Cruz said, his smile pained. "Although if you hadn't been helping me, I would probably have fallen off a lot more, so I'm glad you're going along today to give me some tips."

"It'll be okay," Tommy said, looking pleased at Cruz's praise. "Uncle Rafe is giving you a real slow horse."

Rafe put a hand on Tommy's shoulder and smiled. "I leave the wild ones for you and Josh."

"Well, that's comforting," Laurel said. She looked pointedly at Cort, who only shrugged, leaving Laurel shaking her head and muttering something about Cort not being any better.

Laughing, Jule said, "It's obvious which side of the family Tommy takes after."

Tommy beamed as if Jule had given him the best compliment ever, and Laurel couldn't hide her smile. "The crazy one," she said. "He's definitely his father's son."

"Adventurous," Cort corrected. "Nothing wrong with that."

They were distracted from pursuing the subject any further when one of the ranch hands came up to ask Rafe a question. The group broke up to get last-minute coffee refills, retrieve hats and coats and get ready for the ride. Aria found herself left alone with Cruz, uncertain about what kind of conversation to have with him, especially when he seemed determined not to start one.

"I admire you for volunteering," she finally offered awkwardly, like a gift she expected to be rejected. "It's a long day for someone who's never been on a horse before."

His expression didn't change, except for the twitch of muscle along his jaw. "Rafe and Josh needed the help. I told them I'd probably be more of a hindrance, but they assured me all I have to do is stay in the saddle and follow directions."

"Basically. It's not quite as easy as it sounds. But you're in good shape—you shouldn't have too much trouble."

"Thanks," he drawled, and she flushed.

"I mean it." Damn him, he was making this hard and yet she couldn't fault him for it. She'd hurt him with her refusal to tell him the truth. She could hardly expect any other reaction.

"I wish things were different." She was unaware she'd voiced this closely held wish aloud until Cruz's bitter huff of laughter told her he'd heard.

"They could be. But not when only one of us is willing to try."

"You can't—you don't understand."

"Then make me understand," he urged. They were suddenly closer, the expression in his eyes both frustrated and imploring, and she wanted to spill it all out, there and then, have it done with.

She teetered and maybe she would have fallen except there were so many people, trying to pretend they weren't looking at them when they were. She wasn't about to confess her sins in front of them all.

It was Jed who saved her the anguish of having to tell Cruz once again. Moving slowly into the room, he surveyed the assembled crowd, his gaze resting for a moment on each of his sons in turn. It stayed on Cruz the longest and it was to his oldest son that Jed made his way first.

Jed's only acknowledgment to Aria was a raking glance then he fixed his gaze on Cruz. "Rafe tells me you're goin' along."

"That's the plan," Cruz said. "But don't expect this to suddenly turn me into a rancher. I'll be lucky if I don't spend more of my time on the ground than in the saddle."

"It's in your blood," Jed said, dismissing the idea shortly, as if riding were a genetic trait rather than a learned skill. "Wish I could be out there with you."

He said it almost wistfully and for a moment, Aria almost felt sorry for him. It had to be a kind of hell for a man like Jed Garrett, used to knocking life's obstacles out of his way to get what he wanted, to come up against one that refused to move and had turned his own body into a traitor.

As if he saw some trace of pity in her expression, Jed tossed her a scowl and looked back around the room again, finding his other four sons. "There was a time when I figured I'd die before ever seein' the five of you together," he said gruffly, almost to himself.

Aria looked to Cruz, half expecting him to make some biting comment about it being Jed's fault his sons had been separated.

But whatever he was thinking stayed unsaid and if Jed noticed Cruz's hardened expression he ignored it.

In a way, Cruz was like Jed in that respect. She could see the same resolve to make something out of the nothing they'd been born with, the strength of will that made them both survivors. But where Jed was uncaring of who or what got trampled in his path, Cruz hadn't let his struggle to overcome his past or his successes harden him against caring. It showed in his commitment to his mother, his military service, his willingness to try and find a place for himself in his newfound family, the thought and empathy evident in all the ways he was there for her. It was the reason she knew without a doubt that he would never turn his back on his child; that he would insist on marrying her and would honor that bond until death, even without love and against what he wanted, because it was his responsibility, his duty.

Except she didn't want to be a responsibility, a duty. She wanted to be a passion, a desire that overwhelmed all others, a lover, best friend. She didn't want their child to be a regret, an accident that had to be dealt with, a complication that would breed resentment; for him or her to ever feel that they had been anything else but wanted and loved.

"Aria?"

Cruz's voice jolted her out of her musings and she realized most everyone else was out the door. "I'm sorry," she said, avoiding looking at him as she started to button up her coat. "We should go."

Instead of following her lead, he grasped her upper arm, stopping her, searching her face. Apparently, whatever he saw wasn't what he wanted to find and just as abruptly he let her go, stepping back. "You're right. We should."

Without waiting for her, he strode away and left her to follow. She was certain she missed another opportunity to regain something of what they'd lost and wondered at what point her chances would run out.

As everyone had promised—or threatened—it was a long day that stretched into early evening. It was growing dark when they finally got back to the ranch and Cruz, cold, tired and hungry, thought those new muscles he'd recently discovered were going to be doing a lot of protesting in the morning. Despite that, he'd enjoyed the day's work and more the satisfaction from knowing his being there had made a difference to his brothers. He understood now the appeal of riding and why his brothers had all chosen to settle in this corner of New Mexico. Never more strongly than when he was out in the open expanse of sky and land had he felt its allure, the sense of unfettered freedom.

More than that, Cruz had begun to feel he had a place in his new family. The bond he'd envied his brothers had extended to include him and while it was still largely untried and occasionally uncomfortable, it was strong and undeniable.

He sought Aria out among the group now getting ready for a late dinner. She was there, in the middle of the room, laughing at something Jule was saying and the sound of her voice tightened his chest and throat until it physically hurt. He told himself to look away but he couldn't, all the while wishing like hell things could have been different with her.

Working together today had, if not broken down the barriers between them, at least thinned them so they'd been able to talk and function with an appearance of being on casually friendly terms. But he didn't feel it inside. It wasn't easy to pretend it was all business now, that whatever had gone on before was just a temporary insanity.

"Hey, you okay?" Cort came up to him, handing him a mug of coffee.

"Fine, thanks." Cruz accepted the hot drink gratefully, using it as an excuse to look quickly away from Aria. But he wasn't fast enough.

Cort followed his direction and glanced between her and Cruz. He hesitated then said, "I don't know what happened, and it's none of my business. But for what it's worth, I think I know how you feel. I was to the point once where I was sure Laurel and I were over. I walked around for weeks feeling like part of me had died."

Cruz appreciated his brother's empathy, but found it hard to take. "You apparently worked it out," he said, trying to divert the focus away from an analysis of him and Aria.

"Because of Laurel. I'd given up. She was the one who finally decided to put things right."

"Are you trying to tell me something?" Cruz asked, smiling a little.

"Nothing you don't already know," Cort said. "Except with you and Aria, maybe it's the other way around."

Cruz tried to come up with answer that didn't sound evasive or an outright lie when a loud squeal of "Daddy!" interrupted and two little bodies came hurtling in Cort's direction. Maya and Eliana had arrived with the youngest children and the room suddenly became a lot noisier.

"There's my girls," Cort said, scooping up Angela and Sophie as they cannoned into him. "I missed you guys today."

"We missed you, too," Angela said, wrapping her arms around his neck. "And Mommy."

Sophie tugged at Cort's sweatshirt. "I'm hungry!"

"So am I," Cort said with a laugh. "Let's go find Mommy and Tommy and get some dinner." He turned to Cruz, his smile tempered by a shadow of concern. "Uncle Cruz looks like he could use some, too."

It wasn't food he needed right now; it was Aria. When the others began filing toward the dining room where a buffet had been laid out, he hung back, struggling to gain control over his feelings, determined not to reveal his weakness to her or anyone else.

"It's against the rules to skip dinner after a roundup," Aria said lightly, stepping up to him.

He felt stripped, exposed to her, and it left him struggling with the unfamiliar and unwanted sensation of being out of control. "I was giving the kids the first shot," he responded, saying the first thing that sounded reasonable. "It seemed safer that way."

"You're probably right." She looked around them. "Does this feel weird to you?"

"Most of the time," he said dryly.

She shook her head, smiling ruefully. "No, I mean everyone here, all of you—" she indicated him, his brothers and their families with a vague gesture— "in the same place with Jed and Del, it's not a funeral and there's not been one fight. I think I saw Jed actually smile at something Tommy said, but that could have been a hallucination. Or my brain hasn't quite thawed out yet. Maybe that's why it all looks so...normal."

"Seeing as I don't have a blueprint for *normal* family life, I couldn't really say. It does seem peaceful though," he admitted. "I suppose that is weird, considering the circumstances and everything that's happened in the past."

"It is." Sweeping the room with a glance again, she held his gaze briefly. "You did really well out there today." Then her eyes slid away and he lost her again to her restless searching for anything to look at besides him.

"Thanks." He left it at that, inwardly wincing at the futility of their exchange. He didn't know what else to say to her. He finally settled for safe, polite concern. "You should follow your own rules and get some dinner. You look tired."

"Just what every girl wants to hear," she murmured with a slight grimace. "But you're right, I am tired, we all are. It's been a long day." She did look at him then, straight on, and it hit him, that there were things she wanted to say, troubling things, that she was afraid to put a voice to.

This was his chance to convince her to confide in him, and he wasn't going to waste it. He cupped her face in his palm and she leaned into it with a sigh. "Talk to me," he urged, half demand, half plea. "Tell me what it is. You owe us that much."

"Yes..." It came out uncertainly, tremulous, but it was enough to give Cruz back the hope he'd all but abandoned. "But here—"

He couldn't give her time to change her mind again, not even the time it would take to drive back to her house. Taking her hand, he led her quickly out of the great room, getting out unnoticed, to the back of the house and his rooms. Distance and a closed door muffled the hum of conversation and the single lamp he flicked on left them facing each other in a soft halo of light.

"Aria, I—"

He didn't get any further because she walked straight up to him, put her arms around his neck and kissed him. Holding him to her, she ran her tongue over his lower lip and he accepted her blatant invitation to deepen their kiss until it became an intimate coupling, almost frantic in their mutual need to get closer, to make up for, in one moment, all the time they'd kept their distance.

She tugged at his sweater, pushing her hands up underneath, giving him no time to catch his breath, to think about what they were doing and why. It was fire, unrestrained and wild, and his body was so hard for hers it was painful. But it felt desperate, too, an ending rather than a step forward, and he couldn't ignore it simply for the satisfaction of having her in his arms again.

He tried to pull back, to slow things down enough to force words between them, but she put her fingers over his mouth, stopping him. Her words were jerky, disjointed.

"No. No, not yet," she said fiercely. "I…I need this. I need you to know…there's never been anyone that I… And I want this, I *need* this, before I tell you—"

Gently dragging her fingers away, Cruz pressed a kiss to her palm, closing both their hands around it. "I need you," he said softly. "I love you."

She started back, her face blank with shock, as if that were the last thing she'd expected him to say. He couldn't blame her, because it was the last thing he expected to feel.

"You don't have to say it—because we're…" Her hand sketched a helpless motion, unable to find a description for what they were.

"No," he agreed, "I don't have to say it. But I do. I love you." He spoke the last word against her mouth and she responded, hesitantly at first, and then with growing surety as the urgency from before regained strength.

When they took the first fumbling first steps toward the bed, though, she suddenly stiffened. It took a few moments to pierce the sensual haze fogging his brain before it registered she was pushing back instead of urging him closer. And she was crying, silently, the tears wetting his fingers as he lifted her chin to see her face.

Cruz pulled in a breath, tried to steady the pulse thrumming in his ears, to cool the heat burning through him. It wasn't just unrequited lust; it was a surge of anger at her for doing this to him again, letting him believe they had a chance and then yanking it away.

"Aria, what's wrong?" he said, holding tightly to the leash on his feelings. "And please, don't say it's nothing. We both know that's a lie."

"No, it isn't nothing." Stepping back from him, she briefly pushed her palms over her eyes then swiped the tears from her cheeks before her chin came up and she looked him straight in the face. "It's a pretty big something."

She took a deep breath and Cruz was visited by a sensation that he knew what she was going say, and that it was going to be impossible.

"I'm pregnant."

Chapter Eighteen

Completely blindsided, he just stared.

"Cruz?" When he continued only to look at her, every thought process temporarily frozen, Aria wet her lips and plunged ahead. "Believe me, I never planned on this. It was the last thing I expected. I mean, we used protection but obviously—"

"Aria. Stop." Cruz pushed at his temples in an effort to jump-start his brain. "This is my fault. I should never have—"

"Don't," she snapped. "Please don't say something stupid like you should never have taken advantage of me or come to my house that first night, or even talked to me in the first place." Her mouth thinned to a defiant line. "I chose to make love with you. I don't regret it, although it's pretty obvious at this point, you do. The only thing I regret is not telling you when I found out. I could have spared us both weeks of misunderstanding. We could have settled it by now, had it done and over with."

"*Settled it?* Exactly what is that supposed to mean?" Though unable to believe she would ever give up or harm a child of hers, an irrational fear jabbed at him. Something must have shown on his face, because she jerked back sharply.

"You can't think I would—" She abruptly cut herself short, as if she couldn't bring herself to voice the words. "How can you tell me you love me and then think I would even consider something like…that."

"I don't know what to think," he declared defensively. "You haven't said anything about how you feel about this. You don't bother to tell me, for weeks apparently, that you're expecting my baby and then all you can say is you wish it was done and over with. What am I supposed to think?" He struggled to keep the surge of anger at bay, mixed as it was with emotions he couldn't identify, let alone sort out right now.

"I'm sorry," she said quietly, all the heat in her suddenly dying. "I should have told you sooner. I didn't plan to hide it from you. I just felt …overwhelmed. And I was afraid of how you would react. I know you don't want a family. You didn't know for a long time if you wanted us to be together at all, neither of us did. And now this—this changes everything."

"No. It just makes it more complicated."

Her short laugh was brittle, ragged at the edges. "Now there's an understatement." Then her chin came up and she looked fully at him, the emotion in her face strong and fierce. "I'm keeping my baby."

"There should be a *we* in there somewhere," Cruz said tightly.

"You're right, there should. And in a perfect world, there would be. But we both know this is far from perfect."

"Maybe." Pacing a few steps, he rubbed at the back of his neck, trying to find some thread of rational thought in the chaos of feeling. He turned back to her and she was still watching him with that same expression that dared him to refute her. "You're right, I never expected to have a child. I never expected to have a long-term relationship. I'm still getting used to the idea of loving you."

She stiffened, seemingly holding her breath. He knew she wanted an answer from him that would make it all right. But he didn't have one. It unexpectedly hurt—hurt like hell that she'd kept this from him. Aria, the one person he'd trusted above anyone. Beyond that, he didn't know how to tell her what else he was feeling when he couldn't explain it to himself.

"I need time to…think about it. You say you felt overwhelmed, that's the way I feel right now. But one thing I do know—" The urgent need to convince her of this, if nothing else, gripped him, moved him to take her hands in his. "I won't ever abandon you or this baby."

He'd anticipated, or at least hoped, he could reassure her. But tears pooled in her eyes, reflecting what he could almost call grief. "I know," she said in a voice that broke. "I never thought you would." Gently, she freed her hands and stepped back. "I need to go home."

"Stay here tonight," he urged. "It's not like Jed and Del don't have the room."

"I can't do that. It's too…awkward—after everything."

Cruz closed the distance between them again and took her face in his hands. "I meant what I said. I love you." He got no response; she only continued to look at him, leaving him with the feeling he was stumbling in the dark, without a clue of what emotional traps lay in front of him and no illumination from her on how to avoid them. "I don't want to leave it like this."

"We both need time," she said. "We can talk tomorrow. Tonight—I need to get out of here." Breaking away, she turned toward the door.

He wanted to stop her. But he doubted it would get him any closer to convincing her to stay. Instead, he followed her, keeping to her side and wishing they could circumvent the great room and avoid the questioning glances their disappearance during dinner had caused.

"Why don't you wait and come home with Josh and me?" Eliana offered, walking with Aria and Cruz to the door after Aria had said her goodbyes to the rest of the group. "It's snowing again and you know how bad the roads can get. Sawyer and Maya left early because of it."

"Thanks, but I'm tired and I want to get home and crash," Aria said. She hugged her friend. "I'll be fine. It's not like I haven't driven in snow before."

Eliana looked doubtful and Cruz silently urged his sister-in-law to push the issue, guessing she'd have better luck persuading Aria not to drive than he would right now. But after hesitating, Eliana nodded. "Be careful, okay?"

"Always. You know me."

"I'm following her," Cruz said, shouldering into his own coat. "I'll make sure she gets there."

Aria glanced at him, but didn't say anything until they were outside. The snow was coming thickly now, whipping in eddies of icy wind, white whirls against the flat blackness of the sky. She put a hand to his chest, keeping him at the door. "I don't need you to follow me, really. I am used to driving in this. I'll be fine."

"Keep saying it, if it makes you feel better." He took her arm and started in the direction of her SUV.

"Cruz—"

"I'll be right behind you," he said and then turned quickly to get to his own vehicle.

The weather forced them to keep to a snail's pace, the combination of snow and wind limiting visibility to a few feet. Cruz felt the muscles in his neck and back bunch as he worked to keep her taillights in view while navigating the slippery roads. His every nerve was on alert to the slightest swerve of Aria's SUV. It made him think, briefly, longingly, of Phoenix.

They were about halfway to town when a strong gust of wind blew up a thick flurry of snow, temporarily obscuring his view of the road and her. For a moment his tires lost their purchase and his car fishtailed a little. He compensated, quickly regaining control. But when he peered ahead, there were no points of red light ahead of him.

Cursing under his breath, Cruz crawled up the road, worry eating at his patience. It took ten minutes of inching along before he finally spotted the SUV about fifty feet off the road. Deep ruts in the snow marked where she'd veered off the pavement, narrowly missing a telephone pole, and come to a shuddering stop.

He pulled over, his heart in his throat, feeling more panicked than he could ever remember in his life. Plowing through snow halfway to his knees, he got to the SUV and managed to yank the door open. Aria, still gripping the top of the steering wheel, raised her head from where it had been resting on her clenched hands.

"Are you all right?" Cruz demanded. He fumbled her seat belt off and ran his hands over her, not quite steady but not able to control it.

"I'm fine. I just scared myself. It was stupid. I let myself get distracted and—" Her eyes widened, her mouth working at words that never came. He pulled her into his arms and she was trembling all over, clinging to him like he was her only tether to safety.

Cruz held her for a few moments before scooping her out of the seat, setting her on her feet next to him so he could grab her purse and keys and lock the SUV. Then he picked her up, pretending he didn't hear her instant objection.

"Put me down," she insisted. "I can walk." He continued to ignore her and she gestured back at her SUV. "I can't just leave it there."

"It's not going anywhere tonight. It'll need to be towed."

"Then I'll call—"

"No, you won't." He got her inside his car and then hustled to crank up the heat. Flicking on the dome light, he took a good look at her. Too pale, her breaths coming too fast, the hand protectively cradled against her stomach shaking. He gently brushed the hair back from her face and her skin was cold, a shiver chasing over her at his touch.

"I wasn't paying enough attention," she whispered hoarsely. "I could have—" She put a hand to her mouth, looking as if she was going to be sick.

"Lean back and close your eyes," he ordered. "Take deep breaths." The rhythmic stroke of his hand on her hair seemed to help and after a few minutes, he made sure her seat belt was cinched and then left her curled sideways on the seat as he shifted into gear and resumed the trek into town.

It took him another twenty minutes to make it but he didn't for a second consider driving to her house. She didn't notice, didn't bother opening her eyes, until he pulled to a stop in the emergency room parking lot.

"Oh, please, this is totally unnecessary," she said, though

there was no strength behind her protest. He knew she was scared and refused to admit it; he kept the knowledge to himself, certain she wouldn't appreciate him confronting her with it. "I want to go home. I'm fine. Everything's fine."

"Humor me." He insisted on carrying her inside, over her repeatedly telling him he was overreacting, being ridiculous, and finally, threatening him with various creative forms of violence if he didn't put her down. When he complied, it was to sit her on an examining table in a curtained cubicle and even then, he refused to leave her side until the emergency room doctor kicked him out.

That left him restlessly pacing the waiting room. It felt like hours; the reality was less than half an hour before the doctor came back out.

"Other than a few bruises, she seems to be fine," the doctor told him. "But her blood pressure's a little high. We're going to keep her overnight, just to be on the safe side."

"Did she tell you she's pregnant?"

The doctor nodded. "There doesn't seem to be any harm done. You can go back in now. We're going to be moving her to a room soon."

Half expecting to be greeted with another round of recriminations, Cruz was surprised when Aria appeared almost relieved to see him. They'd put her in a hospital gown, and the whiteness of it and the blanket covering her emphasized her pallor.

"Are you done threatening me with bodily harm?" he asked, smiling a little. He smoothed the hair from her forehead, finding relief in simply touching her.

Her own smile was a ghost. "For the moment. I'm reserving the right to continue later." Dropping her eyes, she plucked nervously at the edge of the blanket. "I was afraid," she said, so softly he scarcely caught the words. "It's stupid. I mean, I just ran off the road. But all I could think about was losing the baby."

Yeah, you just ran off the road. Nearly hit a telephone pole and scared the hell out of me. No big deal. Out loud he said, "It's not going to happen. You're both fine. Everything's okay now. You'll be home tomorrow and this will all seem like a bad dream." He heard himself rattling on, something he never did, but relief made him light-headed.

She let out a huffing sound that might have been a laugh and then sighed. "Is it too much to ask for things to be easy, just once?"

"Apparently so," he said and because he couldn't resist any longer, he rested a hip on the edge of the bed and gathered her into his arms.

When, over an hour later, Aria was finally settled in a room, the nurse gave Cruz an expectant look and opened her mouth, he knew, to tell him he had to leave.

He shook his head. "My fiancée, my baby. She needs me." He said it firmly. "I'm staying."

Aria laced her fingers with his, appealed to the other woman. "Please? For a little while, anyway?"

The nurse's gaze assessed the pair of them and then she nodded. "Not long. You need the rest."

When she'd gone, Cruz resumed his post on the bed next to her and Aria leaned her cheek against his shoulder, closing her eyes. "You shouldn't tell such lies."

"I notice you didn't bother to refute me."

"I wanted you to stay." Her fingers tightened on his. "I do need you."

"Then I'll stay."

"For a little while," she murmured sleepily, the adrenaline rush created by fear finally dissipating, leaving her drowsy.

No, he told her silently as she snuggled closer to his warmth, her breath slowly evening out. *Not for a little while. I'm not letting you go. I'm not going to lose either of you.*

Aria woke slowly from a dream of confused images: of being buried in snow, and Cruz finding her, but when he'd freed her, he'd smiled sadly and walked away, leaving her there, alone in the empty coldness. The sense of loss lingered so strongly, that even when she realized where she was and why, she had a moment's fear that it was true, he had left her, this time for good.

It abated with a turn of her head. He was still at her bedside, slouched in a chair, legs stretched out in front of him, asleep. He looked uncomfortable and rumpled, the shadow of a beard darkening his jaw, and she wondered how much sleep he'd actually gotten, how long he'd simply sat there, watching her as she slept.

As if he sensed her studying him, he shifted in the chair, wincing as he straightened, then caught her gaze. "You're supposed to be sleeping," he said, the sleep-roughened texture of his voice like a lover's touch, deep inside her. He glanced at his watch. "It's not even six yet."

"You were supposed to go home," she countered. "Obviously that didn't happen."

"I wasn't leaving without you." Stretching again, he pushed to his feet and moved to sit on the edge of the bed. He took her hand, searching her face. "How are you feeling?"

Her stomach answered for her, choosing that moment to give an audible rumble. "Um—hungry," she said, returning his amused smile. "Very hungry. I never got my dinner, remember? And definitely ready to get out of here."

"No promises, but I'll see what I can do to hurry things along." Sliding his hand into the hair at her nape, he bent and kissed her, a light, tender caress, imbued with an aching sweetness that inexplicably revived the feeling she was losing him.

But how could she lose someone she'd never really had, she asked herself after Cruz had left to ask a nurse about her leaving. She had been so wary, so certain they could never work out, that she'd nearly pushed him out of her life and then pretty much completed the job by keeping the secret of her pregnancy for so long. Except now, out of responsibility and duty, he would stay, would insist on being a part of her life, their child's life.

My fiancée.

But she wouldn't marry him to satisfy his determination to do the right thing. He said he loved her, and she believed him. And she loved him, deeply and without doubt. When that had happened, she couldn't say; maybe from the beginning, and maybe it had grown slowly, building on those initial moments of intimacy that had formed an undeniable bond between them.

She had never admitted it, to him or herself, yet she knew it it had existed all along, waiting for her to recognize it.

It wouldn't be enough, though, to sustain and nurture a relationship that would be tested early by an unexpected child, a child only one of them truly wanted.

Tears blurred her eyes and she cursed the damned hormones that kept scrambling her emotions and turning her weepy over the smallest things. Hurriedly, she swiped away the dampness and reached deep inside for the resolve she would need when, inevitably, she would have to refuse Cruz's plan for their future.

The inevitable was delayed though, as she waited for Dr. Gonzales to stop by and satisfy herself that Aria hadn't done any damage with her slight mishap. Cruz, so easily shouldering the role of expectant father that Aria could almost believe he was enjoying it, impressed Dr. Gonzales with his questions about what to expect during Aria's pregnancy, and what they needed to do as a couple to prepare for the actual birth.

The whole discussion made Aria uncomfortable because it was cementing his certainty they were going to be in this together, not just through her pregnancy, but in raising their baby. The longer it went on, the more her dread grew at having to tell him it couldn't be.

Finally, when the limits of her patience were tested to the breaking point, Dr. Gonzales agreed she could leave, and after all the paperwork, Cruz drove her home.

"Why don't you grab a shower while I fix you some breakfast?" he said when he'd walked her inside.

Aria considered refusing, telling him she didn't need a babysitter. The thought didn't last long. If there were ever going to be a good time and place for them to hash out the future, this was it. "All right," she gave in, "but I'm warning you, I'm planning on using all the hot water."

Retreating to her bedroom, she called her dad to let him know she wouldn't be able to pick Sully up until tomorrow, making light of her mishap on the road and assuring him she was fine, before indulging in a long, steamy shower. When she'd finally made good on her threat to turn the water lukewarm, she dug out her warmest flannel pants and a long woolly sweater and made her way to the kitchen, finding Cruz there, looking very much at home, as if he spent every morning whipping together breakfast for her.

"I know I took forever, but I didn't think it was long enough for you to run back to the ranch for your suitcase," she said, indicating his sweatshirt and jeans.

He expertly flipped the omelet he'd concocted, sliding it onto a plate. "I always keep a change of clothes in my car. You never know."

"You never told me you were a Boy Scout, too."

"I hope you won't be too disappointed when I tell you the only requirement I can lay claim to in that arena is the 'be prepared' part." Her stomach growled again and he put a mug of herbal tea in her hand and waved away her offer to help. "Sit. I think I can manage this without you."

She sat and for the entire meal, went along with his determination to talk about things that didn't matter, like how she was going to get her SUV out, and whether or not they should call his brothers to let them know what had happened and that she was okay, and how great it was the cattle had gotten moved before another storm set in.

All the while Aria grew more and more restless. Now that her pregnancy was no longer a secret, she wanted to have the conversation, confrontation, argument—whatever it turned out to be—she'd dreaded for weeks. But Cruz seemed equally determined to avoid it, insisting after breakfast that she camp out on the couch and take it easy while he dealt with a few business calls.

"Fine, go ahead. Hide in there," she muttered at the closed door to her office where he'd retreated. Maybe—no probably—he was still angry with her and she couldn't blame him. But if he thought he could wear her down, get her to acquiesce to everything he intended simply by ignoring her, he was going to be disappointed.

She took some paperwork with her to the couch, fiddling with some sketches for the San Francisco project, until finally she couldn't stand the walls between them anymore, both literal and figurative. Pushing everything aside, she got up and shoved open the office door without bothering to knock.

Cruz looked up from the notes he was scribbling and she interrupted him before he could get the first word past his lips. "Don't say it. I'm through resting, and I'm not waiting anymore. We need to talk. Avoiding it isn't going to make it go away." Making it clear she had no intention of leaving, she dropped onto the office couch and fixed him with a hard stare.

"I wasn't avoiding it," he said. He pushed his papers aside and got up to sit beside her. "I wanted to give you a chance to recover from last night. And there were some things I needed to sort out."

She could guess what those things were and she couldn't let him take control, let herself be persuaded into accepting a solution that could only end badly. "Don't. Please don't make plans."

"I would say that's rather unavoidable under the circumstances. But out of curiosity—" he gestured her direction "—would you care to tell me why not?"

"Because I know what you're going to say and I can't go along with it."

"I see." The way he studied her for long, silent seconds, his expression unreadable, had Aria resisting the urge to squirm and wondering exactly what it was he did see. "What is it, exactly, that you think I've decided that's so unacceptable?" he finally asked.

"I know you plan on being a part of this baby's life and I want that," she started slowly, choosing her words carefully. "But I also know you don't want a family and I don't intend on tying you down with one. You'd only end up resenting me and our baby. My life is here, yours isn't. You said yourself you'd gotten used to being a gypsy, and that you'd never want that kind of life for your child. I wouldn't ask you to give it all up, but I can't share it, either. You and me—maybe we could have made it work. But it's not just us anymore. And then there's the whole issue of your mother—" Wincing, she rubbed at her temple and looked sideways at him. "Maybe we shouldn't go there."

Cruz shrugged. "Like you said, avoiding it isn't going to make it go away."

"No, but there's so much else right now…." She drew in a long breath, wished it didn't all have to be so hard. Then again, nothing for them had ever seemed easy, except for the way they had become entangled in each other's lives without either of them wanting or trying. "You're mad at me for not telling you sooner—"

"I was," he interrupted. "We've always been honest with each other, even when we were strangers." He scrubbed a hand over his face and then locked gazes with her again. "That was one of my reasons for coming here to begin with. I was tired of all the lies and secrets. You were the one person I trusted not be like that. So yes, I was angry, all those weeks after Nova's wedding, when I knew you were lying to me about what was wrong. And then yesterday…that hurt."

She started to tell him again how sorry she was, that his admission made the guilt a hundred times worse. He stopped her with a shake of his head.

"We're past it now. I hope," he added.

"I hope, too, but I want you to understand. I told you I didn't say anything about being pregnant because I felt overwhelmed and that's partly true. But I also knew you would insist on us staying together. And I don't want you to stay out of obligation or because you feel responsible. I—I care about you too much to hold you like that."

Now that all her arguments were neatly laid out, minus the messy emotions that she couldn't allow to sway her, Aria looked at Cruz, not sure what she wanted to see in his eyes.

"Okay," he said quietly. "Now that you've told me what I want, how about I tell you what I need?"

"Cruz—"

"Do you love me?"

Oh, there it was. That question she'd hoped he wouldn't ask because it would make all her sensible debate useless. Yet she couldn't lie, not now, when it meant too much. "Yes," she whispered, the one softly spoken syllable full and weighty with layers of feeling.

"Then the rest of it is only details, isn't it?"

"They're pretty big details," she responded dryly.

"They are," he agreed, "and it would be simpler to quit and walk away. Agree to a nice little civilized arrangement where you're the parent and I see my child a few times a year and we pretend all we are is friends who accidentally made a baby. That's your solution, isn't it?"

Aria felt her face grow hot. "You make it sound a lot more cold-blooded than I intended."

"According to you, that's what it is. I only care out of obligation and you're willing to sacrifice us because you're so sure I can't be any better than my father."

"That's not what I meant at all." This was going more badly than she'd imagined. From wanting to have it done with, she now wanted to retreat, to take it all back until she could find a better way out of the tortuous emotional maze she'd trapped herself in. "You would never do what Jed did to you and your brothers. But raising a child shouldn't be something you have to do or you feel like you need to do to prove you're not Jed. We'd all end up miserable," she finished, her voice catching on the emotion welling inside, tightening her throat.

"It doesn't have to be that way," Cruz said softly. Closing the distance between them, he pushed aside the emotional barriers that had kept them at opposite ends and reached out to stroke her hair, her cheek. The tenderness in his touch and his face brought tears to her eyes. And when, very gently, he brushed his fingers over her belly, as if he could touch their child, she couldn't stop them from spilling over. "You were right, before, when you said we've done everything backward. This, too. Maybe it's not the best start. That doesn't mean we can't make it work."

"But you—"

"Have a family now. It took me a while to find them, and it's the last thing I expected to have or thought I would want. But I do, it's what I need. You're what I need." He gathered her into his arms and she went willingly, helpless to do anything else but yield to the most cherished desires of her heart, the ones she had almost given up as impossible. "I love you. And I'll love this baby. Not because I have to, because I can't imagine my life without either of you in it."

She took his face between her hands, wanting him to clearly see in her eyes everything she felt. "I love you, too. So much." She kissed him and thought, of all the times they'd done this, in passion and need, desperation and desire, this was more, an affirmation and a promise of love and life.

"What about your mother?" she asked a few minutes later. "And your business and mine? And—"

Cruz held her away from him a little so he could look into her eyes. "What about us?"

He was right—all those were details. Messy, complicated, even aggravating, but they would find a way to work them out and it would remind them all the more strongly of what really mattered.

"Us? We're probably crazy to try and build something out of all these pieces," she said, shaking her head.

Nuzzling against her throat, Cruz started working his mouth back up toward hers. "I love a good challenge."

"I love you, and you're right—"

"I love you, too. I know that's right."

"It is," Aria murmured before giving herself over to his kiss and the bond that had been between them from the start. This, them together as a family, loving each other, wasn't just good enough.

It was everything.

Epilogue

"It won't be long now." Cruz, his arms in a protective circle around Aria and their soon-to-arrive son, looked with satisfaction at the steel skeleton of the children's ranch. The structures were more promise than actual walls and roof, but they'd laid a strong foundation and by fall, Aria's vision would be reality.

Leaned back against his chest, her arms crossed over his, doubling the embrace, she smiled. "Are you talking about the ranch or Mateo?"

"Both. Although I'm pretty sure Mateo is going to beat the ranch being done by at least a month."

The baby kicked, as if responding to the sound of his name, and this time, it was Cruz who smiled. It continued to be a source of wonder to him that he and Aria, without trying or even imagining, had created something as amazing as their child, and that he, who'd grown up lonely and without roots, had finally come home to the least likely place.

It seemed a lifetime ago, a half-remembered dream, when he had walked into Jed Garrett's house for the first time, a stranger looking for pieces of his past, expecting little and finding everything. Then, he couldn't imagine belonging to a family, having one of his own. Now, he had both.

Despite all the years of separation, the secrets and betrayals that had divided them, he and his brothers had found each other and forged a bond that would never be broken by time or circumstance. He had also come to accept what his father had done, if not to wholly forgive, at least, and even to allow himself to feel a kind of gratitude. His brothers had been doubtful but Aria understood, better than any of them, because without that letter from Jed that had called him to Luna Hermosa, they would never have found each other.

They'd been married for four months and were still working out all those details of moving his company to Taos, shifting a large portion of the business travel to Derek and putting patches on his relationship with his mother.

None of it, not even the expectation of her first grandchild, had settled well with Maria. She continued to flatly refuse to step foot in New Mexico, let alone Luna Hermosa. It had made their wedding plans awkward and in the end he and Aria had followed Sawyer and Maya's example, disappeared to Mexico for two weeks and come back married. Cruz hoped that when Mateo was born, in little more than a month, his mother would relent and at least move closer, to Taos or Santa Fe, but he was prepared to accept that it might be years—or forever—before she would let go the past in favor of a future that included her son and his family.

"You're very quiet all of a sudden," Aria said. She tilted her head back on his shoulder to see him. "Are you all right?"

Cruz bent and lightly kissed her. "I was just thinking about how much everything has changed. If you had asked me that first night where I planned to be in six months, here would never have come up."

Tightening her hold on him, Aria looked at the vista of land and mountains spread around them, golden in the summer sun, and said softly, "Here is good."

They stayed for a few minutes longer, enjoying the quiet and simply being with each other, before keeping their promise to stop by Josh and Eliana's house on their way home.

An hour later, the four of them were sitting on the front porch, talking about the next steps towards the opening of the children's ranch when the sound of a rider approaching drew their attention.

"It's Rafe," Josh said, frowning a little as he got to his feet. "There's gotta be somethin' wrong."

Rafe's expression justified Josh's concern as he swung out of the saddle, walking up to them with the look of a man about to deliver bad news.

"What's happened?" Eliana asked. "Is it Jule or the babies—"

"They're fine," Rafe said, waving off the question foremost with everyone. "They're all at her mother's."

A sense of uneasiness visited Cruz. He too stood up, not sure why he felt the need to be on his feet when Rafe told them what he'd come to say. "What is it then?"

"I was checking the ranch e-mail and found this." Rafe pulled a printout from his shirt pocket. "It was sent to Jed by a Duran Forrester. I figured it was ranch business. I was wrong."

He handed the sheet over to Cruz, who scanned it quickly and then reread it again with the feeling that the words there couldn't possibly make sense. Slowly, he passed it to Josh.

Josh glanced over it and gave a low whistle. "Is this for real?"

"Far as I can tell," Rafe said gruffly.

Aria reached for Cruz's hand. "What is it?"

Cruz looked at his brothers, then back at his wife. "This Duran Forrester—he says he and his brother are Jed's sons. He's coming here—this week—to meet his father."

* * * * *

Turn the page for a sneak preview of
AFTERSHOCK, *a new anthology*
featuring New York Times *bestselling author*
Sharon Sala.

Available October 2008.

n o c t u r n e™

Dramatic and sensual tales of paranormal romance.

Chapter 1

Nicole Masters was sitting cross-legged on her sofa while a cold autumn rain peppered the windows of her fourth-floor apartment. She was poking at the ice cream in her bowl and trying not to be in a mood.

Six weeks ago, a simple trip to her neighborhood pharmacy had turned into a nightmare. She'd walked into the middle of a robbery. She never even saw the man who shot her in the head and left her for dead. She'd survived, but some of her senses had not. She was dealing with short-term memory loss and a tendency to stagger. Even though she'd been told the problems were most likely temporary, she waged a daily battle with depression.

Her parents had been killed in a car wreck when she was twenty-one. And except for a few friends—and most recently her boyfriend, Dominic Tucci, who lived in the apartment right above hers, she was alone. Her doctor kept reminding her that she should be grateful to be alive, and on one level she knew he was right. But he wasn't living in her shoes.

If she'd been anywhere else but at that pharmacy when the robbery happened, she wouldn't have died twice on the way to the hospital. Instead of being grateful that she'd survived, she couldn't stop thinking of what she'd lost.

But that wasn't the end of her troubles. On top of everything else, something strange was happening inside her head. She'd begun to hear odd things: sounds, not voices—at least, she didn't think it was voices. It was more like the distant noise of rapids—a rush of wind and water inside her head that, when it came, blocked out everything around her. It didn't happen often, but when it did, it was frightening, and it was driving her crazy.

The blank moments, which is what she called them, even had a rhythm. First there came that sound, then a cold sweat, then panic with no reason. Part of her feared it was the beginning of an emotional breakdown. And part of her feared it wasn't—that it was going to turn out to be a permanent souvenir of her resurrection.

Frustrated with herself and the situation as it stood, she upped the sound on the TV remote. But instead of *Wheel of Fortune,* an announcer broke in with a special bulletin.

"This just in. Police are on the scene of a kidnapping that occurred only hours ago at The Dakota. Molly Dane, the six-year-old daughter of one of Hollywood's blockbuster stars, Lyla Dane, was taken by force from the family apartment. At this time they have yet to receive a ransom demand. The housekeeper was seriously injured during the abduction, and is, at the present time, in surgery. Police are hoping to be able to talk to her once she regains consciousness. In the meantime, we are going now to a press conference with Lyla Dane."

Horrified, Nicole stilled as the cameras went live to where the actress was speaking before a bank of microphones. The shock and terror in Lyla Dane's voice were physically painful to watch.

But even though Nicole kept upping the volume, the sound continued to fade.

Just when she was beginning to think something was wrong with her set, the broadcast suddenly switched from the Dane press conference to what appeared to be footage of the kidnapping, beginning with footage from inside the apartment.

When the front door suddenly flew back against the wall and four men rushed in, Nicole gasped. Horrified, she quickly realized that this must have been caught on a security camera inside the Dane apartment.

As Nicole continued to watch, a small Asian woman, who she guessed was the maid, rushed forward in an effort to keep them out. When one of the men hit her in the face with his gun, Nicole moaned. The violence was too reminiscent of what she'd lived through. Sick to her stomach, she fisted her hands against her belly, wishing it was over, but unable to tear her gaze away.

When the maid dropped to the carpet, the same man followed with a vicious kick to the little woman's midsection that lifted her off the floor.

"Oh, my God," Nicole said. When blood began to pool beneath the maid's head, she started to cry.

As the tape played on, the four men split up in different directions. The camera caught one running down a long marble hallway, then disappearing into a room. Moments later he reappeared, carrying a little girl, who Nicole assumed was Molly Dane. The child was wearing a pair of red pants and a white turtleneck sweater, and her hair was partially blocking her abductor's face as he carried her down the hall. She was kicking and screaming in his arms, and when he slapped her, it elicited an agonized scream that brought the other three running. Nicole watched in horror as one of them ran up and put his hand over Molly's face. Seconds later, she went limp.

One moment they were in the foyer, then they were gone.

Nicole jumped to her feet, then staggered drunkenly. The bowl of ice cream she'd absentmindedly placed in her lap shattered at her feet, splattering glass and melting ice cream everywhere.

The picture on the screen abruptly switched from the kidnapping to what Nicole assumed was a rerun of Lyla Dane's plea for her daughter's safe return, but she was numb.

Before she could think what to do next, the doorbell rang. Startled by the unexpected sound, she shakily swiped at the tears and took a step forward. She didn't feel the glass shards piercing her feet until she took the second step. At that point, sharp pains shot through her foot. She gasped, then looked down in confusion. Her legs looked as if she'd been running through mud, and she was standing in broken glass and ice cream, while a thin ribbon of blood seeped out from beneath her toes.

"Oh, no," Nicole mumbled, then stifled a second moan of pain.

The doorbell rang again. She shivered, then clutched her head in confusion.

"Just a minute!" she yelled, then tried to sidestep the rest of the debris as she hobbled to the door.

When she looked through the peephole in the door, she didn't know whether to be relieved or regretful.

It was Dominic, and as usual, she was a mess.

Nicole smiled a little self-consciously as she opened the door to let him in. "I just don't know what's happening to me. I think I'm losing my mind."

"Hey, don't talk about my woman like that."

Nicole rode the surge of delight his words brought. "So I'm still your woman?"

Dominic lowered his head.

Their lips met.

The kiss proceeded.

Slowly.

Thoroughly.

* * * * *

Be sure to look for the AFTERSHOCK *anthology next month,*
as well as other exciting paranormal stories
from Silhouette Nocturne.
Available in October wherever books are sold.

nocturne™

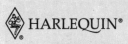

REQUEST YOUR FREE BOOKS!

2 FREE NOVELS PLUS 2 FREE GIFTS!

SPECIAL EDITION®

Life, Love and Family!

YES! Please send me 2 FREE Silhouette Special Edition® novels and my 2 FREE gifts (gifts are worth about $10). After receiving them, if I don't wish to receive any more books, I can return the shipping statement marked "cancel." If I don't cancel, I will receive 6 brand-new novels every month and be billed just $4.24 per book in the U.S. or $4.99 per book in Canada, plus 25¢ shipping and handling per book and applicable taxes, if any*. That's a savings of at least 15% off the cover price! I understand that accepting the 2 free books and gifts places me under no obligation to buy anything. I can always return a shipment and cancel at any time. Even if I never buy another book from Silhouette, the two free books and gifts are mine to keep forever.

235 SDN EEYU   335 SDN EEY6

Name	(PLEASE PRINT)
Address	Apt. #
City	State/Prov.	Zip/Postal Code

Signature (if under 18, a parent or guardian must sign)

Mail to the Silhouette Reader Service:
IN U.S.A.: P.O. Box 1867, Buffalo, NY 14240-1867
IN CANADA: P.O. Box 609, Fort Erie, Ontario L2A 5X3

Not valid to current subscribers of Silhouette Special Edition books.

Want to try two free books from another line?
Call 1-800-873-8635 or visit www.morefreebooks.com.

* Terms and prices subject to change without notice. N.Y. residents add applicable sales tax. Canadian residents will be charged applicable provincial taxes and GST. Offer not valid in Quebec. This offer is limited to one order per household. All orders subject to approval. Credit or debit balances in a customer's account(s) may be offset by any other outstanding balance owed by or to the customer. Please allow 4 to 6 weeks for delivery. Offer available while quantities last.

Your Privacy: Silhouette is committed to protecting your privacy. Our Privacy Policy is available online at www.eHarlequin.com or upon request from the Reader Service. From time to time we make our lists of customers available to reputable third parties who may have a product or service of interest to you. If you would prefer we not share your name and address, please check here. ☐

SSE08R

#1927 HAVING TANNER BRAVO'S BABY—Christine Rimmer
Bravo Family Ties
Tanner Bravo and Crystal Cerise had it bad for each other, though
they couldn't be more different. Tanner was the type to settle down;
free-spirited Crystal wouldn't hear of it. Now that Crystal was
pregnant, would Tanner have his way after all?

#1928 FAMILY IN PROGRESS—Brenda Harlen
Back in Business
Restoring classic cars was widowed dad Steven Warren's stock in
trade. And when magazine photographer Samara Kenzo showed up
to snap his masterpieces, her focus was squarely on the handsome
mechanic. But the closer they got, the more Steven's preteen
daughter objected to this interloper....

#1929 HOMETOWN SWEETHEART—Victoria Pade
Northbridge Nuptials
When Wyatt Grayson's elderly grandmother showed up, disoriented
and raving, in her hometown, it was social worker Neily Pratt to
the rescue. And while her job was to determine if Wyatt was a fit
guardian for his grandmother, Neily knew right away that she'd
appoint him guardian of her own heart any day!

#1930 THE SINGLE DAD'S VIRGIN WIFE—Susan Crosby
Wives for Hire
Tricia McBride was in the mood for adventure, and that's just what
she got when she agreed to homeschool Noah Falcon's two sets
of twins. As she warmed to the charms of this single dad, Tricia
realized that what started out strictly business was turning into pure
pleasure....

#1931 ACCIDENTAL PRINCESS—Nancy Robards Thompson
Most little girls dream of being a princess—single mom Sophie
Baldwin's world turned upside down when she found out she was
one! As this social-worker-turned-sovereign rightfully claimed
the throne of St. Michel, little did she know she was claiming the
heart of St. Michel's Minister of Security, Philippe Lejardin, in the
process.

#1932 FALLING FOR THE LONE WOLF—Crystal Green
The Suds Club
Her friends at the Suds Club Laundromat noticed that something was
up with Jenny Hunter—especially Web consultant Liam McCree,
who had designs on the businesswoman. Would serial-dating Jenny
end up with this secret admirer? Or would a looming health crisis
stand in their way? It would all come out in the wash....

SSECNM0908

SPECIAL EDITION